CLAIMED

DECADENCE AFTER DARK BOOK TWO

M. NEVER

CLAIMED
Copyright © M. NEVER 2014
All rights reserved

Names, characters and incidents depicted in this book are products of the author's imagination, or are used fictitiously. Any resemblance to actual events, locales, organizations, or persons, living or dead, is entirely coincidental and beyond the intent of the author or the publisher. No part of this book may be reproduced or shared by any electronic or mechanical means, including but not limited to printing, file sharing, and email, without prior written permission from author M. Never.

Cover Design By:
Marisa Shor, Cover Me, Darling

Editing By:
Jenny Carlsrud Sims, Editing 4 Indies

Proofreading By:
Nichole Strauss, Perfectly Publishable

Interior Design and Formatting By:
Christine Borgford, Perfectly Publishable

Your naked body should only belong to those who fall in love with your naked soul. ~ unknown

JETT

PROLOGUE

I KNOW WHO IT IS before I even answer the phone.

"What's up, Jimmy?"

"Your boy is at it again. Gettin' belligerent and disrupting my customers."

"Awesome," I groan under my breath. "I'll be there in ten minutes."

"Five minutes. This is my last courtesy call. Next time, I'm calling the cops."

"I hear ya loud and clear."

"Good." Click.

Fuck. I shrug on a pair of jeans and run my fingers through my hair. The first time I can sleep through the night in six years and this jackass repeatedly picks three a.m. to self-destruct. If it were anyone else, I'd have told Jimmy to toss him in the gutter and let him sleep off his load. But I can't do that, not to Kayne. At least not this time, but possibly the next. This shit is getting old.

It takes me exactly seven minutes to drive to the hole Kayne has taken up residence in the last three months. Transition into the civilian world has been significantly harder for him than myself. Losing Ellie destroyed him, more so than even I could have predicted. He was fucked up when it came to women to begin with, and getting wrapped up with her only magnified his issues twentyfold. Sometimes I worry he's reached a point of no return.

I walk into the dark little bar with a rainbow of shady characters. No, Kayne couldn't just pick any bar to get drunk in; he had to pick the one where the baddest motherfuckers in town hang out. A place where the wrong look can get you stabbed or the wrong word will earn you a bottle smashed over your head.

I spot him in the corner being corralled by two linebackers in motorcycle jackets. *Just fucking great.* He's swaying on his feet with his bottom lip busted wide open. But it's the look in his eyes that has me worried. His stare is dark and removed like his soul has disappeared.

"You're late," Jimmy sneers from behind the bar.

"Keep your shirt on. I'm here, aren't I? What happened?" I ask as we walk the length of the room side by side toward Kayne.

"What happened is your friend came, got shitfaced, and started a fight. Again," he snarls. "I've had it. He's out, and if he shows his face in here one more time, I'm not going to intervene when he gets what's coming to him. Got me?" the burly man asks with his arms crossed and a glare that can make the average person piss themselves.

"I got it." I wave my hand. I'm sure if I was anyone else, I'd be intimidated. But I don't have time for hard-asses who think they're tough shit. If Kayne wasn't fucked up, we could wipe the floor with every douchebag in this entire place.

I squeeze through the two mountains blocking him. "Excuse me, fellas. I got it from here." I grab Kayne's arm, and he growls at me. "Easy, killer. Just taking you to get some air." I pull him through the bar, stumbling drunk, and cursing like a sailor. To be honest, I'm impressed he has the ability to speak given the condition he's in.

Once outside, I haul off and punch him in the gut. Why? Because the last thing I need is a ticking time bomb. Which is exactly what Kayne is at the moment—what he's been since the moment Ellie walked out of his life. And the only way for him to come to terms with what he's feeling is to face it head on. I have learned this about him the hard way.

Kayne hunches over, caught off guard for a second, and then retaliates by tackling me against the car. "Come on, cocksucker, get it all out." I continue with the kidney shots as he crushes me against the driver's side door. "She's gone! She's gone! And you have to fucking accept that!" I scream at him.

"I can't!" Kayne howls like a wounded animal then slumps to the ground, trying—and failing miserably—to hide the emotion leaking out of his eyes. Ughhhh, messed-up motherfucker. I prop him up on the sidewalk. He hits my soft spot every time.

"You can't keep doing this to yourself." I clasp his shoulder as he clumsily sits on the curb, pulling his legs up to steady himself. "You're going to wind up getting hurt, or worse, getting dead. Is that what you worked so hard for? Sacrificed so much of your life for?" I shake him. "To be buried six feet under?"

"I'd be better off dead." He wipes his cheeks roughly with the palms of his hands, his elbows resting on his knees.

"That's the alcohol talking."

"No, it's not. What's the point of living if you have nothing to live for?" He looks up at me with bloodshot eyes.

My flesh actually heats.

"You selfish scumbag. You have nothing to live for? What the fuck am I? I don't count just because you can't fuck me?"

"What?" His expression falls. "No . . . That's not . . . You're my best friend. My brother . . . The only family I have." He stumbles over his words.

"Well, how do you think your brother would feel if you end up dead?" I get in his face.

Kayne shrugs. "Shitty?"

"Yeah. Pretty. Fucking. Shitty," I snap.

Kayne stares at me blankly. I know he's in there *somewhere*. Then he drops his head in his hands pathetically. "I just miss her so damn much."

"I know."

"Is there ever going to be a woman in my life who doesn't break my heart?"

Aww shit, he's going there. "You can't blame Ellie for

breaking your heart. We both knew the possible outcome when we took her."

"I just can't stand her being gone. It's killing me." His voice cracks as he buries his face in the crook of his arm and recoils into a ball.

"For now," I assert. "She's gone for now. That doesn't mean she'll be gone forever."

"How can you possibly know that?" He raises his head and sniffs.

I roll my eyes. "Haven't you learned yet? I know everything."

Kayne actually chuckles. It's a deranged sound, but at least he's connecting with me on some coherent level.

We stare at each other for some time before I concede. It's late, I'm tired, and he's smashed.

"Come on, big man. Let's get you home and cleaned up. You bled all over yourself." Splattered red stains are covering his white shirt.

"Not my blood." He grins up at me. "It's the fucker's who was stupid enough to fight me. He never got a shot in."

"Then what happened to your lip?"

"Fell off the barstool."

"You what?" Oh, for Christ's sake, he can throw down in a bar fight, but he can't take a damn leak.

"Let's go." I hold out my hand exasperated.

Kayne teeters a bit before his palm finally connects with mine. I haul him to his feet, and it feels like I'm pulling on a steel anchor. Once standing, I rest him against the car and manually unlock the doors. My 1966 Chevelle didn't exactly come equipped with keyless entry. After I dump him in the front seat, I slide behind the wheel and start the engine. My red devil purrs to life, and I can't help but think there's only one other kind of hum that's better than this car's.

I glance over at Kayne; he looks green and is barely conscious. "Listen man, you puke in here, and I'm tossing you out while we're still moving."

Kayne smirks, his head bobbing all over the place as I pull away. In no time at all, he's passed out and breathing loudly.

What am I going to do with his dumbass? He's a wreck.

I can't fault the guy completely for all his fuckedupness; he's had a rough life. Abused, neglected, and cast aside; not to mention abandoned by the one person who was supposed to love him the most. It's tragic, really. And then, when he finally gets one tiny flicker of happiness, what happens? It's corrupted by evil and shrouded in darkness. Sometimes, you just can't win for trying.

"Ellie," Kayne moans miserably beside me while grabbing his crotch in his drunken sleep.

All I can do is shake my head.

Oy, what a fucking hot mess.

ELLIE

"NO MATTER WHERE YOU GO *or who you're with, you'll always be mine.*" His voice echoes in the darkness. "*Mine, Ellie.*" I hurl myself up out of a dead sleep, panting. My hair is sticking to my forehead from sweat, and my tank top is clinging to my chest. I catch my breath and remind myself it was only a dream.

Only a dream. Only a dream.

The tropical nighttime breeze flutters through the half-open window and cools my burning skin. I fall back down onto my pillow and try to banish the vision of majestic blue eyes haunting my mind. Not only his eyes—his voice, his scent, his words. "*I'd much rather shower you with pleasure than torture you with pain . . . but I'll do what I have to do to make you submit.*"

It's been a year since I left him—the man who abducted me, trained me, used me, owned me, *deceived* me. A whole year since I found out I was free.

Immediately after I left Mansion, I was held in a safe house for three days. Jett stayed with me the whole time. He laid with me while I slept, held my hand while I was debriefed by a very shady man in a black suit threatening me with jail time if I divulged one word about the classified operation, and held me when I fell to pieces night after night. He was my sanity. Which is crazy, when you think about it. He was one-half of the duo who held me captive, forced me to submit, and conformed me into a slave. A sex slave. But no matter how low I felt, it was Jett who lifted me up. When the curtain fell, he was the only one I could trust. Warped as it may have been.

I look up at my apartment building. It looks exactly the same. Red brick and concrete stairs.

"Last stop on the crazy train," Jett says grinning.

I feel the anxiety stampede through me as I gaze out the tinted window of the truck. Do I look different? I definitely feel different. I wonder if everyone will be able to see the scars of my experiences sliced all over my skin. I guess I'm about to find out.

I barely allowed myself to miss anyone while I was gone, and all that suppressed emotion is threatening to break through the surface of my facade. I'm finally home. My eyes burn as I fight back tears.

"Remember what we talked about. Only recount very vague details. You were kidnapped, drugged, and you don't remember much of your time in captivity."

I frown and nod.

"It's important you keep the accounts of what happened to yourself."

I nod some more. I understand. I really do.

"Am I ever going to see you again?" *I ask Jett with a shaky voice.*

"Maybe. It's up to you."

"If I forgive Kayne?" *I narrow my eyes.*

He shrugs. "We're a package deal."

The tears I'm trying to contain fall. I sadly realize that I'm never going to see Jett again. It feels like my soul has been ripped from my body, and now I'm losing my best friend in the process.

"No tears, sweet thing." *He wipes my cheek with his thumb.* "Time to be the strong girl I know you are. This is your decision."

And I stand by it.

"Where are you going now that this is all over?"

"I have some unfinished business of my own to take care of." *He fiddles with the cuff of his sleeve.* "But don't miss me too much; I might not be as far as you think." *He winks.*

"What does that mean?"

"It means just because I'm leaving now it doesn't mean I'll be gone forever."

I look at him like the crazy man he is. I'm too tired for riddles.

"Go on." *he nudges me.* "Time to go home."

I hug him one last time and step out of the car.

Time to go home.

After my very teary return, I spent months trying to acclimate back into some semblance of a 'normal' life. I quit Expo (despite Mark's protests), started seeing a psychiatrist, and spent most of the summer down the shore—away from the city and the reminders of the past. Reminders of *him*.

I meant it when I said I never wanted to see him again, and when I finally felt like I was moving on, a package arrived on August twenty-eighth, my twenty-third birthday. It was a large, rectangular, white box with a plain white card and a simple white bow. When I opened the card, I nearly fell apart. One word was inscribed on the inside:

CUPCAKE

I ripped open the box with overflowing tears to find two dozen miniature red velvet cupcakes. I cried even harder. I didn't even know why. I vowed to put Kayne Roberts behind me, and up until that moment, I thought I had. But one look at that word and a whole world of emotion let loose. I tore up the card and chucked the cupcakes in the dumpster on the side of my building. I just couldn't. I was leaving for school, and that's where my focus had to stay. I would never again let someone take my hopes and dreams and future away. Never. I had no idea who Kayne was. He deceived me from the very moment I met him. How do you care about someone you don't know at all? On a basic human level, maybe. But to love someone, expose yourself to them, and trust them with your entire heart?

Hell no.

I left for Hawaii the very next day.

If I had ever wished to see paradise, I had finally arrived. Oahu is beyond beautiful—the landscape, the flowers, the ocean. Being five thousand miles away from New York, I could breathe. It was a new beginning, and I took complete advantage. I learned to surf on the beaches of Waikiki, hiked to the top of Diamond Head, and snorkeled with tropical fish and sea turtles in Hanauma Bay.

The dark clouds had finally separated. Or so I thought.

I didn't even realize it was happening. It was like a tiny tear in your favorite shirt that you never even notice until there is a gaping hole in the seam. I tried to ignore it, tried to keep myself busy with classes and extracurricular activities, but it was always there. The heaviness in my chest weighing me down. Thoughts of him fogging my mind. And once I acknowledged the feelings sprouting inside me, they grew rapidly, like radioactive flowers.

You can't love him, I kept telling myself. He kidnapped you, held you captive, forced you to wear a collar and be his slave. And he did it all under false pretenses. None of it was real. I pounded that mantra into my head. None of it was real. *"I would kill for you."*

Was it?

That brings me to present day.

My freshman year of college is almost over. I'm living the life I thought I wanted and second-guessing myself every day.

I close my eyes and try not to think, try to ignore the heat my body is missing, and the way a certain pair of hands used to touch me, hold me, subdue me until I was coming undone at his command. Nights like these are the worst because nothing can satisfy the need. Trust me, I've tried relentlessly to fulfill it—but my desire only wants one thing. Or only one person, I should say. My body is still a lecherous traitor even after all this time. I slip my hands into my underwear and massage the ungodly ache.

"Every morsel of food you eat, every breath of air you take is because of me. Because I allow it . . . You live because of me. You live for me. Remember that when you fall asleep with my come inside you."

IT'S A BEAUTIFUL, CLEAR MORNING.

I have a cup of Starbucks in my hand and the roof off my Jeep. I bought it the first week I was here. An obnoxious yellow Wrangler I am absolutely in love with. With the money I saved over the years, some grants, and a very large severance package from Mark, my finances are sitting pretty for the foreseeable future. I don't need much, a one-bedroom apartment, my car, and some groceries keep me living modestly, but happy. The fact that all those things are located in the middle of paradise doesn't hurt, either.

I take a seat in my English class, prepared to ace my last final.

"Morning, good looking." Michael slips into the seat next to me.

"Morning yourself," I reply as I take a sip of my blonde roast.

"Ready to crush this test?" he asks with a cute grin and huge dimples. He's adorable. I met Michael in this very seat at the beginning of the semester. He's in the same boat I am; he started college late, and is immersed in a sea of barely legal adults. Being a twenty-three-year-old freshman can have its downfalls. Like cradle robbing.

Michael wasn't shy; he sat right next to me, struck up a conversation, and we haven't stopped talking since. We started hanging out after class, then on the weekends, and what started out as an innocent friendship snowballed into something more. Something fun and physical and completely carefree. At least for me. I know Michael wants more, but there's just no way I'm ready for that. I'm perfectly happy getting drunk, having sex, and leaving it at that.

"Up for a little surfing after this?" Michael asks with his big brown eyes as the tests are handed out.

I shrug. "The rest of the day looks pretty wide open."

"That's what I like to hear." He grins, picks up his pen, and starts writing.

I WATCH FROM THE BEACH as Michael rides in his last wave of the day. He's quite the hottie—all tan skin, dark hair, and flat stomach. Michael was a military brat and lived all over the world, but he says Hawaii is home. When he was seventeen, his mother relocated to California, but Michael refused to leave. So, family friends took him in until he was able to support himself on his own. We're kindreds like that. He put off school until he had enough money stashed away to work part time and still live comfortably. By the looks of him, his plan is working out just fine.

He runs up the beach with his surfboard under his arm and his body dotted with water droplets. As I watch him approach, I can't stop myself from imagining another face grinning at me from the shoreline—one with crystal-blue eyes, a seductive mouth, and tattoos on his skin. A face that haunts me when I sleep, and is impossible to find when I'm awake.

"Ellie? El? Where'd you go?" Michael asks pulling me out of my daydream. I smile, hiding the embarrassment of being caught.

"Nowhere, I'm right here."

"Sure about that, gorgeous? You looked like you were visiting la-la land."

"The ocean must have put me in a trance."

"The ocean, huh?" he pokes fun.

I smack his stomach. "Okay, maybe it was a totally hot surfer. But he's gone now." I pout.

"You think you're funny?" Michael raises his eyebrows devilishly.

"I think I'm hilarious." I start to giggle nervously.

"Let's see how funny you are after I throw you in." He lunges at me.

"Michael!" I screech as he hauls me over his shoulder and jogs toward the water's edge.

He then tosses me in and wrestles with me under the water. I come up for air, gasping and laughing all at the same time.

"You're a jerk." I splash him.

"And you're hilarious, remember?"

"Yes. And now very wet." I wade back to the shore.

"Is there a better way to be?" he asks salaciously.

I roll my eyes and splash him again. Men.

Once dry, Michael picks up both boards. "I'm going to the North Shore to surf tomorrow," he tells me as we walk to our cars. "Want to come? There's supposed to be a kickass party on the beach, too."

"That sounds like fun," I tell him as he slides my surfboard into the backseat of my Jeep.

"Perfect. I'll pick you up around noon. I have to work in the morning."

"I'll be ready." I smile. I am nowhere near skilled enough to surf North Shore waves, but I like hanging out on the beach and watching everyone else. Especially Michael.

"You know, I can come over later tonight if you want." He steps closer to me and puts his hands on my hips, smelling of salt and sand. "That way I don't have to wait a whole twenty-four hours to see you again."

"Is that such a torturous amount of time?" I flirt.

"For me, yes. You, I wonder sometimes."

"What is that supposed to mean?" I question him.

Michael doesn't answer; instead, he leans in and presses his lips firmly against mine. I kiss him back, but the fire doesn't burn as brightly on my end. I'm trying, I really am, but the past and all these crazy feelings I have are holding me back.

Michael sighs when I pull away, pressing his forehead against mine. "One day, whatever demons are inside of you are going to have to come out. And when they do, I'll be right next to you."

I stare into Michael's big brown eyes. They're so sweet and kind. I almost feel guilty for keeping all my secrets from him. But what would he think if he found out about my past? That I was owned? Or that there's an hysteria of conflicting desires inside me that I can't make heads or tails of? I don't respond because what can I possibly say? I can't make him any promises or give him any guarantees.

"I'll see you tomorrow." I kiss him chastely on the lips.

"I'm counting on it." He spanks me playfully on the ass, and I'm flooded with a million emotions, and way too many memories to even count. My breathing speeds up and my head feels light as I climb into my Jeep. *"You've been such a good kitten; it spared you from ten."* I try to hide everything I'm feeling as I turn on the car, unsure if Michael senses anything is off. I say one last goodbye, and then speed away with the ghost of Kayne's hands stinging my ass.

I drive around until it's dark, just letting my idle thoughts wonder. *"You are so sexy. I can't tear my hands or my lips or my eyes off of you. You're my most prized possession. I meant it when I said I would kill for you, Ellie. I'd do anything for you."*

I pull into my little apartment complex a few hours later, park, and then just sit in the car under the cover of night. I clutch the steering wheel and rest my forehead on my hands. How would I even begin to look for him? Someone who doesn't exist, at least on paper. Maybe I should put an ad on Craigslist. Desperately seeking slave owner.

It's official. I've completely lost my mind.

I think what I really need is a big glass of wine, a bath, and a sleeping pill. Maybe a dozen of them.

As I get out and walk to the front door of my duplex, I resolve to put Kayne Roberts behind me. Right now, this second. My life is good, I'm living out my dreams, and I have an amazingly sweet guy who is trying his damnedest to be everything I need. What more can one person ask for? *"No matter where you go or who you're with. You'll always be mine."*

I walk up the steps to the second floor landing like I'm dragging rocks. I've been bugging the super for weeks to fix the porch light. I hate coming home late and not being able to see my front door.

"You know, Ellie," a male voice says from behind me, and I nearly jump out of my skin. "The first rule of protection is self-awareness. And a young, beautiful girl like yourself, sitting in her open Jeep all alone in the dark, just begs for some sick pervert to pounce." Jett emerges from the shadows, the small light from his phone illuminating his features. I freeze in place for a split second before I tackle him. "Jett!" It's an involuntary reaction.

"I missed you, too, sweet thing." He chuckles, squeezing me hard. I'm overwhelmed with emotion as Jett holds me in his arms. And in Jett fashion, he hugs me for as long as I need.

"Do you make a habit of lurking around dark porches?" I ask shakily, "Or just mine?"

"Depends," he answers flippantly, releasing me. I can't see much of his face, but I can make out the shadow of his smile.

"What are you doing here?" I gain my wits while wiping away the stray happy tear from the corner of my eye.

"Do you want me to tell you while we're standing in the dark, or shall we go inside and talk?"

"Inside." I quickly unlock the door and flick on the lights with Jett right behind me. My apartment isn't anything extravagant, it's nothing like the opulent room Kayne kept me in. My most expensive piece of furniture is a Pottery Barn couch. I figured I was going to be doing a lot of studying in my little living room, so I might as well be comfortable. I haven't regretted my purchase for one minute.

"Do you want something to drink?" I ask nervously. Why am I suddenly nervous?

Jett watches me with entertained eyes as I fidget around my apartment, opening and closing the refrigerator door like I have OCD.

"I'm good, Ellie, but maybe you should have one?" He raises his eyebrows suggestively. I grab a water from the fridge and sit down on the couch. Jett follows, plopping down beside me. "Hmmm." He bounces a few times. "Comfy."

I nearly burst out laughing.

"It's good to see you smile," Jett says.

"It feels good to smile," I tell him. There's a few seconds' pause.

"Why are you here, Jett? Not that I'm not happy to see you, it's just so out of the blue." I'm not complaining, trust me.

"I've come to deliver a message."

"A message?"

"From Kayne." He pulls an envelope out of the back pocket of his jeans and hands it to me.

I take it, inspecting it curiously.

"Open it," he urges.

My hands start to tremble, and my heart starts to pound as I rip it open. *You wanted this,* I remind myself—repeatedly. I pull out the contents of the envelope, and am now thoroughly confused. "A plane ticket?"

"There's something else," Jett informs me. I look inside the envelope again, and pull out the thin piece of paper that was hiding under the ticket. I unfold it to read its contents, and just like before, only one word is scribbled:

CUPCAKE

I can't explain what seeing that word does to me. It unleashes so many sparring emotions, it feels like they're trying to kill me.

"Ellie?" Jett's voice sounds far away. I look up at him not

even realizing I started to cry.

Jett takes my hand. "I know you went through a lot. We all did. But if there is any chance you can forgive him, get on that plane tomorrow."

"Tomorrow?" I study the ticket. Yup, tomorrow's date, to "Bora Bora?"

Jett shrugs.

"How is he?" I ask guardedly.

Jett shoots me a sad smile. "Better, now that he stopped drinking and started showering again."

"Did he really take me leaving that hard?"

"You have no idea, Ellie." His tone is bleak.

"Why didn't he come himself?"

"He didn't want you to feel pressured or uncomfortable. Although, personally, I think he's just afraid of your right hook." Jett winks.

I roll my eyes. "It probably didn't even hurt."

"Ellie, you slapped him so hard, *I* felt it."

"He deserved it." I defend my actions.

"I suppose on some level he did. But what he really deserves now is your forgiveness," Jett implores me. "Not just what he deserves, but what he needs."

I crush the envelope, ticket, and piece of paper to my chest conflicted. This is what I wanted, so why am I having such a hard time coming to terms?

"I can't make any promises I'll be on that plane." It's the truth. It's time to pull the trigger, and I'm hesitating. I'm pretty sure instances like that can get you killed.

Jett just nods. "It's your choice. A car will be here to pick you up at noon. Think about it, Ellie." He puts his hand on my knee and then stands up.

"Are you leaving?" I follow his movements worried.

Jett nods. He looks the same — A shock of blond hair, turquoise eyes, and a quiet air of authority.

"But you just got here."

"I did what I came to do. Now it's time to go."

I frown.

"If you make the right decision, you'll see me again," he says with one finger under my chin.

I look away. I have a lot of thinking to do, and not a whole lot of time to do it. I stand up and reluctantly walk Jett to the door.

He stops just before he leaves, looking at me with those with penetrating eyes. "This is his last attempt, Ellie. If you don't show up, he's disappearing, and this time it will be for good."

I respond silently with a confused expression. He kisses me on the cheek then vanishes into the darkness.

Disappearing for good?

KAYNE

I WAIT IMPATIENTLY IN THE car while Jett and Ellie's silhouettes move slowly around her apartment. I can't stop my leg from shaking or my heart from hammering. As soon as I saw her pull up, I wanted to rip her out of the car and crush her body against mine. I wanted to feel her lips and smell her skin and taste her sweetness. I want what we had back, every single thread of it.

It feels like hours have passed by the time Jett leaves Ellie's apartment. He slips into the driver's seat and turns on the engine without a word. I wait for a report, but he just throws the car into drive and pulls away. I burn a hole through the side of his head as he rolls the window down and plays with the radio.

"Are you fucking serious right now?"

"What?" Jett asks aloofly as his hair flutters in the wind.

"Are you going to tell me what she said, or do I have to beat it out of you?" I ask crazily.

"First of all, you wish you could kick my ass. Secondly, all you had to do was ask me nicely."

"Jett," I growl. "This is not the time for fucking around. Is she coming or not?"

"I don't know," he answers directly, and my heart drops out of my chest.

"She still doesn't want to see me?"

"I don't know that, either."

"Well, what the fuck do you know?" I erupt.

"Jesus, chill out. I know if you keep acting like this you're going to be minus one girl and one friend."

I put my hand over my face and let out a frustrated sigh. I don't think I can survive living one more day without Ellie.

"Please, Jett," I say as calmly as possible. "Tell me what you do know."

"Much better, cocksucker."

I glare at him out of the corner of my eye.

"I think she wants to see you. She still seems conflicted. But she did ask about you."

"What did she ask?" I'm starving for any morsel of information I can get.

"She asked if you were okay. And why didn't you come yourself."

"That's good, right?"

"It's anyone's guess."

"For fuck's sake, you read women like tarot cards, and you can't tell if she wants to see me or not?"

"I think she does. I also think she's scared."

"Of what?"

"Oh, I don't know, maybe you slapping a collar on her and locking her in a dark room?"

"That isn't fucking funny." I can't stop myself from smirking. "I did love her in that collar, though."

"Didn't we all."

Jett pulls up to our destination. I stare idly at the plane. "Let's do this." He slaps me on the arm.

I nod with a knot the size of Texas in my throat. I'm half considering driving back to Ellie's house and throwing her over my shoulder so she has no choice but to come with me, but I don't think that scenario will fly. I don't want her to feel forced or like she's being backed into a corner. I want her to come because she wants to. I want her to see for herself that I'm not the tyrant she believes me to be. Yes, I love dominance and submission, but I also love Ellie in any way I can have her. She controls the playing field, and I'll abide by her rules. Even if that means changing who I am. For her, I would do it. For her, I'd do anything.

"Clock's ticking, Kayne." Jett slams on the hood of his Chevelle.

I take a deep breath and get out of the car, carrying with me the most lethal arsenal on the planet.

Hope.

ELLIE

I LAY AWAKE STARING OUT the window at yet another clear blue Hawaiian morning.

After Jett left last night, I skipped the bath, and went straight for the wine and sleeping pills. They helped me relax, but in no way provided the restful night's sleep I was hoping for. I tossed and turned, dreaming about majestic blue eyes, a firm hand, and clashing feelings. Throwing the covers off, I get out of bed. In the kitchen, I pick up the envelope that has the plane ticket and note stuffed inside. I pull out the white folded piece of paper and stare at the word written in his handwriting: Cupcake. That one single word holds so much power it could be deemed a deadly weapon. *"I'll use it so you know you mean more to me than just sex.*

"Do I?"

"Yes, baby. So much more."

It's amazing how you can get handed exactly what you want and not feel anything like you thought you would. I thought this would make me happy, make me excited, but all it makes me is anxious. I stare at the word for what feels like forever, finally deciding I have to see him. I need to figure out if what I'm feeling is real or just a psychotic episode. And if I'm going to do this, I need to go shopping! A girl can't reconnect with her ex-slave owner wearing the tattered old rags she calls clothes hanging in her closet.

In record time, I change into a denim miniskirt and tank top, throw my hair into a ponytail, and grab my keys off the kitchen counter. I've given myself exactly four hours to shop, shower, and pack, leaving one hour to hyperventilate before the car picks me up.

I DUMP MY HAUL OF sexy little sundresses, underwear, and bikinis onto my bed. Not bad for a few hours' work. I pack in a hurry, leaving out the white tube dress with hot pink embroidery on the hem and the strappy wedge heels I fell in love with at first sight. I shower and blow-dry my hair then attempt to apply some makeup. Where is Jett when I really need him? Luckily, I received a crash course at the MAC counter after one of the makeup artists witnessed me trying to apply eyeliner. After she had rubbed the crooked lines off my eyelids, she informed me that all I really needed was a little eye shadow and a few thick coats of mascara. Then she applied a shimmery brown powder all over my face and stained my lips a bright pink. She said the secret to makeup is using just enough to enhance my natural beauty. I believed her, because when I looked in the mirror, I still felt like myself only sexed up a bit. It really is amazing what a little makeup can do.

I've come pretty damn close to recreating her masterpiece.

I'm barely finished getting ready when there's a knock at my door. My heart freefalls into my stomach. It's time to go. I open the door to a tall, nice looking man dressed in black with a driver's hat on. "Miss Stevens," he addresses me professionally.

"Yes." My voice is small.

"All set to go, ma'am? Can I carry your bags?"

I can't see his eyes behind the dark glasses he's wearing, but his wavy brown hair is tousled at the nape of his neck and his grin is relaxed, mischievous almost.

He seems harmless enough.

"Yes, please." I step aside and allow him to retrieve my one and only suitcase. Steeling my nerves, I lock the door behind me, and follow the driver to the black Town Car parked in the visitor's space outside my building. Just as he places my suitcase in the trunk, a familiar pickup pulls up behind us.

Shit. I completely forgot.

Michael steps out of his truck with a confused expression. Shit. Shit. Shit. Jett's visit completely scrambled my brain.

"Going somewhere?" He eyes the car and the driver, who is suddenly standing uncomfortably close to me.

"Bora Bora," I reply nervously.

"Tahiti?" His eyebrows shoot up.

"Yes."

"Why?"

What do I tell him? I'm going to see the man who abducted me, chained me to a bed for over a month, and used me as a living, breathing sex toy? The man who—though ruthless, intense and merciless at times—somehow penetrated my soul, and may now be irreversibly connected to?

"Exorcise some demons," is my response. It's the God's honest truth.

Michael stares at me with multiple expressions playing across his face, and for the first time since we met, I'm having trouble reading him.

"Ma'am." The driver interrupts our silent exchange.

"I have to go," I say softly.

Michael nods, and then unexpectedly grabs my arm. He yanks me to him, then forcefully crushes his lips against mine. *Whoa.* I barely kiss him back as my emotions wage war. Michael is the one I should want. He's sweet and kind and generous—not to mention gorgeous—but the spark between us pales in comparison to what just thinking about Kayne does to me. It lights my entire world on fire, burning everything around me to ash.

"Stay," he presses. "I know you've been harboring something bad. Stay with me and we can work it out together."

I look at Michael sadly. I should want to stay, but I don't. What I want, deep down, is to see Kayne.

It's an incurable urge.

"I can't." I kiss him on the cheek and free myself from his death grip.

"Ellie," he protests my leaving with some bite.

"Sorry." I slip into the backseat of the sedan with Michael's dark-brown eyes searing into me the whole time. Once the door shuts, I exhale the breath I didn't even realize I was holding.

The ride to the airport was silent and the flight uneventful, minus the hour delay. Kayne didn't spare one expense; I flew first class, pampered with hot towels and bubbly champagne the whole four-hour trip. Some girls might feel guilty that a man is spending ridiculous amounts of money on them. Not me — at least not in this scenario. After everything he put me through, I deserve to be spoiled. And by the looks of it so far, he agrees.

The airport is ultra-bright from the sunlight pouring in through the windows. If living on an island has taught me anything, it's come prepared with dark sunglasses. After I retrieve my suitcase, I follow the crowd outside where I am struck by the most beautiful turquoise-blue water I have ever seen. I then find Jett holding a little sign that says 'Stevens.'

I can't stop the grin from spreading across my face as I approach him. I don't know what it is, but Jett always feels comfortable. Like Southern cooking and fresh-squeezed lemonade. Just standing next to him puts me at ease and assures me everything is going to be okay, even when I doubt all my decisions.

"You look delicious," he whispers in my ear as he hugs me.

"Thank you?" I giggle. He has such an odd way with compliments.

"You're welcome." Jett releases me and picks up my suitcase. "You smell delicious, too. This way," he motions with his head.

Jett leads me up the dock until we get to a small speedboat tied up near the end.

"Your chariot." He hops in first, then grabs my suitcase and motions to the bag on my arm. Once all my items are in the boat, he extends his hands to me. I'm definitely not wearing the right shoes for this; I carefully place my hands in his and hold my breath as I step down. Before I realize it, Jett has one arm hooked around me and is gingerly placing me on my feet. He winks. "Think I would let you break an ankle?"

"I'd hope not."

"Never. Kayne would castrate me for even a scratch."

My stomach flips from just the mere mention of his name. Fuck, I'm really doing this.

"Ellie, are you okay? You just went pale," Jett asks with

concerned eyes.

"I'm fine. Just a little nervous, I guess." I put on my bravest smile.

"Sweet thing, just a word to the wise." Jett places his hands on my shoulders. "This can be as easy or as hard as you make it. When I told you that you held all the power, I wasn't lying. It's still true. The ball is in your court. What you choose to do with it will determine the outcome. Okay?"

"Okay," I reply, although I'm not exactly sure I understand. At the moment, I'm not sure I understand anything; my thoughts and emotions are just a great big jumbled mess. There are so many interconnecting wires, my insides feel like one big knot.

Jett motions for me to sit, unties the ropes, and then starts the engine. The little boat purrs to life, and a few seconds later, we take off. I concentrate on the scenery to distract me from my nerves—the crystal-blue lagoon, the lush greenery of Mount Otemanu, and the rainbow beaming through the clouds over the volcano. I'll never deny Hawaii is magnificent, but Bora Bora's beauty is indescribable. The landscape almost gleams like a fairy tale.

The boat ride is short and silent which, in all honesty, I'm grateful for. I'm not sure how engaging my small talk would be. All my thoughts are gravitating to *him*. My heart is beating and my palms are sweating. I keep asking myself if this is the right thing. Do I still have time to change my mind? What would happen if I did? I know the answer to that question. The nagging regret would eventually eat me alive. I have to see him. I have to know. *Was it real?* And if it was, do we just start over? I can get past the whips and chains and fuckings, but the lying? The deceiving? Even if it was for the right reason, I still question his sincerity. Not to mention my sanity.

Jett cuts the engine, and I snap out of my wandering thoughts. We've arrived at a resort. A very posh, exclusive resort from the looks of it.

"Showtime," Jett says as he lifts me out of the boat and onto dry land. There's a tall man standing in front of the lobby doors watching us intently. It sort of makes me uncomfortable. I move a little closer to Jett once he's grabbed my luggage and secured the boat. The man then approaches us with a kind smile.

"Monsieur." He addresses Jett with a pleasant French accent.

"Matias." He and Jett shake hands then Matias immediately turns his attention to me. "Mademoiselle." He kisses my hand. I think I actually blush.

"Ellie, Matias," Jett formally introduces us. "He'll escort you from here."

"Oui." Matias grabs my suitcase dutifully. "Monsieur Andrews is quite anxious for your arrival."

"Andrews?" I repeat as Matias places my bag in the backseat of a golf cart parked off to the side.

"Alias," Jett leans in discreetly and whispers in my ear. "Just go with it."

I nod silently, fortifying my nerves. He needs an alias?

"Kayne will explain. Now go."

I frown. "Why aren't you taking me?"

Jett flashes me a smile. "This is my stop, sweet thing."

I eye Matias standing next to the golf cart waiting expectantly.

"You're in good hands. And you'll be in even better ones once you see Kayne. Now go." He slaps me on the ass.

"Jett!" I scold him. He just winks at me. "If you need me, I'm in bungalow forty-six. Scoot."

"Fine," I huff, rubbing my backside. I'm going! Holy shit! I walk to Matias, and he helps me into the cart. He hops in next to me and turns on the engine. A moment later, a soft breeze is flipping my light-brown hair as we drive down a little pathway, away from the lobby and toward the beach.

"Your first time in Tahiti?" Matias asks casually with one hand draped over the steering wheel.

"Yes," I answer as we pull onto a boarded pathway stretching out over the aquamarine water. Oversized tiki huts are situated on both sides of us, each with straw-covered roofs and unobstructed views.

"And what do you think so far?"

"Well, considering I've only seen the airport and lagoon, I'd say it's amazing."

Matias laughs lightly. I'm glad someone is relaxed. Every overwater bungalow we pass jacks my unease up another level. I'm going to be a string ready to snap by the time we reach our destination.

We travel as far as we can on the boardwalk path until we reach the very end. Three very large two-story bungalows hug the round boardwalk.

Matias parks in front of the one in the middle.

"Arrived." He smiles brightly and my heart actually stops beating. I'm nervous, excited, anxious, and terrified. I feel like I'm strapped into a rollercoaster fearfully awaiting the ride.

And that's exactly what Kayne is, the Kingda Ka—a man who can launch your body and mind one hundred, twenty-eight miles per hour in three point five seconds.

Once Matias helps me out of the cart, I nervously smooth my dress and fidget with my hair. He rolls my suitcase behind him, and opens the front door; that's when I freefall from four hundred, fifty feet in the air. Matias stands at the entrance of the villa naive to my hesitation. He has no idea; no idea what I've been through, or what the person inside subjected me to.

"Miss?" He raises his eyebrows concerned.

I smile weakly and command my feet to move, one foot in front of the other until I cross the threshold. My basic motor functions cease to exist as the man who has haunted my dreams and consumed my thoughts stands across the room looking like the demonic perfection I remember him to be. The two of us just stare, the tension so thick it feels like we're trapped in the middle of an Amazon rainforest, and need a machete to hack through the brush. Matias emerges from a room to my left, minus my bags. I didn't even notice him disappear; I'm so engrossed by the human being standing in front of me.

Matias stands between us, glancing from me to Kayne and then back again. He has to feel it, the unstable energy smothering the elegantly decorated room.

"Let me show you around," Matias says. Following him in a haze, he shows me the living area with a couch, television, wet bar, and small working desk. The bedroom he placed my things in and the sundeck with private pool. Upstairs is the 'well-being room' with twin massage tables, balcony, and sauna. This freaking place is bigger than my apartment and my parents' combined. Matias chatters nonstop as we make our way back downstairs.

" . . . And as Mr. Andrews knows, I am here for whatever you need, whenever you need it." He smiles, the skin wrinkling around his kind eyes.

"Thank you."

"*Monsieur?* Will there be anything else?" He turns to Kayne, who hasn't moved from his spot.

"No, that will be all," he answers, and his voice feels like an oversized tuning fork vibrating against my body.

"Ring me when you are ready to leave for dinner," Matias responds in a hurry.

Kayne nods, never taking his eyes off me — those majestic blue eyes with the brown lightning bolt that have the ability to cut me right in half. Once Matias is gone, it's just me, Kayne, and a whole shitload of awkward silence.

"How was your flight?" Kayne finally asks, breaking the ice.

"Fine," I answer flatly.

"The boat ride?"

"Fine."

"What do you think of the island?"

"It's fine."

"Is there anything that isn't fine?"

"No."

Kayne smirks, and I wonder what the fuck is so amusing.

Awkward silence regains control of the room.

"Ellie, I—" Kayne takes a few steps forward, and I take a few steps back. He freezes with a frown.

"I've arranged dinner for us," he informs me, and then continues to approach me.

I nod, persistently backing up as he stalks across the room. I bump into a wall, and can only watch with wide eyes as he closes the distance between us. He crowds me, coming so close that I can feel the heat of his body and inhale the fresh scent of his cologne. He can still make me weak, even after all this time. *After everything.*

Kayne lifts his hand to my face and skims his thumb across my cheek. I stand paralyzed, caught by his touch and the hypnotic look in his eyes.

"I'm glad you're here, Ellie." He leans in, inching closer and closer to my mouth. My heartbeat speeds up, and my brain function slows down as he brushes his lips against mine. Then he does it again, this time adding more pressure and swiping his tongue between my lips. I nearly fall apart. The third time, he full-blown kisses me with no hesitation or second thought. He takes full possession of my mouth, trapping my face in his hands, and pinning my body flat against the wall. I kiss him back with even more force than I knew I was capable of. Our tongues twist together as we both fight for air. The longer we kiss, the more aware I become of heightening sensations and overflowing feelings. I start to spin out of control, trying frantically to untangle the strings of my emotions.

"Kayne—" I pull away.

"Ellie." He returns with so much need it nearly cripples me. I have to think, and that's not going to happen while he detains me with his oppressive presence.

"Please stop." I grab onto his linen shirt for dear life.

He takes a deep breath, fighting the urge I know we're both feeling. But I'm not just going to fall into his bed, or get tangled up in his seductive web. There are issues that need to be worked out, and questions that need to be answered.

"I'd like to freshen up." I try to move away from him, but he cages me in by planting both hands on the wall.

"I have missed you every single second of every single day that we have been apart."

And it's quite clear his words are true. His sharp stare and rock hard erection digging into my stomach convey as much.

"Kayne, please." Cocksucker has me begging already.

He hesitates for a beat then pushes off the wall, giving me the room I so desperately need.

"Whatever you want, Ellie." His words send both a chill and a tingle down my spine. They're as menacing as they are promising.

Kayne watches me with a guarded expression as I escape into the bedroom and slam the door behind me.

Once inside, I sink to the floor, breathing for the very first time since I stepped foot on this island.

KAYNE

THE DOOR SLAMS, AND I think I actually jump.

My dick is hard, my heart is hammering, and lips are tingling. That kiss was nothing but a fucking cock tease. Ellie and her monosyllables. I forgot how much I missed them—although, I'll admit, I much prefer them when we're having sex. I couldn't control myself with her standing there all sexy and doe-eyed and completely irresistible. I wasn't lying when I said I missed her every single second of every single day. It's been excruciating living without her. And now that she's here, under the same roof, she still feels just as unattainable as when we were apart. For now.

I hope.

Pray?

Okay, beg.

I rest my forehead against her door, silently pleading for her to come out. I contemplate going in, but I'll give her space. I know that's what she needs. Jett has been preaching it to me for almost a year. That's why I didn't pursue her sooner, even though I wanted to.

Every single second of every single day.

I sent the cupcakes to test the water, to see where her head was. Which, to my great disappointment, was nowhere near forgiving me, since she trashed them a nanosecond after she opened the box. How do I know that? I'm a black operative — spying is what I do. And I've been spying on Ellie since the day she left me. I know everything there is to know about her, right down to her little boy toy.

I pace the bungalow so many times I think I wear through the hardwood floor. I have a drink, and then another. I take a piss, and then wait some more. I'm about to go mad, so I finally say fuck it and knock on her door.

"Ellie?"

No answer.

"Ellie?" I jiggle the door handle.

"I'll be out in a sec," she yells. I wonder how long that is in girl time. I decide to call Matias and arrange for our ride. Here's hoping, right?

After I hang up with the butler, Ellie finally emerges. She's changed. No longer wearing the white little dress she arrived in. She's transformed into a dark angel. Her light-brown hair is pulled back into a low ponytail and her eye makeup is heavy, but it's her dress that makes my jaw drop. It's a loose fitting, shiny material that drapes over her body. It almost reminds me of a piece of lingerie, something Jett would dress her in just to entice me. The black strings curving over her shoulders so thin I could floss my freakin' teeth with them. I think she's trying to kill me.

"You look . . . amazing." Yes, I sound just like a love-struck fool because that's exactly what I am; a man stupidly in love with a sultry little kitten who holds his beating heart in the palm of her hand.

"Thank you." She fidgets slightly.

There's a knock at the door a moment later.

"Our ride is here." I smile as genuinely as possible. Ellie exits first, brushing against me in the doorway. Her sweet smell is heady, and her contact makes me horny. Holy hell. This may just be the most trying night of my life. As Matias assists Ellie into the golf cart, I catch the hem of her dress riding up so far it makes my cock kick.

Damn.

I climb in next to her, and my big body crowds her small

frame in the backseat. Our legs touch and shoulders bump. Ellie folds her arms over her chest and crosses her legs, withdrawing into herself. Typical body language for someone who is clearly uncomfortable. I hate that I make her feel that way. I hate that she recoils and is anxious around me. But I'm not exactly sure how to fix it. Fix us. I'm sure if I were Jett, I would think of something clever to say, get her talking, have her laughing and be completely open by the time we sat down to dinner. But here is where I lack finesse. I know how to speak with my body, but words are more difficult.

"Where are we going anyway?" she asks as we pass bungalow after bungalow.

"I set up a private dinner. So we can talk."

Ironic, I know.

"Private?" The word dances warily on her tongue.

"Yes."

"Will there be a seat for me at this dinner or will I be dining between your knees?" she asks caustically.

I can't stop my lip from twitching with amusement. God, I didn't realize how much I loved her fire until it was taken away from me. I glance at Matias. He is happily driving through the resort, not giving away if he heard Ellie's statement or not. If he did, he is smart not to acknowledge it. In response, I dip my head, bringing my mouth as close to her ear as possible. Ellie stiffens as I inhale her scent. "Tonight, you have a chair, but I'll never object to you dining between my knees."

I may be a desperate man, but I am still me, and the image of Ellie naked, kneeling, and taking food from my hand is enough to send me right into sexual orbit.

She glares at me with my face an inch away from hers. "Keep dreaming," she spits. "I'll never kneel for you again." There's so much fight in in her voice, but there's also doubt, too. People often rebel against the things that make them vulnerable, while at the same time tempting them like sin. Maybe Ellie will never kneel for me again, and that's okay. I've made peace with that fact. Changing my ways is a sacrifice I'm willing to make. A year apart has altered so many things; it's given me perspective and time to think. I have never wanted a woman the way I want Ellie. Never wanted to pursue a relationship or take that scary step of caring for another human being. I had no example to learn from so what good would I have been at it? That's what I thought my whole life until I met Ellie—until I was forced to care, to protect, to feel. And I don't want to give that up because I as much as I believed I could live without love, in a second flat she proved me wrong. The moment she was put in danger, the moment there was a chance I could lose her forever. That single moment I knew I could be more. Give more. To her.

We pull up to a secluded part of the resort with a sandy pathway leading to the beach.

"When you said dinner, I was expecting a restaurant," she says as she slips out of the golf cart. She stops short just before we step onto the sand.

"Ellie?"

"One sec." She puts her hand on my arm then pulls off the black stiletto heels from her feet. The ones that are as deadly as they are sexy.

My mind explodes with images of what I could do to her while wearing those shoes.

Behave.

We walk toward the water, around some palm trees, and through some light brush until we come to a clearing. There, tucked away, is our own private table lit with white candles, and pink paper lanterns dangling overhead. I can't take credit for the romantic setting, that's all Jett. I just told him to create something Ellie would love. I watch her out of the corner of my eye as we slowly approach the table. Her arms are still wrapped defensively around her upper body, the hem of her dress is rippling slightly in the wind.

"This is very nice," she says once we're standing next to the table, and for the life of me I can't figure out what her melancholy tone is about.

"Shall we?" I pull out her chair, and Ellie sits. Then I take my seat adjacent to hers. The table is dressed with a white tablecloth, porcelain plates, and shiny silverware. The centerpiece is three multitiered cylinder vases with submerged orchids and candles floating on top. There are more orchids situated on the mirrored base, and even some wrapped around our napkins, like holders. Ellie fiddles with hers, inspecting the delicate white flower that is just as beautiful as she is.

"Wine, mademoiselle?" Matias appears with two bottles in his hands, pulling Ellie out of her wandering thoughts.

"Oh, yes. Red, please." She smiles. He pours her glass and then turns to me.

"The same." Before Matias is even done pouring my glass, Ellie has guzzled down half of her own.

"Easy there, killer. This night is going to be over for you before it even begins if you keep up that pace."

"Are you always going to be in the business of telling me what to do?"

I put my hands up in surrender. "I wasn't trying to tell you what to do. I was merely making an observation. If you want to get shitfaced, by all means do so. I'll hold your hair back while you puke."

"Would you?" she asks sharply.

"Of course, I would. If you needed me, I'd be there."

She breathes heavily as she stares at me like she's trying to stab me to death with just her pupils. Did I say something wrong?

I wait for her to speak, but it seems she has nothing to say. That unnerves me. "Ellie, what are you thinking?" I ask delicately. It feels like I'm suddenly walking over a field of landmines.

"I'm wondering why you brought me here."

"To dinner? We're both humans. We need to eat."

"That's not what I meant. Why did you beckon me to Tahiti?"

"You said you wanted to see paradise," I answer honestly.

"I live in Hawaii," she responds flatly, placing her wine down and crossing her arms.

"Neutral ground?" I try again.

Ellie shakes her head sternly, completely unconvinced.

I huff. "Fine." She wants to do this, then we'll do this. "I brought you here to reclaim what's mine," I tell her straight out.

Her jaw drops. "You still think I'm yours?"

"Not think," I correct her. "Know."

Ellie looks at me beyond irritated. Her mossy-green eyes flashing with disbelief.

"I was never yours."

"Now, we both know that's not true." I take a sip of the Pinot noir arrogantly.

Ellie's irritated expression morphs into anger.

"What do you want from me?"

I laugh, more to myself than at her. "What do I want?" I muse. "Probably too much."

"And what exactly is too much?"

"What did I want before?"

Ellie frowns. "My obedience, my submission, and my body."

"And your love," I stipulate. "What I want most is your love. But what I want is irrelevant. It's what you're willing to give me that's important."

"Why should I give you anything?" The question sounds more sad and hurtful than anything else.

I shrug. "Maybe you shouldn't. But I'm holding out hope that one day you might consider forgiving me and let what was happening between us continue into something more."

"More?" she says exasperated. This conversation is going beautifully. Exactly where I hoped. Right down the fucking toilet.

"Yes, more," I continue.

"And what exactly would be more?"

"I already told you. Love." I add ardently.

"You use that word quite freely."

"It's because I know what I feel. And even though I'm terrified of it, I'm not going to run from it."

"You have no idea what fear is," she replies bitterly.

"Of course, I do. I've lived in fear my whole life, and I've caused it. I know *exactly* what fear is."

"No wonder you were so good at dishing it out."

"Do what you know," I respond sharply, echoing a conversation we once had forever ago.

I can actually feel the rage radiating off Ellie. I don't mean to be so petulant, but when I feel threatened, my defenses go up, especially when it comes to a woman; and Ellie is definitely gunning for me tonight.

I have to keep reminding myself that she's different from all the rest, that her anger is warranted, but I'm afraid it will consume her. Consume us.

"Ellie, I don't want to fight. I want to talk."

"About love?" she fumes. It's like that word is acid to her.

"That can be the first topic of conversation, and once we get that squared away, we can move on to a more titillating subject." I smile impishly, attempting to cut away from the disastrous turn our talk has taken.

"And what subject would that be?"

"Your body." I gulp down another mouthful of wine as Ellie shakes her head incredulously. I'm sure there are a boatload of other topics I could have picked, but I panicked.

"My body?" she repeats, gazing at me shrewdly.

"Mmm hmm."

"And what exactly would you do to my body if you had it?"

"So many wonderful things." I lick my bottom lip.

"Oh really?" She stands seductively and takes a sip of wine like she's trying to entice me. Which, she is.

"Would you pleasure it?" she asks holding the glass to her chest.

"Yes," I answer looking up at her with only my eyes.

"How?" She places the wineglass down on the table and inches toward me.

"However you would let me."

"Would you lick me?" She crosses her ankles all sultry like. I know what she's doing; I'm not an idiot. I know when I'm being goaded. But at the moment, I just don't care.

"Yes." I drink her in—every sexy, dangerous inch of her.

"Suck me?"

"Yes." I sweep my eyes over her five-foot-four frame.

"Finger me?"

"Yes."

"Fuck me?" she taunts, coming closer until our bodies are touching.

"Hell, yes." I look up, breathing heavy. "There isn't anything I want more."

"Would you spank me?" Her voice suddenly turns hard. "Would you spank me until I cried? Beat me while I begged you to stop? Chain me to the bed and use me as you saw fit all while you lied to me? Make me think I actually mean something when all I really am is a plaything?" she lashes out.

I freeze. Hold up. She may be pissed, but I'm not going to let her believe things that just aren't true.

"You were never just a plaything," I growl, standing up so I tower over her. "You don't put your life on the line for a *plaything*. You don't risk six years of work, an entire household full of people, and your own fucking heart for a *plaything*. You may be angry with me, Ellie, but I did what I did for a reason, and I would do it again without blinking an eye. Not only because I loved dominating you, but because you are here, standing in front of me, alive and mentally sound."

Something sparks in her eyes. Hatred maybe?

"Says you!" She picks up a glass of wine and throws it in my face, staining the front of my white shirt red. Then she runs off.

"Ellie!" Goddamn it, I wipe my face with my hand. This is definitely not how I saw dinner going. I start to go after her, determined to toss her over my shoulder and spank some sense into her, but Jett's words ring in my ears, stopping me from moving. *She needs space.*

Ughhhh! I punch the table, rattling the entire thing.

Can I just tell you how fucking over space I am.

ELLIE

I RUN BAREFOOT THROUGH THE resort with my emotions in a stir.

"You don't put your life on the line for a plaything. You don't risk six years of work, a house full of people, and your own heart for a plaything." His words echo resoundingly.

Before I know it, I'm standing in front of bungalow number forty-six, knocking—more like pounding—on the door. *Jett, please be here.* I urgently wipe away the tears from under my eyes, black streaks staining my fingers from my watery mascara.

"Hang on!" I hear him shout from behind the door. Thank God! A moment later, it swings open to a half-naked Jett. I nearly choke on my tears. "Ellie?" He looks at me with a perplexed expression. It's half-confused, half-concerned.

Holy shit. I can't respond because my jaw has unhinged from my face. Jett is ripped, like completely shredded.

"Ellie?" he repeats again, but I can't draw my eyes away from his body, his glinting nipple ring, or the brightly colored tattoos running over his collarbone and down his chest like a wave crashing over the shoreline. All the time Jett and I spent together, I never so much as saw him without a shirt, and now I sort of feel shortchanged. He saw me naked every day and deprived me of the view in return.

"See something you like, sweet thing?" Jett asks flirtatiously, grabbing onto the doorframe above his head. The cuts of his muscles rippling, becoming more defined.

Um, hell yes.

"Ahhhh . . ." I finally look up into his eyes and they are dancing with humor, and possibly something else. Something hot and completely forbidden.

"What are you doing here, Ellie? Shouldn't you be trying to reconcile with Kayne?" he asks suggestively. Oh, how little does he know. Kayne and I are nowhere near reconciling. Like not even a little.

"We got into a fight." I bite my lip.

"A fight?"

"I threw wine in his face."

Jett frowns. "I see."

"I'm so confused."

"About what?" he asks concerned.

"Everything," I answer exasperated.

"Oh boy." Jett releases the doorframe and steps outside. "Let's talk."

I nod.

Jett and I sit on the side of the wooden walkway, our feet dangling over the edge. I fiddle with my fingers silently not knowing where to start.

"Ellie." Jett takes one of my hands in his, and I tighten my grip. I feel grounded when I'm with him. "Tell me what's going on."

I heave a sigh, looking over at him. You know it's really not fair to the rest of the men in this world. Jett is too pretty and nice and intuitive for his own good. He has me gawking like a fool at his cut muscles and light eyes accentuated in the moonlight.

"What's going on?" I repeat. "Great question."

I gnaw on my lip, hard, nearly drawing blood as I try to figure out where to start.

"Um?" I struggle, trying to pinpoint exactly where everything went wrong. Probably when I got on the plane.

"Okay," Jett senses my dilemma, "let's start at the very beginning. How did you feel when you saw him again?"

"Confused."

"Confused how?"

"I didn't know how to act," I admit ridiculously. "I wasn't sure if I should kneel at his feet or spit in his face. I don't know who to be around him."

"Ellie," Jett's voice pitches. "You don't need to be anyone but yourself. That's who Kayne wants."

"Myself?" I scoff. "I barely know who that is. I'm nothing but a twenty-three-year-old college freshman trying to figure out her life. That's who he wants?"

"Sweet thing," Jett squeezes my hand, "I'll let you in on a little secret, we are all just twenty-three-year-old college freshman trying to figure out our lives. Kayne especially."

I give him a skeptical look.

"I wouldn't lie to you, Ellie. Kayne is in the same place you are. He's just as confused, and borderline desperate."

"Desperate?"

"Mmm hmm. Desperate to get you back."

"What if I can't . . ."

"Forgive him?"

"Trust him."

Jett studies me like a science experiment, those turquoise-blue eyes poking me like probes.

"Trust him not to lie to you?"

I look up at the stars and take a deep breath. "In a way. I'm afraid he's always going to see me as an object. I'm afraid his feelings aren't real, and I'm afraid if I open myself up I'm just going to get hurt again."

Jett puts his arm around my shoulders comforting me. "I get it, Ellie. I do. You and Kayne have a very sordid past. Your fears are justified, but I can tell you with absolute certainty that Kayne's feelings are real." He lifts my chin so I'm looking at him in the eyes. I'm convinced they are the most genuine eyes on the planet. "Let me tell you something about Kayne. Trusting women is a hard limit for him."

I sit up straight, surprised. "Why?"

"It stems from his upbringing. I'll let him give you the gory details. You should hear it from him anyway. It's his story to tell. But I can say confidently, with you, he's shattering all his insecurities. And it's making him vulnerable."

"Vulnerable?" I question skeptically. Are we talking about the same alpha male who stripped me naked, forced me to submit, and controlled my entire existence without one bat of an eyelash?

"Yes," Jett confirms, "and that's a very dangerous place for Kayne."

"Why?"

"Because it makes him lose control."

"Control of what?"

"His life."

"Oh." I frown.

"Ellie, let me paint you a picture to try and help you understand.

Imagine what it would be like to live your entire life in the dark, and then one day suddenly experience the sun. To feel its warmth and bask in its light, to feed off it and become dependent on it. And then in a flash have it ripped away leaving you in the cold dark place you once were.

"Kayne lived in the dark. And then you came. You were his sun, and his light, and his warmth. The moment you left, he was thrust back into the darkness. An abysmal place where he drowns in the demons of his past. He needs the light now more than ever. He needs you. Don't doubt the sincerity of his feelings. They're more real than you and me, and the air that we breathe. Trust me, I would never lie to you about something as delicate as Kayne's feelings.

"He'll never intentionally hurt you. Of that, I'm sure. The man is more loyal than a dog. But I'll be honest, Kayne is intense and sometimes hard to handle, especially when his emotions get involved. That's why he was so over the top when it came to you, in all aspects," he insinuates, and I nod, understanding. "He wanted you to feel what he was feeling. And it was the only way he knew how to show it."

My cheeks suddenly heat. The man does know what he's doing between the sheets. I can still feel every orgasm like they were branded between my legs.

"Ellie?" Jett wiggles my hand.

"Hmmm?"

"Where did you go?"

I feel my cheeks burn brighter.

Jett eyes me knowingly. "Oh, I know. Taking a little trip down memory lane?"

"There is nothing little about it," I smile.

Jett rolls his eyes playfully. "Incorrigible."

"Definitely," I confirm with a shameless smile, and we both laugh.

"It's good to see you smile."

"It feels good to smile." I sigh, relaxed for the first time since I stepped foot on this island.

"How about you go give Kayne one of those smiles, and put him out of his misery."

"Maybe I should let him suffer just a little while longer," I joke.

"Ellie, Kayne has been suffering his whole life. He needs some peace, and you're it."

"You really know how to work a girl over." I elbow him.

"And proud of it." Jett kisses me on the cheek then hauls me to my feet. "Where do you think Kayne learned it from? I taught him everything he knows," Jett whispers in my ear, sending chills down my spine.

"Everything?" I question.

Jett nods sternly. His aqua eyes so bright they're crackling like live wires.

Holy shit. I'm suddenly overheating from just the mere thought of what Kayne and Jett are capable of.

"Now, go get your man." Jett smacks me on the ass. "I know he's waiting for you. Probably has a search party out right now."

"Jett, you're so dramatic."

He shoots me a deadpan look.

"Oh, no."

"Oh, yes."

Oh, shit. My nerves re-emerge with a vengeance.

"Think he'll forgive me for throwing wine in his face?" It's a rhetorical question.

"Probably, but you can always make it up to him."

"How?"

"Do you remember the conversation we had when I told you I know what all men like? And you so colorfully answered a blowjob?"

"Yes."

He pops his eyebrows at me.

"Ugh, guys are such cavemen."

"Perhaps, but it works every time," he smiles widely, "do you want me to walk you back to your bungalow?"

"No, I think I can manage," I smirk.

"Okay. Good. Now, if we're finished, I have to go club a beautiful redhead and drag her to bed."

I roll my eyes.

Cavemen. Definitely cavemen.

KAYNE

I AM WALLOWING IN MY misery. Yes, wallowing, because I see now Ellie will never be able to forgive me. I took it too far and ruined any small chance I had with her.

I won't beg her to stay when she walks into this room and demands to go home. I won't crack or crumble until she's gone. I did this. And I'll face the consequences. My heart sinks a little further. Tomorrow, I'll disappear. Go so deep undercover that I'll forget this life, and any other life ever existed, and hopefully one day forget Ellie exists, too. Because the memory of her will slowly destroy me. Like it is now. She'll never understand the effect of those few precious weeks. How she changed me. How I loved her. *Love* her.

I hear the front door creak open, and my insides petrify. I can't allow myself to feel anything or I'll never survive her leaving again. I'm on the brink of a meltdown already.

"Hi," she says unsurely as she stands in the darkness on the edge of the room.

"Hi," I respond desolately.

The silence stretches for a long time before Ellie takes a deep breath and crosses the living room to where I'm sitting on the couch, the moonlight spilling through the windows highlighting her slim body and bare feet.

"Can I sit?" she asks, fiddling with her fingers nervously.

I gaze up at her with just my eyes, hoping she sees a steely look instead of a dying man.

"Of course."

Ellie climbs onto the couch, tucking her legs underneath her, sitting much closer than I expect.

"Kayne, I'm sorry."

"For what?" I ask floored. The last thing I expected from Ellie was an apology.

"For getting upset and throwing wine at you. I think I was harboring some residual anger."

I actually laugh. "Ellie, you have nothing to be sorry for. I deserved it. That, and so much more. I just wish . . ." I swallow the emotion that's trying to choke me. " . . . I just wish you could find a way to forgive me."

"Forgive you? I forgave you a long time ago. Trust is the problem. I trusted you." Her voice strains and my heart twists. "After everything you put me through, I still trusted you, and then you betrayed me. I didn't know what to believe anymore. First, you were one person, then you were another, and then you were someone entirely different. I felt so used. So humiliated. So stupid." Angry tears start to well in her eyes. It's clear she had already been crying from her smudged mascara, and here she is about to do it again. I wonder if I'll ever be able to make her smile as much as I've made her cry.

"Ellie, I'm sorry." I try to reach for her, but she pushes me away.

"Please let me finish. You were right when you said I liked being yours." It sounds like that was very hard to admit. "And after you pulled the rug out from under me, I hated myself for it. I hated you. I was ready to give up everything for you. I was content," she says tormented.

I have no idea how to respond to that, so I just apologize again. "I'm sorry."

"Don't be sorry," she snaps frustrated. "Just tell me why. Why did you feel the need to take it to such an extreme?"

"Why did I need to take it to such an extreme?" I repeat her question, running through the thousands of answers I had come up with over the last year because I knew this conversation was inevitable. "Part necessity, part appearance, part selfish desire," I answer truthfully. Because right now, the truth is all I have to give.

Ellie looks at me confounded.

"I didn't know you'd become so important in such a short amount of time." Now I'm the one who sounds tormented.

"What?" She shakes her head not understanding.

"Those few hours sitting together on the couch during Mark's party." I start to recount. "Talking, laughing, flirting. I didn't want the night to end, and I never wanted to let you go. But my life was so complicated, I wasn't sure how much I could give. Then Javier showed up and everything spun out of control. I knew what he was capable of, I'd seen it firsthand."

I tighten my fists from the traumatic memories.

"Women, so many women . . ." I get a headache just thinking about it. "Crawling around the floor like animals. Stuffed into cages so small they were hunched in a ball, all of them starved and abused."

"What? Why?" Ellie asks horrified.

"Money. Some of them were for his personal use. Most were to be sold off as sex slaves." Ellie turns pale. The light may be dim in the room, but the color of her skin unmistakable. "But that's not the worst part," I continue, on a mission to make her understand. "I visited his home once. Three months before he came to the States. While I was there, he made a habit of abusing one of them nightly. Screams . . . all night I heard them scream, like he wanted to make a point. He wanted me to know exactly who I was dealing with, and unfortunately, he made an impression. I'll never deny it. The sounds still haunt me.

"But the last night was the worst. God, what he put that poor girl through." I still get sick thinking about it. "She screamed for hours until I finally couldn't take it anymore. If there was ever a time I was going to chuck it all, it was that moment. But just as I was about to leave my room and go on a murderous rampage slash suicide mission, it all stopped. A little while later, I heard digging in the backyard. That's when I saw her, lying dead on the ground, mutilated beyond recognition. Her bloody and contorted body looked like a prop in a horror movie. She almost didn't even seem real. I watched sickly while one of his thugs dug her shallow grave."

Ellie turns from white to green. That's the right reaction; I nearly puked just retelling the story myself.

"That night I vowed that girl's death wouldn't be in vain. Her blood will always be on my hands because I did nothing to stop him. I will have to live with that until the day I die. It's also why I was so hell-bent on not blowing my cover. Why I went to such an extreme. There was so much riding on that operation, so many lives at stake. Including yours.

"When Javier said he wanted you, all I could see was your face next to that grave. He had to believe that you were mine. He had to believe that I was taking a page from his book. It was the only way to keep him away."

"He didn't stay away." Angry tears fall.

"I know." I cup her cheek in my hand. "And I'm sorry. I did my best to protect you. But he got what he deserved. He's dead. And I swear to God, Ellie, I would have killed him right there in front of you that night if it were under any other circumstances. *I swear.* Everything would have been different." I wipe away the wetness on her face. "I didn't know how serious he was when he said he wanted you. If I made you disappear, it might have looked suspicious, and possibly blown my cover. If I did nothing, I ran the risk of Javier pursuing you. The only thing I was truly sure of is that somehow you'd become more important to me than my own life. I'd fallen in love with you and didn't even know it. Or maybe I did and just didn't know how to recognize it. Either way, I made a split-second decision and claimed you before he could."

She clutches my wrist as she listens to me speak, like it's anchoring her to the ground. I know it's anchoring me.

"I just wanted to do what I thought was right for everyone. It may have been deceitful, and felt like I misled you, but it delivered the outcome I was hoping for. So, please tell me, Ellie, now that you know everything, which is the bigger betrayal? Handing you over to the monster so you could die, or becoming the monster so you could live?"

Not a peep leaves Ellie's mouth, not even a flow of air.

"What happened to the other girls? Did you save them?" She finally blinks, causing more tears to fall.

"Yes. Seventeen of them. And Javier's house was burned to the ground."

"Good." She wipes her eyes roughly with the tips of her fingers. When she's finished, I take her hand and lick up every last drop of her tears. She watches me thoughtfully, as if being reminded of a memory. They taste the same now as they did then, salty and sad.

"Did you like doing all those things to me?" She sniffs. "Hurting me? Making me cry?"

I pause, breathing heavily. "That's a complicated answer."

"Why?" She looks at me so intensely, like she wants to pick me apart.

"Because . . . I did." I lower her hand and tangle her fingers with mine. "But I wish we did those things under different circumstances."

"What kind of different circumstances?" She's enthralled now.

"Ellie, the only women I have ever been with have been submissive. They expected certain treatment, and I expected certain behavior. Spanking, whipping, and punishment is what we were both accustomed to. You, as far as I was aware, knew nothing of the sort so I had to teach you. If you were going to truly be my slave, you needed to act a certain way, portray a certain persona. And you did. You surprised everyone, especially me. You endured everything I threw at you, facing it head on. I never forced a woman before. To be honest, I didn't even know if I had it in me. But being with you was like a drug, I couldn't stop myself from pushing you, wanting to find out just how far I could go. How far you would go."

"You pushed me pretty far." She admits.

"You pushed me pretty far, too."

"I did?"

"Yes. You're the strongest person I've ever met."

"And you would want that with me again? To be submissive?" Her tone tells me she doesn't like that idea, but the question opens all kinds of promise.

"I told you that I'll take whatever you're willing to give me. I've made peace with giving up that lifestyle. You're what's important."

"What happened to kink being king in your world?"

"That world doesn't exist anymore."

"You expect me to believe you're okay with walking away from everything you know just so we can be together?"

I nod, confidently.

I can see the indecisiveness in her smoky-green eyes. The ones I've gotten lost in so many times. "I've never had love in my life, Ellie. Never thought I wanted it or needed it, or even deserved it. Then I met you, and everything changed. I don't know how or why, I just knew you were different.

"I know I can't force you to love me. I just thought if I could make you see *me*, see that I'm not the monster you think I am, maybe there could still be a chance." I pull her closer so her body is pressed up against mine. She feels so good and so perfect, I pray to God I'm saying the right things to convince her to say. "I want you in my life," I plead with her. "You just need to be brave enough to want me back."

She takes a long deep breath, clearly battling with the demons inside her.

"I don't want to go," she expels softly. "But it's going to be hard to trust you again."

Hope swells inside of me. "We'll take it slow. We have this place for two weeks. We can spend it getting to know each other. No pressure."

Ellie just flicks the collar of my shirt thoughtfully, not agreeing to anything. That tiny bit of hope rising inside me suddenly becomes a violent cyclone of water escaping down a drain.

"I ruined your shirt," she says.

"I don't give two shits about my shirt." I grab her, straddling her legs over my lap, serious now. "You can get mad, scream, hit me, beat me, torture me if you want. I'll endure it all if it means you'll stay." I hold onto her hips tightly, vulnerability seeping out of every pore in my body. "I don't think I can survive another day without you in my life."

She stares deeply into my eyes with her hands resting on my chest, so wrackingly quiet.

"Please," I beg. Yes, me. I beg.

"Okay." Her response is so soft I barely hear it.

"Okay?" I repeat just to make sure I didn't dream it.

"Okay. I'll stay."

"Really?"

Ellie cracks a smile. "Yes, really. But we go slowly."

"I can do slow." *Yeah, right.* But I'll try.

Ellie brushes her hands over my chest, separating my shirt. I unbuttoned it with the intention of changing, but I never made it past the couch or the last two buttons. I struggle to sit still while she reacquaints herself with my body, running her palms over my skin and stopping at my tattoo. She always was fascinated by the large colorful compass over my heart.

"Look hard," I tell her.

"At what?"

"The ink."

She stares at the tattoo, then gasps. Written in very tiny script is her name on the needle pointing North.

"You're crazy."

"Without a doubt," I chuckle.

Her expression softens as she rubs the tip of her finger over her name. I have no control over what happens next. She feels so fucking good straddled on top of me, touching me the way she is. I tuck a piece of hair that's come loose from her ponytail behind her ear and the contact is magnetic. I lean forward, starving for just one tiny taste. She allows me to brush my lips against hers, never closing her eyes. I do it again, our gazes still locked. The third time, I apply more pressure, wrapping my arm around her waist. She kisses me back with just as much ferocity as this afternoon, and soon our slow, simple act becomes passionately charged.

I slide my hands eagerly under her dress and palm her ass while I swipe my tongue between her lips. She opens her mouth, allowing me in while simultaneously wrapping her arms around my neck. I crush her down against my erection, the two of us moaning as our hips clash together. With my heart starting to race, I slip my thumb under the silky material of her thong desperate to play with her, tickle her, lick her, fuck her. All the things she dangled in front of my face earlier tonight. Just as I begin to massage small circles over her folds, eager to sink my finger into the wet heat I've been dreaming about for the last twelve months, Ellie grabs my wrist.

"Kayne, no."

"No?" I halt. "Why no?" I test the waters by trying to move my hand.

Ellie pants. "Because I need to know that no is an option." She rests her forehead against mine.

"Of course, it is. I never want to take anything away from you. Ever again. I want to give you everything. Make you happy any way I can." I look up at her. "I would lie, cheat, steal, *kill* to keep you happy, Ellie. I would kill for you." I grab her neck. "I meant it then, and I mean it even more now. I would kill for you." I stress the words, caught up in her penetrating stare.

With a small smile, she drops a kiss on my lips. "Tonight," she breathes, "I need you to just lay with me."

ELLIE

I WAKE UP WITH KAYNE'S arm locked around my waist. His hold is so tight it's nearly suffocating me.

Last night was one of the longest of my life. So much information shared, so many questions answered, and an abundance of emotion soaring to the surface. Jett was right; Kayne has some deep-seated insecurities and has been severely deprived. But he also showed me how passionate and strong his convictions lie. Yes, what he did was monumentally fucked up, but there's no denying it bonded us. The pull is so strong it feels unbreakable. And that's scary as hell.

I don't know where I found the strength to deny him last night, but I needed to do it. I needed to know that he would never force me again. And he didn't, despite his raging hard on and the unbridled lust in his eyes. He just carried me to bed, wrapped me in his arms, and fell asleep. Almost too easily. Too naturally.

He feels so good pressed up against me. So right and wrong.

I'm in such a dangerous place. I know all too well what he's capable of, and yet at the same time, I barely know him at all. I'm certain exploring this path will lead to one of two things. An epic love, or my calamitous self-destruction.

Kayne stirs in his sleep as the early-morning sun brightens the room and the glorious view on display before us. He couldn't have picked a dreamier destination. I could lay here all day and just admire the tranquil turquoise-blue of the water.

"Mmmm." Kayne stirs again, this time sliding his hand over my stomach, pulling the hem of my dress up as he goes. "You stayed."

"Why wouldn't I?"

"Don't know. I guess I expect the worst."

I put my hand over his, lacing his fingers with mine. He hugs me tighter, digging his erection into my back, making my blood flow increase in speed.

"What would help ease your mind?" I ask softly.

"Knowing last night made a difference." He skims our entwined fingers down my bare thigh, and kisses me behind my ear.

"It did." I tilt my head, giving him better access to my neck.

"Good." He sucks hard on my skin, spurring my whole body to come alive. I let go of his hand as it explores my body, sliding from my hip to my torso then straight up to my breast. He squeezes it roughly over the fabric, pinching my nipple until it pebbles.

"Ellie," Kayne utters my name painfully, and I know there's no turning back now. Not that I want to. "I need you so much."

"I need you, too." I turn in his arms, desperate for him just to kiss me. And kiss me he does. Like a starving man who's never tasted sugar before, he invades my mouth, sucking my tongue, forcefully pushing my head into the pillow.

I'm drowning already, and he's barely even touched me. Kayne breaks our kiss just long enough to rip the lacey panties off my body then reclaims my mouth. I meet him roll for roll and thrust for thrust as our tongues tangle together. "I want to show you," he says between kisses. "I want to show you how much I missed you."

Before I even have a chance to respond, he's repositioning us, sliding off the bed and onto the floor, dragging my lower body with him until my legs are dangling over the side of the mattress. He pulls me up into a sitting position and situates himself between my knees. This is a first, Kayne kneeling before me.

Kayne sucks on his lower lip as he gazes at me, his eyes hungry and his body ready. He takes both thin straps of my dress between his fingers and slowly lowers them down my arms, exposing my breasts. The hunger in his eyes quickly morphs into famine as he drinks in my naked chest, my nipples hardening just from his stare. He leans forward, and I brace myself for his touch, for his lips to find my skin, his mouth to find my aching points. But he only grazes his teeth against my neck and runs his hands up the outside of my thighs. "Can I touch you, Ellie?"

"Yes." I drop my head back and moan as he kisses my neck and massages my breasts.

"Can I taste you, baby? Can I put my mouth on your pussy and lick you until you come?" Kayne swirls his tongue against my skin mimicking exactly what he would do if I say yes. I'm panting before I know it, his words as illicit as his actions. "Can I?"

"Yes." I force out the word as he rolls my rock hard nipples between his fingers. God, the effect this man has on me. It's inhuman and maddening and utterly blissful. Kayne kisses his way down my body, sucking on each of my breasts and stopping short just below my navel. I'm so tuned up I can barely stand it. I almost beg, but I refrain. Anticipating his next move, I watch engrossed as he hooks his arms around my thighs and spreads me wide, locking my legs in place.

"Lean back, Ellie." He pulls my lower body closer to the edge of the bed just so a bit of my ass is hovering off the side. Resting back on my hands, I grab onto the sheet for support, the two of us breathing raggedly as we stare into each other's eyes. "I want you to watch. I want you to see how much I missed you." Kayne tightens his arms and drops his head, and all I can do is hold my breath as his tongue darts out to take its first taste. The contact feels electric as Kayne launches a full-on assault, making sure I see every circle and every thrust. Pink flesh meeting pink flesh, both glistening with my arousal.

Kayne moans against me as he sucks vigorously on my clit.

"You really do taste like cupcakes." He laps me up like sugary frosting, and all I can do is quiver uncontrollably. He isn't wasting a moment pushing me to the brink.

"Kayne." I moan his name, close my eyes, and drop my head back as the sensations completely take over.

"Don't take your eyes off me, Ellie." He halts all movement, and I snap my head up. "I want you to see. I want you to watch me make you come." His stare is sharp as a knife and dark with desire. I know that look. It's his unyielding need for control—his dominant side waking from a yearlong slumber. It makes me shiver in all the right ways. It's such a fucking turn on that I almost hate myself for loving it. But it's his dominance that made me realize what we were both capable of. I drop my gaze as Kayne leans back down, trapping my swollen clit between his teeth and gently bites. I try to buck my hips as a zap of pleasure courses through my body, but his hold has my lower half restrained.

Oh God, I'm so close—watching him, feeling him, succumbing to him.

"Kayne, please," I cry out as he brushes his tongue over the entire length of my slit, driving me mad.

I've had just about all I can take when he finally decides to take pity on me and apply the pressure I need. Forced to watch as he fucks me with his mouth, stabbing my entrance repeatedly with his masterful tongue, everything south tightens and tingles. "Oh God, please."

I gasp. "Please, Kayne, may I come?"

As soon as the words leave my lips, the energy in the room changes. He looks up at me as I stare down, my heart pounding in my ears as he slows his strokes.

"Ellie, you just made me hard as fuck, but you don't have to ask my permission anymore," he says gruffly, between licks. "You're free to come whenever you want."

Embarrassment washes over me like I have never known, deflating my orgasm like a vented hot air balloon, and suddenly all I want to do is escape.

"Come for me, baby." He continues to lick me, but I grab his hair.

"No. Stop. Let go. Stop." I fight to jerk my legs out of his iron tight hold.

Kayne releases me, thankfully, with a worried expression.

"Ellie?" He tries to touch me, but all I want to do is disappear. I bolt up and retreat into the bathroom, locking the door behind me. Such a fucking idiot! I asked his permission!

I kick away my dress that is now pooling at my feet and turn on the shower, wanting to scrub the last five minutes away. I step into the freezing cold spray and bury my face in my hands.

"Ellie?" Kayne bangs on the door as I slowly die of mortification. "Ellie, please let me in." I can't tell the frame of mind he's in over the running water. On some level, I'm afraid he's mad and will want to punish me. On another, I know that's ludicrous given the conversation we had last night. My head is just too screwed up to think straight, and it's all thanks to Kayne.

"Ellie!" He bangs on the door harder, and I jump.

"Can you just give me a minute?" I snap.

This reunion is going spectacularly. For the first time, I strongly believe I made the wrong decision coming here. Maybe I wasn't ready. Maybe I'll never be ready. Maybe I'll always believe I'm nothing more than just a slave.

Just as I turn under the showerhead to wet my hair, I catch Kayne climbing through the window.

"What the fuck are you doing?" I ask as he drops his pants, shrugs out of his stained shirt and steps into the shower with me.

"Your minute is up." He stalks forward and pins me against the tiled wall.

"Kayne," I protest not meeting his eyes.

"Ellie." He grabs my chin and forces me to look at him. "Let's get a few things straight. First, no more running from me. That shit's over. You've had over a year to come to terms with everything. I'm done waiting. You run, and I'll come after you."

I stare into his eyes silently, my chest heaving, water dotting my face as the stream ricochets off his body. Part of me wants to fight him, to tell him to fuck off, and the other wants to melt into his arms and submit. It's a constant tug-of-war battling inside me.

"Second," his voice turns velvety soft, "if you want to ask my permission to come, be my guest. It makes me fucking hard as a rock." He pushes his erection against my belly.

"I don't want to ask your permission. I never want you to control me again." But even as I say the words, I know they're only partly true. Kayne's dominance is what makes him so seductive, what draws me to him like a dancing flame, and that's exactly the problem—one tiny touch and I get burned.

"I'll never do anything you don't want me to do, but I'm not going to let you walk all over me, either. I want to be with you,

Ellie, however I can have you," he repeats his words from last night. The same ones that won me over. One simple sentence that sealed my fate.

I take a deep breath and pull myself together. I want to be here, with him.

"I just hate that I'm conditioned," I tell him honestly.

Kayne smirks and cups my face in his hand. "Well, we'll just have to recondition you." He closes his mouth over mine, flicking his tongue against my teeth. "Starting now." He embraces me more urgently, pressing his big body flush against mine. There are so many promises in that kiss; it's like a swear, an oath, an affirmation.

"How do you want me to make you come? Do you want me to lick or fuck an orgasm out of you?"

My worried thoughts become nothing but a haze as he manipulates my mind with his profane words.

"Ellie, tell me," he urges gently, sucking my earlobe into his mouth.

I search for my voice, finding it behind the searing need shooting through my system. "Both?" I struggle to answer.

I feel Kayne smirk against my cheek. "That's my girl." He doesn't waste a second kissing his way down my body until he's settled on his knees. "Hang on, baby." That's my only warning as he hooks his arms under my thighs and hoists me right off the ground.

"Oh!" I steady myself with one hand against the wall as Kayne buries his face between my legs and licks until I'm writhing and moaning, fisting his hair, and squaring off with the orgasm that eluded me just a short while ago. "Oh God, oh God." My voice pitches as I slump in his arms, my climax grabbing hold and yanking me down into a spiraling black abyss.

I come around cocooned in Kayne's arms, the warm spray of the shower tickling my skin and the even hotter caress of his lips traveling down my neck.

"Welcome back."

"Mmm."

"How was your trip?"

"Too short."

"We can go again." He squeezes me in his arms, his erection

digging into my thigh. "I need you so bad, Ellie," he says strained.

"You can have me," I reply without even opening my eyes. At this very moment, he could do anything he wanted to me and I wouldn't protest.

Kayne growls in my ear. "Turn around. Put your hands over your head."

I do as he says, placing my hands against the wall. A moment later, he's pinning my wrists together with his fingers, like a zip tie. He splays his free hand on my lower abdomen and juts my hips out. I'm stretched and tethered and in seemingly familiar territory.

Kayne teases my pussy with the length of his erection, skimming through my wet folds before he fully penetrates me. I know what he's doing, drawing out my desire until I'm desperate again. He plays that game so well.

I moan as he grazes my sensitive slit, winding me up.

"I thought you said you needed me?" I rock against his steel-hard erection.

"I do, I just want to make sure you need me back." He keeps up the leisurely pace between my legs.

"Do you? Do you need me, baby?" he rasps in my ear, and as much as it pains me to admit it, I do.

"Yes, I need you," I whisper.

"I need you, too." With that, he thrusts into me, filling me to the brim. His fingers tighten around my wrists as my muscles clench around his cock. Kayne groans, burying his face in my neck while stalling inside me for a few heat-induced seconds. "Fuck," he spits as he starts to move, pulling all the way out then driving back in, each thrust a little more urgent than the last. "God, I missed you." He picks up the pace, keeping me positioned exactly how he wants me, hands pinned, hips out. Hitting my sweet spot over and over until everything inside me gravitates to the pulsing sensation between my legs. The ache is unbearable, but at the same time so deliciously good.

"Ellie, come with me," he grinds out as he slams into me so hard he lifts me right off the ground. "Come."

"Oh God!" I'm almost there, barreling down the last lengths, as Kayne clouds my mind the same way the steam is clouding the shower. When he drops his hand from my abdomen and circles my swollen clit with his finger, I detonate, crying out and coming hard all over his cock.

Kayne pulls out at the tail end of my orgasm and jerks off all over my ass, warm semen coating my skin as he groans like a dying man. He drops his head onto my shoulder and breathes the word 'mine' so softly I don't think I was meant to hear; but I did, and the declaration sends chills down my spine and hot lava through my veins.

Kayne releases my wrists and grabs onto my waist. I rest my hands on the shower wall, thankful for the reprieve, and peek at him over my shoulder. I'm still slightly bent over, and he's still slightly lust drunk. He rubs his come into my skin, making small circles down my behind until he's cupping one of my ass cheeks in his hand. I tense as he squeezes it, not hard enough to hurt, but in a way that tells me he's tempted to spank me. I brace myself for the blow, but it never comes. Instead, he just looks up into my eyes. "I needed that," he says sedately, right before the corners of his mouth curve up into a devilish smile.

"So you said," I mock, and the heavy energy between us cracks as we both start laughing.

Kayne hauls me into his arms with happiness radiating from his body.

"I also need you." He kisses me sweetly as he positions me under the spray washing away his sticky remnants from my backside.

"*So you said.*" I sigh, kissing him back.

"I'll say it as many times as I have to until you believe it."

KAYNE'S PHONE BUZZES ON THE nightstand. I ignore it the first time, but it persistently vibrates for several minutes while I lay in bed — Kayne's bed — recuperating and processing the events of the morning. I glance around our vacation bungalow. The one with a view of Bora Bora to die for, expensive furnishings, and glass floors where fish swim beneath us. This is definitely paradise, and he's spared no expense.

His phone goes off again, and now I think it might be

important. I grab the towel off the floor, wrap it around my naked self, and then pick up the phone. I walk into the bathroom to find him standing in front of the sink brushing his teeth. I pause in the doorway and just watch. Kayne catches me staring through the mirror. He spits, wipes his mouth, and then asks, "What's up, Ellie?"

"Oh, um." I snap out of my suspended state and walk over to him. "Your phone kept buzzing. I thought it might be important."

Kayne pulls me against him while he takes the phone. "Why were you looking at me funny before?" He glances at his screen with his arm securely around my waist.

"I've never seen you brush your teeth before," I admit. "It's so . . . normal."

Kayne laughs. "I'm not an alien, Ellie," he says as he types something with his free hand.

"To me you are," I giggle. "Ever since I met you, you've always had this persona that felt way bigger than me. First wealthy businessman, and then . . . well . . . you know," I fidget and blush. *The controlling Dom.* "Then undercover super spy."

Kayne laughs dropping his face closer to mine. "I'm just a man, Ellie. I put my pants on one leg at a time just like everyone else."

Yeah, right! Kayne is way more than just a man. He can try to convince me, and himself, and the world that he's just like everyone else, but that's so far from the truth it's actually comical. He's a force, half angel, half demon, wrapped up in a package of male perfection. No, he's no alien; he's a predator. He entices you with his charm, lures you with his appeal, traps you with his will, then pounces on you when you least expect it, ready to kill.

Just a man, my ass.

Kayne's phone buzzes in his hand again.

"You're popular," I comment.

"Not really." He looks down at the screen and frowns.

"Everything okay?"

"Fine." He pastes on a fake smile. "Just work."

"Just work?" I repeat. He refers to his job so nonchalantly, like he's a computer programmer instead of an international man of mystery.

"Yes, work. And it's fine."

"So fine you have to use an alias?"

He looks at me slyly. "The alias is just for precaution. You don't take down one of the most dangerous drug lords in the world and not take necessary steps to protect yourself."

"Are you in danger?" I ask concerned.

"No, at least none that we know of."

"We?"

"Yes, I have a twenty-four-hour surveillance team scanning for threats. And there aren't any that we're aware of at the moment."

"But there could be?"

"There's always a possibility of retribution."

"Kayne—"

"Ellie," he interrupts me, "I will tell you this. You have nothing to worry about. I would die before I let something bad happen to you."

"I don't think it's me I'm worried about."

Kayne smiles. His facial expression is endearing, but his eyes tell a completely different story. They're deadly and cold, and actually scare me. "Baby," he says almost threateningly. "If someone is stupid enough to come after me, they better have their funeral arrangements made. Got me?"

"Yes."

"Good." He drops a kiss on my lips, but doesn't let go of me.

"Do you have to go back undercover?" I ask.

"There's a possibility I could be activated again, but the probability of me running an operation is slim to none. I'm too high profile now, so I would most likely be backup support."

I blink rapidly; it's so strange to hear him talk like this. It's just one more layer of this complicated man.

"I'm not sure what means exactly."

"Different operatives have different responsibilities." He finally let's go of me. "I was a field operative, so my face was out there on the front lines. There are cyber, communications, linguists, and administrative operatives who work behind the scenes."

"For the government?"

"Yes and no. I was trained by the government, but work for an independent contractor."

"You're losing me," I say clearly confused.

"That's probably a good thing. The less you know about my occupation, the better."

"So, you're not a government spook?"

Kayne chuckles. "I'm not even sure what that means. What I am is a former U.S. soldier who was recruited for a special operations program because I possessed certain personality traits."

"And those traits are?" I'm engrossed by every ounce of information he feeds me.

"Low morality and no identity. I didn't mind killing people, and I didn't care if I got killed. That's the most lethal kind of agent. It's also the kind of agent the government doesn't like to associate themselves with directly, which is why I'm employed by a privately funded contractor. It gives us, and them, flexibility to go around the law so to speak."

"Do you still feel that way?" I frown.

"What way?"

"That you don't care if you get killed?"

Kayne's face softens. "I'll let you know at the end of our vacation." He runs his thumb down my cheek. "Enough shop talk. Let me worry about protecting the free world and you not worry at all. How does getting out of here for a little while sound? We can go check out the white sand beaches and down a dozen fruity drinks with those stupid little umbrellas in them."

"Sounds like a plan," I laugh, "and the recipe for a really bad hangover."

I DECIDE ON ONE OF my new bathing suits for the beach. The strapless stringy two-piece that barely covers my ass. I was going to save this one, but the idea of seeing Kayne's face when I wear it is too tempting to pass up. He's either going to love it, hate it, or—and my money's on this one—hate the fact that he loves me wearing it. Either way, I win on all accounts.

I walk out into the living room where Kayne is waiting for

me, and his expression falls. "Ellie, what are you wearing?"

I look down at my body. "A bathing suit?" I reply innocently.

Kayne raises his eyebrows. "Ellie, that isn't a bathing suit; that is a string wrapped around your body." He clearly disapproves. I smile to myself. "I have a cover-up." I show him the sheer white shirt that's practically see-through.

He grimaces. Too bad.

"Are we going?" I walk past him toward the front door. "I want to see the island."

Just as I turn the knob and crack the door open, it slams shut. I glance behind me.

"You can't go out like that."

"Why not?"

"Why not?" he asks exasperated. "Because you're indecent!"

"It's a bathing suit," I argue.

"That is not a bathing suit," he reiterates. "It's something Jett would dress you in to entice me."

"Who says that's not what I'm trying to do?" I bat my eyelashes at him.

"Baby, I'm already enticed. Now, please go change."

"No."

"Ellie." His patience is wearing thin. Good.

"Kayne," I mimic his tone, "my father doesn't even tell me how to dress, so don't think you're going to."

"I think if your father saw you wearing that he might have something to say."

"Well, he's not here. And you don't own me," I remind him. "I can do what I want. So move your hand, and let's go." I stare him down, just daring him to challenge me.

Kayne glares back at me with an ice-cold expression, the blue in his eyes as vibrant as a winter sky. He can try to intimidate me all he wants. I'm not backing down. It's my body and my life. After a few long heated beats, he gives in. "Fine."

Victory, I sing to myself. He really is a smart man. He knows if he argues with me it's going to get him nowhere fast. I was curious to see just how serious he was when he said he wasn't interested in controlling me. I will admit his jealousy kind of turns me on. I love how protective he is.

Although I won't tell him that.

Yet.

Kayne removes his hand from the door. "Can you please wear your cover-up at least?" he asks, straining for composure.

"Okay." I slip the loose fitting shirt over my head and cover myself.

"Happy?" I ask.

"No," he replies sourly.

I giggle uncontrollably. This is gonna be fun.

We climb into the golf cart where Matias is already waiting behind the wheel. I snuggle up next to Kayne in the tiny seat. I don't want him to be upset, but I do want him to know that I'm through taking orders and following commands. He immediately puts his arm around me and nuzzles his nose into my hair. It makes me tingle. Matias glances at us and smirks as he drives off. We're a far cry from the couple who first climbed into his cart nearly twenty-four hours ago.

"Kayne?" I whisper in his ear.

"Mmm hmm?" he answers, holding me tightly.

"What happened to your house and the business?"

He looks quickly at Matias before he answers me. Maybe I should have waited until we were in private to ask, but our conversation this morning has me wondering.

Kayne drops his head, pressing his lips to my ear. "Gone," he murmurs so only I can hear. "Everything was liquidated."

"Oh," I reply surprised, and he shakes his head sternly. I take the hint. This conversation is over.

"Later," he whispers while skimming my neck with his teeth.

"Sorry."

"Don't be." He drops a kiss on my lips just as Matias pulls up to our destination. The resort's private beach — complete with crystal-blue lagoon, cushioned lounge chairs, and tiki bar.

"Ring when you need me, sir," Matias says to Kayne as they shake hands.

"Will do."

Kayne and I walk the short distance to the bar when I suddenly spot a familiar face dressed in board shorts and a smile heading our way.

"Jett!" I nearly jump into his arms. "I didn't think we were going to see you."

"I'm always around." He hugs me.

"Thank you for last night," I whisper in his ear right before he releases me.

"Anytime. You know that," he whispers back.

"Ellie, do you want something to drink?" Kayne asks from behind me. It's such a simple question, but his flat tone implies something so much more. Is he jealous of Jett? I couldn't fathom it. He was the one who took care of me all that time. The only one he trusted me with.

"Yes, please." I turn and walk over to him. I can't see his eyes behind those brown aviator sunglasses he always wears, but I can see the curve of his lips, and the way they're turned down.

"Downing a dozen, remember?" I slide up against him.

"I didn't forget." He puts his arm around me and kisses the top of my head.

"One for me, too." Jett casually leans against the bar beside us, arms folded, eyes bright, the color almost a perfect match to the turquoise water.

"Three Mai Tais," Kayne orders as I steal glimpses of the two hottest men I have ever met.

Jett cocks his eyebrow at me, acknowledging how perfectly content I am with Kayne's protective arm around me. I pull down my sunglasses and exaggerate an eye roll at him.

He chuckles, his nipple ring glinting in the sun.

"What's so funny?" Kayne asks Jett over my head.

"The image of you holding a girlie drink with a pink umbrella."

"I'm channeling my inner bitch just for you."

I glance up at Kayne.

"Sorry. Was that offensive?"

I smile. "Maybe if I was anyone else. But my sense of humor is pretty liberal."

"Perfect, you'll fit right in with the perverts," Jett jokes.

"Speak for yourself." Kayne scoffs.

"Hmmm, I don't think Jett is too far out of line. Birds of a feather . . ." I point out. I know firsthand just how perverted Kayne can be.

"I love her," Jett laughs.

Kayne leers at me, sucking his bottom lip between his teeth. His eyes just barely visible behind the brown lenses.

"Ellie, why don't you go grab us a seat. I need to talk to Jett for a minute," he says, running his hand down my back and over my behind. "I'll bring your drink when it's ready."

"Okay," I frown. "Sure." Why does it feel like I'm suddenly being dismissed?

Kayne drops a kiss on my lips and spanks my ass lightly, sending me on my way.

Fine, then.

I saunter down to where the sand meets the water. It's a glorious day. The beach itself is quiet, but there are people snorkeling several yards away and jet skiing in the distance.

I discard my cover-up, and then glance behind me. Jett and Kayne look like they're talking casually, but I can feel both of their heated stares searing into my skin.

KAYNE

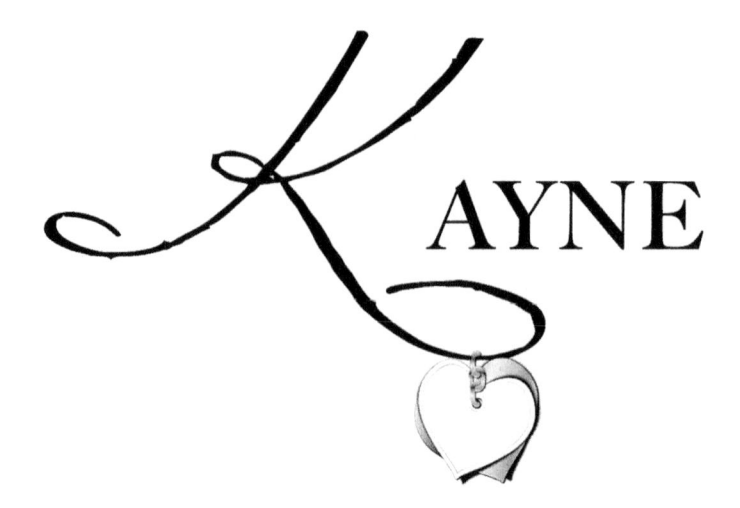

I WATCH ELLIE SHIMMY AWAY wearing nothing more than an R-rated bikini and a sorry excuse for a cover-up. It took everything I had to let her walk out of the bungalow like that without leaving handprints on her ass. I have to keep reminding myself our dynamic has changed. She is no longer my slave, and I am no longer her Master, which really fucking sucks sometimes. Like now. I have a feeling she is going to test me at every turn.

"You got laid." Jett shifts his eyes to me.

"How could you possibly know that?" I respond flatly.

"Because, for the first time in almost twelve months, your energy isn't hostile and Ellie is the perfect shade of post-coital peach."

"You need to lay off the Zen. And yes, we had sex."

"So you two are working things out?"

"Looks like it. She's still here. Although she is hell-bent on making sure I understand she is independent and won't take any shit from me."

Jett grins, and then immediately frowns. "Is that bathing suit part of her independence?" he asks as Ellie disrobes, catching every single eye on the beach. Including ours.

"Yup."

"You let her out in that?"

"She didn't give me much of a choice. Tough little thing." I smile to myself.

"That she is."

The bartender serves us our drinks. Finally. Paradise service takes forever. It's annoying.

"You read that text this morning?" I ask Jett as I take a sip of my drink. Looks like we were both wrong. No pink umbrellas, just red hibiscus garnishing our Mai Tais. Much more manly.

"Yup."

"Were you able to get any more information?"

"Yeah. I figured you'd be busy, so I checked in."

"And?"

"It was confirmed the Jackal landed in Honolulu this morning via private jet."

"Do we know what he wants?" I ask softly, standing as casually as possible, watching Ellie dip her toes in the water.

"Negative. Could be nothing. Could be one of Javier's most dangerous American allies' just wants to listen to some authentic Hawaiian music and dine on kalua pig."

"Right, with me doing the hula in a grass skirt," I retort cynically, tracking Ellie's every move.

"You have the abs for it."

"Yeah, well, the only way he's going to get close enough to see my abs is if I have him in a headlock."

"No need for violence if it isn't necessary."

"Violence is always necessary," I contest.

Jett snickers. We have always butted heads on this subject. He believes in avoiding a mess. I always take the bloody way out. I believe it leaves more of an impression.

"Juice has eyes on him. We'll know soon enough if he's up to something."

"Good." My pulse beats double time in my neck. "The last thing I want to do is upset Ellie with reminders of Javier."

"Amen, brother." Jett taps his cup against mine. "Um, Kayne, speaking of reminders, did you happen to tell Ellie about Sugar?"

"You haven't called her that since Mansion."

"I know, but it's the only name Ellie knows her by," Jett says as Sugar approaches Ellie on the beach. All we can do is watch the train wreck happen as we walk quickly down to the girls.

They speak briefly, like for a split second, before Ellie starts walking backward, then bumps into a lounge chair, and ends up falling flat on her ass.

"Ooo," Jett and I both collectively respond.

"Oh! Are you okay?" we hear Sugar ask, reaching for her.

Ellie just nods stunned. She looks embarrassed, uneasy, and disoriented all at the same time.

"Ellie." Jett slips his arms around Sugar's—or I should say London's—waist. That's her real name. "I see you two are getting reacquainted."

She glances silently between Jett, London, and me.

"You look confused, Ellie," I comment offhandedly. It's clear she's been blindsided and doesn't know how to react. I probably should have warned her about the two of them. But, to be honest, it was the last thing on my mind.

"I am." She eyes me irately.

"London is here with me," Jett clarifies. "We're together."

"Together?"

"Yeah, you know, like dating," I chime in.

"I know dating." Her answer is short.

"I figured. Mai Tai?" I shove a drink in her face.

"Just the one? I think I need all twelve."

"YOU DIDN'T THINK TO WARN me that Jett was dating a ghost from our sordid past?" Ellie fumes, half a mile down the beach, away from where London and Jett can hear.

"Didn't seem like such a big deal," I shrug.

"Maybe to you."

"Are you ashamed of what happened between the three of us?"

"No, yes, no . . . ugh." Ellie turns red. "It's just . . . Just."

"Just?"

"I just didn't think I was ever going to see her again," she finally admits, frustrated.

"Well, she was excited to see you if that makes you feel any better."

"I don't know how that makes me feel." She crosses her arms and looks up at me with just her gorgeous green eyes.

"It really isn't a big deal." I try to reassure her.

"To you, maybe."

"Can you just give it a chance? I know the dynamic is different. It's something we all have to get used to. But she's a great girl, and Jett is head over heels, stupidly in love with her." *Sort of the exact same way I feel about you.*

"Were they together when we were together?" she asks uncomfortably, plucking the string on her bikini bottom.

"I'm not sure, honestly. Something was going on, I think, but they didn't hook up officially until after everything cooled down."

Ellie frowns, wringing her fingers together. "Did you sleep with her?"

"Ah . . ." Oh, shit. I wasn't expecting her to ask that.

"I'll take that as a yes. Of course you did. She was one of your 'girls.'" She makes air quotes.

"It's not what you think."

"Then please tell me what to think."

Fuck, I wasn't ready for this conversation so early in the day.

"Yes, I slept with her," I admit. "A few times, but only when Jett wanted to share her."

"Excuse me?" Her head tilts as she looks up at me puzzled.

"Jett and I had a threesome with London," I speak slowly, clarifying my sentence.

"Oh." Her eyes widen.

"Really, we're all even if you think about it. Jett and I have been with London, and you and I have been with London, so it's all good." I try to rationalize.

"That's not how I see it at all. If I sleep with Jett, then we'd be all good." She counters with her own rationale. It ain't flying.

"Over my fucking dead body. Jett may get off on sharing his women, but I don't. Unless it's with another woman." I slip that in there.

Ellie folds her arms and smirks. "Yes, I remember how much you enjoyed seeing me with another woman."

"If I recall, you enjoyed it, too." I cautiously slide my arm around her waist.

"I did." She embraces my subtle surrender, running her nails down my biceps, over my barbed-wire tattoo, giving me the chills.

"But you still could have warned me."

"I'm sorry. Please forgive my oversight. Only one woman has been on my mind."

"Oh, yeah? Who's that?" she asks seductively, skimming the tip of her tongue up my neck.

"Like you don't know." I grab her ass and crush her body against mine. "If you don't quit that I'm going to have to drag you into the lagoon and tear that tiny bikini off you."

She giggles, "No way, I'm still mad at you. You'll have to suffer." She sucks on my skin.

"Would it have really made that much a difference if you knew or not?" Her mouth feels so good I'm starting to unravel.

"Possibly. I could have avoided looking like a blindsided idiot."

"It was cute."

"It definitely wasn't."

"It definitely was. And what I say goes."

"Mmm hmm. Keep thinking that."

"I will." I squeeze Ellie's ass cheek and nearly lift her off the ground. She lets out a little half scream, and I can't help but think that's not the only way I'm going to make her scream. "Can we go try and make nice?" I set her down and take her hand. I need to walk off my waking arousal, and walk it off right now.

"I guess I don't really have a choice," she resigns.

Once back, Ellie and I snuggle up in the lounge chair next to Jett and London. Jett throws me a look as Ellie situates herself between my legs and lays back on my chest.

I return a head nod indicating things are all good, even though Ellie still feels a little tense. I rub her shoulders in an attempt to relax her, and after a few minutes, she inhales deeply and melts against me. I smile to myself, feeding off her energy. She'll never understand the effect she has on me.

For the next hour, the four of us just lounge like fat cats, soaking up the sun and sucking down drinks.

I can't remember the last time I sat around and did nothing, and actually enjoyed myself.

"Oh!" Ellie sits up as two people standing on surfboards float by. "Do you want to go paddleboarding? I learned how to do it in Hawaii. It's fun!"

I curl my lip. "Fun? No engine, no pedal, no throttle. How much fun could it be?"

Ellie's eyebrows shoot up. "Oh, well, excuse me, Mr. Adrenaline Junkie." She pushes me playfully. "You can just watch me then."

"It would be my pleasure," I answer as she gets up haughtily, and walks down the beach to the man sitting under a straw umbrella signing out water sports equipment.

"How much fun could it be?" Jett punches me in the arm out of the blue.

"Hey! What the fuck was that for?" I rub my arm.

"You are an idiot," he snaps.

"What? Why?"

"Do *you* know how much fun it could be?" he gets in my face. "*I'll* show you how much fun it can be."

I gape at him silently. "What's got your nuts in a twist?"

"You, you moron." With that, he takes off in the same direction as Ellie.

I glance over at London cluelessly. She just shrugs.

I watch as Jett and Ellie walk their boards out into the water, then quickly and effortlessly mount them by kneeling first then standing. Ellie impresses me by how comfortably she can move in that skimpy little bikini I plan on burning once we get back to the bungalow.

Jett and Ellie push off with their sticks, sending them gliding over the crystal-blue lagoon, both keeping pace with each other. I still don't see how this is supposed to be fun. I want to yawn just watching them. I place my hands behind head, close my eyes, and relax. That's when I hear Ellie scream. My heart nearly jumps out of my throat. I pop up to find Jett on Ellie's surfboard. They're play fighting, Jett attempting to push her off the board and then catching her just before she falls into the water. Ellie is laughing hysterically trying her damnedest to fend him off. I glare, my blood heating, as he puts his hands all over her mostly exposed body.

Okay, he's made his point. Repeatedly. Especially over Ellie's back, sides, and thighs.

"The man sure knows how to send a message," London comments behind her large black sunglasses.

"That he fucking does," I gripe just as he grabs her ass with both hands and presses her against him.

"Jett!" Ellie cries out laughing even harder wiggling in his arms.

That's it. Jett may be my best friend and all, but he is crossing the line. My girl, my body, and only my hands touch it.

I toss my aviators down and storm off into the water, wading out to Jett and Ellie. She doesn't see me coming because her back is turned, but Jett and I lock eyes. Just as I get a foot away, Jett pushes Ellie with some force, knocking her back right into my arms.

"Oh!" she startles when I catch her. "Where did you come from?" she asks laughing.

"I'm always around," I tell her, tightening my grip.

"Good to know."

"You're having too much fun with Jett." I hiss.

"Jett was the only one who wanted to have any fun."

"That's not true. We had fun this morning," I whisper in her ear.

"Yes, we did." Ellie's cheeks burn bright pink.

Jett clears his throat. "My work here is done." He jumps off the board and into the water.

"Work?" Ellie repeats.

"Ignore him, he has Tourette's. Bogus shit just flies out of his mouth."

"Keep telling yourself that, bro," Jett digs.

"Get fucking lost." I turn my full attention to Ellie.

"With pleasure, cranky pants," Jett says as he swims off.

Ellie just looks at me with a strange expression.

"What?"

"I think that was the first conversation I've ever heard the two of you have."

"And?"

"Enlightening."

"Yeah, well, you almost lose your life with a person a few

times, you come to appreciate them."

"Oh? That's how you talk to someone you appreciate? And how many times have you almost lost your life?" she says, sidetracked.

"A few." I press my forehead against hers. "That's all you need to know. I'm here, and that's what's important."

"Yes, it is." She kisses me softly on the lips.

I return the kiss, adding a little more pressure before I pull away.

"I'm sorry," I apologize earnestly.

"For what?"

"Blowing you off."

"You didn't blow me off."

"I should have come paddleboarding with you."

"Why? I don't expect us to like all the same things. That's unrealistic."

"Are you a realist, Ellie?" I tease her.

"No, I just have common sense."

"Glad one of us does."

"You admit to your flaws?" she jests.

"My honesty is all I have left."

"Says the black operative."

"You got me there." I curl her in my arms.

"Kayne?"

"Yeah?"

"Did Jett make you jealous?"

"Baby, when it comes to you, everyone makes me jealous."

"You don't have anything to worry about with Jett. We're just friends."

"Yes," I reflect. "I know all about Jett and his *friends.*"

I place Ellie on the board. "Enough talk about Jett. Show me." I climb on after her. She smiles brightly. Happily. It makes my chest hurt. All I've wanted was to see that expression, and I'm such an idiot I didn't realize it'd take something as simple as paddleboarding to put it there.

Once we stand, she positions the stick in the water steadying herself. I firmly place both my hands on her abdomen, pressing her back against my front. "Let's see your skills, beach bunny."

ELLIE

I WASN'T EXACTLY UPSET THAT Kayne didn't want to paddleboard, but it was nice to spend time with him doing something other than having sex.

After an hour of quality time, we spent the rest of the day on the beach consuming copious amounts of alcohol and talking about a variety of subjects. School, my family, Mark. Such mundane things to the average person, but so critical to our fragile relationship.

"Why don't we all have dinner?" London asks as Kayne and I stand to leave.

Both Kayne and Jett look at me. No pressure or anything.

"Um, sure." I smile as genuinely as possible. "That sounds fun."

I think.

"Good!" London responds excitedly. "The sushi restaurant here is supposed to be amazing."

"Sushi it is, then." I pull on my cover-up.

"You eat sushi?" Kayne asks me.

"Of course, I do. I'm from New York. It's one of my five food groups."

"Perfect! Mine, too." London's big blue eyes sparkle. I stole glances at her and Jett all throughout the day. They make one beautiful couple. "She could live off the stuff," Jett chimes in.

"Eight o'clock?" I ask.

London nods zealously.

"See you then," I say as Kayne laces our fingers together and leads me away from the beach. I tighten my grip, still getting used to him holding my hand. Still getting used to him holding me period—not ashamed to admit that I like the way it feels.

"Do you eat sushi?" I ask him, realizing I have no idea if he likes raw fish or not. Or if he has any allergies or likes to sleep on the right or left side of the bed. Besides how he takes his coffee and his sexual preferences, I really don't know much about him.

"Yes. If I'm forced to." He grins down at me.

"Oh, no." I stop walking.

"It's fine, Ellie." He tugs me along. "There will be something on the menu that I'll eat. I'm not picky. Trust me. It's a meal, I'll never pass it up."

"Okay. Well, what do you like to eat?"

"Simple stuff. I'm a meat and potatoes guy. I could live off rare steak and cold beer."

"I'll keep that in mind. Is there a preferred dessert I should know about?"

"Cupcakes, of course. And before you ask, my favorite flavor is between your legs." He informs me lewdly.

"Kayne." I smack him playfully right on his washboard abs.

"It's the truth." He hugs me against him as we walk toward the long line of bungalows stretching out over the water. Ours is far off in the distance.

"Where did you grow up?" I ask.

"Detroit."

"Tough city."

"You have no idea."

"Tigers fan?"

"Not in the least."

"Yankees fan?"

"I'm not much into baseball. More a hockey guy. I like confrontation."

"Why does that not surprise me?"

He shrugs, "You've seen my aggressive side?"

"I don't think I even scratched the surface."

"Let's hope you never have to, either."

We stroll a few minutes in comfortable silence, taking in the scenery. It's crazy, but Mount Otemanu almost looks blue this time of day.

"So, now that you have whisked me away, whatever shall you do with me?" I toy as our bungalow comes into view.

"I have dozens of ideas," his voice vibrates with desire. "The question is what do you want to do?"

I bite my lip before I speak. "I want to rent a Jeep and explore. And go snorkeling and learn to kite surf," I say excitedly. "I read about this awesome tour guide who takes you on a private excursion around the island on his boat then makes you dinner on a secluded beach from the fish he catches that day."

"Had some time to do some research, have we?" Kayne asks highly amused.

"Yes! I was googling on the plane. I get excited going to new places!" I say enthusiastically.

"Do you always bounce?" Kayne laughs as I pop up and down on my toes.

"No, not usually," I giggle, planting my feet back on the ground. I'm probably making the biggest ass of myself. I am a severely deprived world traveler. "I only get hyper when you feed me too many sugary drinks."

"Good to know. I'll make sure you stick to vodka and tonics with a lemon from now on."

"You remember?" I stop walking.

"I remember everything, Ellie."

I can't stop myself from smiling.

"Maybe I should just stick to wine. Too many vodka and tonics make me horny."

"And we have a winner." Kayne makes a fist over his head.

I pepper Kayne with more questions as we get closer and closer to the bungalow.

"Favorite color?"

"Green."

"Favorite city?"

"Amsterdam."

"You've been to Holland?"

"I've been all over the world."

"All over?"

"All over," he confirms.

"The Middle East?" I ask cautiously.

"Yes."

"For business or pleasure?"

"Both. Dubai is nice, but I wouldn't recommend Bagram nowadays."

It's sobering to hear him say that.

"Ellie? Did I say something to upset you?" Kayne's face drops.

"Why were you there? Can you tell me?"

"Training exercises mostly. We were dropped in the baddest of the bad and left to find our way back to home station."

"But you don't have to go back, right?"

"No, not at the moment. But there's always a possibility. Does that worry you?"

"Maybe." I chew the inside of my cheek. It makes me think long and hard about what it's like caring for a man who puts himself in danger as his day job.

"Hey. Whatever you're thinking about, please stop. I don't like that look."

"I'm sorry." I blink rapidly out of my silent thoughts. "I'm not thinking about anything."

"Ellie, please. Let's get something straight. You'll never be able to lie to me. No matter how hard you try. So if something is on your mind, just say it."

I'm not sure I'm ready to tell him that putting his life in danger terrifies me. That after only spending one day together, I'm already getting attached. Or that old feelings are resurfacing faster than I expected. No, I'm not ready to tell him any of that yet, because I'm just coming to terms with it myself.

"It's just scary, that's all."

"What's scary?"

"The thought of you being in a place that's so dangerous."

"You get used to it after a while." He starts ushering me along.

"How about we sit down with Matias and set up some excursions. This vacation is all about fun, and I think we can both use a huge dose of that." He does a good job of spinning the topic of conversation.

"Agreed," I relent, wrapping my arms around his waist and squeezing tightly. A healthy dose of fun is exactly what I need.

We walk arm in arm until we reach our butler's office, then spend over an hour plotting out activities for the next week.

"I AM SO READY FOR a shower." I head straight for the bathroom once we get back to the bungalow.

"Sounds like a plan to me." Kayne rips off his shirt and follows close behind me.

"I don't remember inviting you." I coquettishly look over my shoulder at him.

"I didn't think I needed an invitation." Kayne wraps his arms around me and kisses my cheek. It's a sexy, lust-fueled gesture.

"What if I said no?"

"I would respect that, and then just stand here and watch you lather up all my favorite parts of your body. I enjoy watching you touch yourself just as much as I enjoy touching you." He slides my bathing suit top over my head.

"Oh, really?"

"Yup." My bottoms are gone a second later.

He drops my bikini into the sink.

"I'm never going to see that again, am I?" I ask him.

"Nope. Now get in the shower." He taps me lightly on the ass.

I step into the cream-colored stone stall with Kayne right behind me.

"Stay there," he orders. Mr. Bossy is never far away.

With my back to him, I'm suddenly very aware of what can happen in situations like these. I brace myself for his hands. Not in a bad way, but in a domineering, I'm going to take you right here right now and you have nothing to say about it way. But Kayne surprises me. Instead of going straight for the kill like I'm expecting, he starts to wash my hair. Massaging my scalp in such a way it almost doesn't feel like him. Or does it? I remember those times. Those faint moments when he touched me with such tenderness it actually felt like he loved me. Back then, I couldn't decipher, but now his intentions are very clear.

"How does that feel?"

"So good." I close my eyes and get lost in the ministrations of his fingers.

"It's longer."

"What's longer?"

"Your hair. It's lighter and longer. I like it."

"More of it for you to pull," I tease.

"That's not what I was getting at." He tugs gently.

"You couldn't resist."

"You planted the seed. I was trying to be nice."

"And you are," I moan as he presses harder.

"Good to know I can elicit sounds from you the *nice* way."

"It's a pleasant surprise for me, too."

"I'm hoping to surprise you a lot during this vacation." He spins me around and tips my head back to rinse out the soap.

"I'm keeping an open mind," I speak with my eyes closed.

"I'm very thankful for that." He drops a kiss on my lips, and then starts to lather my body, making sure he covers every curve.

I glance up at him through my wet eyelashes, darting my eyes away shyly once they meet his.

"Ask, Ellie." Kayne brushes over my breasts, his hands sliding easily from the soap.

"How did you know?"

"I'm trained to read people, and I've made it my business to read you like a book."

"What's my tell?" I put my hand on my hip. I didn't think I was that easy to pick apart.

"It's your eyes. They're too inquisitive, especially when something is on your mind. So ask me whatever you want to know. I'll answer as honestly as I can."

"Your honest side is refreshing." I run my fingertips over his stomach, tracing the words etched on his ribs. *A certain kind of darkness is needed to see the stars.*

"I told you, I don't want to keep anything from you. I only kept secrets for a reason. A very important reason," he stipulates.

"I know."

"Do you?" He lifts my chin with his finger.

"Yes. Now, I do."

"Good. So ask already."

I chew on my lip, then fire away. "What happened to the women who worked for you?"

"They were compensated for their services and sent on their way."

"Sent where?"

"Wherever they wanted to go," he says breezily. "Some stayed in the life. Some started fresh. I'm not exactly sure what happened to each and every one of them, but I do know they're safe and doing what they want."

"Did you sleep with all of them?"

Kayne freezes with his hands on my backside.

"No, Ellie, I didn't."

"How many then?"

"Does it really matter?" he questions stiffly. "You're the only one I want to sleep with now."

"I want to know. How many women have you been with?"

Kayne huffs, staring at me intensely. "Seven women."

"Seven? That's it?" I can't hide the surprise in my voice.

"You were expecting a higher number?"

"Honestly, yes."

"Why?"

"Because . . ."

"Because why?" he presses

"Because . . . you're you."

"What does that mean?" He's clearly uncomfortable now.

"You know exactly what that means."

"No, I don't." His eyes narrow.

"Yes, you do. Don't play dumb."

"Are you saying you like the way I touch you?" His mood morphs from touchy to feely. He can still give me whiplash.

"I'm saying you are very skilled with your body. That's all."

"So, you do like the way I touch you?" he asks again with a shameless grin, and I come to realize he hides behind sex when he feels insecure.

"I liked it when you were massaging my scalp."

"Are you dancing around my question on purpose?" He squeezes my ass.

"Maybe."

"Maybe I'll show you what my body can really do."

"I think I already have an idea." I grab the bottle of soap and squirt some into my hands. "My turn."

"Be my guest."

I rub Kayne's chest, working a thick lather over his skin, and then moving my hands down his stomach.

"You can go lower if you want." He releases my waist and takes a small step back.

"I'm happy right where I am." I circle my hands over his rock-hard abs, which incidentally aren't the only thing that's rock-hard on him at the moment.

"Don't you want to know how many men I've been with?" I ask as I wash him.

"No," he scoffs. "As far as I'm concerned, I'm the only man you've ever been with."

That makes me laugh.

"Why so few?" I keep probing.

Kayne's muscles tense under my fingertips. I look up into his eyes and see hesitation there.

"Is there something I should know?" I query.

"No."

"You sure?"

"Yes. Now who's trying to read who?" His voice is firm. Not threatening, just cautious. There is definitely a side of him he doesn't want to show.

"Jett told me that trusting women is a hard limit for you," I state with sensitivity.

"And when did he tell you that?" His eyes smolder.

"Last night."

"Oh, really?"

"Yes. I was upset and confused. He was just trying to help."

"Right," he sneers.

"You once said that you wanted me to understand you."

Kayne sighs, then runs his hands down my face and kisses me lightly. "I know," he replies pained. It nearly breaks my heart. "And I really want you to."

"So tell me why so few women."

Steam clouds around us as Kayne stares down at me. He wavers before answering.

"I need to feel comfortable with a woman in order to have sex with her."

"Comfortable? Like in a relationship?"

"No. No relationships. That was the last thing I wanted. I had a few girls on retainer who I slept with. Sex with no strings. Simpler that way."

"And no emotion," I frown.

"Emotion was expendable at the time."

"And now?"

"Now it's essential." He swipes his thumb across my cheek. It feels like it leaves a trail of fire in its wake.

"Did you keep those women on retainer while we were apart?" I ask without looking at him, circling my hands over his chest.

"No. I haven't been with anyone since you."

My eyes fly to his. I know they're as wide as saucers. It's been a year.

"It's true. I could break a steel plate with my forearm. You were, and are, the only person I want," he says resolutely. The statement makes my heart flutter.

"Why me?" I ask the burning question.

Kayne shrugs, pulling me into his body. "I don't know why exactly. You never intimidated me. You were always happy and smiling, and when you looked at me, it wasn't anything but warm."

"Oh, I was warm all right," I laugh. "I overheated every time I saw you."

"I guess I liked it." He leans in to kiss me.

"How old were you when you lost your virginity?" I ask right before his lips touch mine.

"What does it matter?"

"Just another piece of the puzzle." I rub up against his erection in an attempt to relax him.

Kayne closes his eyes and moans softly.

"Nineteen. I was nineteen when I lost it," he answers absentmindedly, getting lost in the friction of our bodies.

"Did you love her?"

"No. I have never been interested in love until I met you. If it wasn't for Jett, I might still be a virgin."

"Did he introduce the two of you or something?"

Kayne grabs hold of my waist and stops all movements. He's breathing hard, his eyes are dilated, and water is spilling down his face.

"It's not like that. Jett was there with me, Ellie. We were on leave, and since I didn't have any place to go, I went home to California with him. I don't know if Jett ever told you the business his family runs or who his mother is—"

"He told me," I interrupt him.

That last night at Mansion I pried Jett for information and he gave it to me, divulging his mother is a Madame, and why he grew up around a lot of women.

"So you know what I'm talking about?" Kayne asks, and I nod. "It's not like I got there, and he threw me into a bedroom with a random girl. It's like he handpicked her specifically for me. She spent a few days warming up to me, getting to know me, and then one night we all went out and got drunk. Jett instigated the whole thing. Like he knew I wouldn't go through with it unless I had moral support. He was probably right. So we did it. All three of us. Together."

"She became my first submissive, but I never loved her. And she never loved me, either. But you I love, whether you're submissive or not."

"You sure about that?" I test him.

"Absolutely, one-hundred-percent." With that, he pins me against the wall and crushes his lips against mine. The kiss nearly steals the air right out of my lungs.

"I want things to be different with you." He rubs his nose against my cheek.

"Different how?" I press my chest against his as my core becomes as hot as the running water.

"I'll show you." He closes the distance between our mouths, and I brace for another soul shattering connection, but Kayne switches gears and kisses me unlike any way he has ever kissed me before—passionately, affectionately, devotedly, reverently—every word that could possibly describe an all-consuming, unstoppable love. And I know it's too fast, too soon, but the weight of his affection overwhelms me to the point I can no longer think, or see, or even breathe. So I just kiss him back, pouring whatever amount of emotion I'm capable of giving him at the moment into the embrace.

Kayne lifts me off the floor, forcing my legs around his hips as he steps under the steaming spray of water, rinsing off whatever suds are left on us. Then he turns the shower off. We never break our kiss as he steps out of the stall and walks into the bedroom, the two of us dripping wet.

Not even bothering with a towel, he lays me down on the bed, trapping my body beneath his.

"Hold onto me. Whatever you do, don't let go." He positions his erection between my legs, the head pushing at my entrance gently. He's not even inside me, and I'm already responding, flooding with desire as the tip of his cock slides easily between my wet folds.

Then, in one fluid motion, he sinks into me so perfectly slow that I nearly split in two.

"Oh, God." I dig my face into his neck as my arms and legs and pussy all tighten painfully around him.

"Ellie," he moans, nudging my cheek with his nose coaxing me to look up at him. He drops kisses on my lips over and over as he rocks in and out of me.

"You feel so good." Kayne dips his tongue into my mouth, pressing his body harder against mine, his pelvis repeatedly brushing over my throbbing clit as our wet bodies slide easily against each other from the thin residue of soap still left on our skin.

"So do you." I get lost in the feel of him, the way his long, measured thrusts stretch and fill me, producing not only a physical response but an emotional one. My heart and pussy constrict at the same time as the orgasm inside me grows fast and furiously, threatening to unleash.

"You're going to make me come." I squirm breathless underneath him, unable to control it.

"Not yet, Ellie. Hold onto it." He hugs me tighter and thrusts deeper. My body spasms. "You feel too fucking good."

But I can't hold on, because he feels the exact same way, so thick and hard and overpowering.

"Oh God, oh God, oh God." I chant against his neck without a prayer. "Kayne!" My orgasm steamrolls me, and I tumble over the edge, my clit aching and muscles contracting violently.

A few moments later, at the tail end of my internal frenzy, Kayne grabs my thigh with one hand and slams into me, groaning in what sounds like unbearable pleasure.

He collapses on top of me once his orgasm subsides, wrapping me in his arms and breathing heavily.

"I love you." The words flow out in a whisper as he hugs me tightly. I flutter my eyes open and stare up at the thin white fabric covering the canopy bed, a whirlwind of emotions running through me.

"I know," I kiss the side of his face. It's the only response I have. I'm not ready to go there. He's so sure about how he feels. And although I want to be here, with him, I'm still coming to terms with what I want and how much I can give.

"Good, always remember that." He kisses my forehead and then rolls off me, pulling me into his side so I am snuggled in the crook of his arm. I lay my head on his chest and listen to his heartbeat. It's such a strong, soothing sound, almost hypnotic. I put my hand next to my ear to feel it.

"It beats because of you."

"What?"

"It never beat until I met you." He puts his hand over mine.

"I find that hard to believe."

"It's true. I never had a reason to live until you, Ellie."

I blush and hide my face. How can he be so open? I thought men were supposed to be closed off and devoid of all emotion?

"Did I say something to upset you?"

"No," I snuggle closer to him, "you're just making it very hard to resist you."

"Baby, that's the idea." He kisses my head and laughs.

I doze off warm and content in Kayne's arms as the last bit of light fades away from the day.

"HEY, SLEEPYHEAD," KAYNE SHAKES ME lightly. "We're going to be late for dinner."

I crack open my eyes to find him showered and dressed.

He smells good, like shaving cream. "I let you sleep as long as I could."

"Do we have to go?" I stretch sleepily.

"Yes. We promised." It sounds like there's no getting out of it.

"Fine." If my stomach wasn't rumbling, I would throw the covers over my head and protest.

"Up you go, sleeping beauty." Kayne picks me up off the bed and I go limp in his arms. "Funny," he mocks. "Are you always such a lazy riser?"

"No. Only when I'm interrupted from such a comfortable sleep." He carries me into the bathroom.

"A hot bath should help wake you up." I look down to see the tub full of water and overflowing with bubbles.

I look up and smile at him. "Now you're just sucking up."

"Maybe a little." He grins, his blue eyes shining.

I kiss him on the cheek, his skin smooth against my lips. He presses his face into the kiss and moans softly. Not a 'you're making me hot' kind of moan. An 'I love that gesture' kind of moan. It makes me all warm and tingly inside.

"We have to hurry." Kayne places me on my feet in the tub. "Ten minutes enough time to soak?"

"Yes." I drop down into the water, the bubbles covering up my body. "I'm surprised you're letting me bathe alone."

"I figured you might want some time to yourself. Am I wrong?"

"Yes and no," I answer, leaving it at that. "I'll be out in a few."

Kayne nods then walks out, closing the door behind him. I lean against the edge of tub and gaze out the picture window into the dark. I daydream about this afternoon. The way Kayne touched me, the things he said. "*I love you.*" It's never been like that between us before. It felt like he was trying to give me everything. Every part of him. It's overwhelming in a good and bad way. I don't want to rush into anything, and I don't want to feel too much, but Kayne is a force to be reckoned with; especially when it comes to sex, love, even emotion.

"Ellie?" Kayne knocks.

"Times up?" I answer.

"For now."

I climb out of the tub and dry off. I walk out of the bathroom and head for my bedroom, thinking about what I should wear.

"Where are you going?" Kayne asks from the chair in the corner of the room. He's holding his phone, regarding me smugly.

"To get dressed. My clothes are in the other room."

"Not anymore." He nods his head toward the door behind him.

I walk cautiously by him and through the doorway. I'll be damned, he moved me in. Everything I stuffed into my suitcase is now hanging on one side of the closet, opposite his clothes, which are situated just as neatly.

"Been busy have you?" I ask as he stands behind me.

"I didn't think you'd mind." He kisses my bare shoulder.

"I don't, but only because I hate unpacking."

"See? I'm good for something."

"You're good for a few things. Like telling me where you hid my underwear." I walk into the closet. It's as big as the bathroom in my apartment.

Kayne follows me in and pulls open a drawer.

"Underwear and bras." He opens the next one down. "Shirts." And then the last, grazing my arm with his lips as he goes. "Bathing suits."

"Are you always so organized?" I sigh from the heat of his mouth.

"Yes. Repercussion of military life. I'm always on time, too. So get dressed," he hisses in my ear playfully then leaves.

Fine then.

I dress quickly in a black miniskirt and midriff top with a flowy sheer overlay stitched with a funky black, white, and peach pattern. It was an impulse buy, but I like it. Kayne will hate it. I don't regret the rash purchase one bit. I throw my damp hair into a high bun and attempt some makeup. Lastly, I rub some shimmery lotion on my arms and legs to moisturize and highlight my tanned skin.

I walk out of the bedroom exactly twenty minutes later and Kayne's jaw drops.

"Like my outfit?" I spin.

"No."

I laugh. Didn't think so.

"Not a patterns guy?" I curl my lip.

He growls. "No, I'm not a 'my girlfriend's skirt is so short she's flashing the world her ass' kind of guy."

"Hmm," I muse. "I must have missed the conversation where we established labels."

He glares at me.

"Are we going? I know how much you hate to be late." I walk out of the bedroom.

"Brat," he snaps from behind me.

I smirk devilishly and saunter out the front door. I can actually feel the frustration radiating from Kayne's body. It's increasing the island's already tropical temperature. I love it.

After a silent ride with a brooding Kayne, we make it to the restaurant right on time. He steps out first then escorts me. Matias smiles at us. I smile back, Kayne just grimaces.

"Have a nice evening," he says jovially and drives away. Apparently, I'm not the only one amused by Kayne's annoyance.

I grab his hand and bat my eyelashes at him. "Are you going to be pissy all night?"

"Maybe," he answers flatly.

This evening should be fun, sitting across from my bisexual one-night stand trying to make nice, while my ex-slave owner acts like a petulant child beside me. Awesome.

I heave a breath and start walking for the door, but am stopped abruptly by Kayne's statue-like stance. He yanks me into his chest and locks me against him with one arm.

"I hate that outfit," he growls. "I hate that I have to figure out a way to walk in front of you and behind you all at the same time while resisting the urge to stab out every single eye that ogles you. How's that for honesty?"

"You did say you didn't want to keep anything from me." I inhale sharply as he tightens his hold.

"You look so hot my cock is on fire," he whispers in my ear while people pass by us. "I don't want you making any other man feel that way." He slips his finger between my legs and strokes my clit.

"Kayne!" I gasp, grabbing his wrist. "We're in public."

"I know." He grabs my ass. "Mine."

I look up at him with flushed cheeks and a racing heart. For a fleeting second, he holds my stare.

"Yours or not, you still don't get to tell me what to wear."

"We'll see." He releases me, and I stumble a little. Jerk still has the power to immobilize me. "You're missing something."

"I'm wearing underwear," I huff.

He smiles, trying desperately to contain his composure. "That's not what I meant."

"Oh. What did you mean?" I pull down the hem of my skirt. Kayne reaches into his pocket and pulls something out. He opens his hand and inside are a small pair of stud earrings.

I look up at him. "For me?"

"Well, I don't have my ears pierced, and I think they might clash with this shirt."

"You sound like Jett now." I take the earrings after he offers them to me. They're so different. Not a common pair of studs. These look like tiny balls of tangled platinum yarn. Sort of appropriate considering that's how my insides felt when I got here.

"The jeweler called them love knots," he says aloof, almost as if he's embarrassed. "I took a chance. Jett suggested diamonds."

"I love them," I say as I put them on. "How do they look?"

"Perfect."

"Thank you. They're a very thoughtful gift," I say, touching my earlobe.

"You're welcome." He kisses me softly on the lips and my emotions soar. It's one thing for a man to buy you jewelry; it's something entirely different when he puts thought and effort into the meaning. It makes me love them even more.

I catch a quick glimpse of my new earrings in the reflection of the door. They shine brightly in the light.

Kayne pushes me slightly in front of him as we walk through the restaurant, his arm placed firmly around my waist. I think he's attempting to protect his assets. Or what he thinks are his assets.

That's still to be determined.

Jett and London are already at the bar waiting for us. The room is dimly lit with amber up-lighting and gold accents. Very posh. Feels like New York, and I love it.

Jett stands and hugs me as soon as I'm in arm's reach.

"Nice earrings," he murmurs in my ear.

"How did you know? Kayne show you?"

"Nope. A girl only smiles the way you are when she receives something extra special. Looks good on you."

"What? The earrings or the smile?"

"Both."

"Alright," Kayne nearly rips me out of Jett's arms. "What are you two going for, the world record for longest hug?"

I roll my eyes at him. Dramatic much?

"Just being friendly," Jett responds.

"Uh-huh," Kayne returns flippantly.

"Hey, Ellie." London chirps from her chair while she sips on a red drink in a martini glass. She's dressed very similar to me, short skirt, high heels, and skimpy light pink top made of a satiny material. The most notable difference is she's gorgeous on a whole other level with her long red hair, big breasts, and sparkling blue eyes. It's official. She and Jett make one seriously intimidating couple.

"Hey, London." I try to smile naturally, but I'm still a little uncomfortable around her. I keep picturing her naked, wearing a collar, and feeling me up. I glance at Kayne; I wonder if that's what he sees when he looks at us.

Is it suddenly hot in here?

"Ellie?" Kayne gives me a strange look. I blush.

"I need to use the restroom," I announce spontaneously.

"Everything okay?" he asks worried.

"Fine."

"Well, our table is ready," Jett tells me. "Do you want us to wait for you?"

"No. I'll find you. The place isn't very big." I begin to step away.

"You sure?" Kayne presses.

"Positive."

"You know what?" London puts her drink down. "I'll come with you." She hops off her seat and smiles. "We can use some girl time." She hooks her arm into mine, and both Jett and Kayne's eyes glaze over. Maybe she should have used a different term.

London leads me away from the two drooling men. If they weren't picturing us together before, they definitely are now.

We walk into the bathroom still arm and arm just as an older woman exits. She eyes us judgmentally as she passes by. Is it that obvious something conspired between us? Or am I just being paranoid. It feels like there is a huge flashing sign hovering over our heads that reads 'We Had Sex.'

The bathroom is small with only two stalls, wooden doors, and a marble vanity with double sinks. London lets go of my arm and settles her hip on the sink, standing closer to me than a normal girlfriend would.

"I'm glad we have a second alone. I've really wanted to talk to you," she begins.

"About what?"

"Look, Ellie," she sighs. "I don't want things to be weird between us because of what happened. I was only doing my job." London bites down on her bottom lip.

I frown. Am I the only one who finds this conversation totally fucked up?

"Oh, no, please don't think I didn't enjoy it." She puts her hand on my arm reassuringly. "That night was one of the hottest of my life."

I can't lie—mine, too.

"Jett still gets upset that he missed it."

"What?"

"Yeah, he wishes he was there," she smirks.

"Were you two together when . . . *we were together?*" I clear my throat.

"No, not exactly. It was complicated. After everything happened, I didn't think I was ever going to see him again. Boy, was I wrong."

"I didn't think I was ever going to see either of them again. Or you." I laugh.

"Well, I'm glad you're here. Kayne was so miserable for such a long time. I think if you didn't show up, it would have destroyed him. Like, literally killed him."

"Well, I'm here, and we're working on things."

"Good. He really is a good man."

"Did you know who Kayne and Jett really were?"

"Nope, no idea. Not until after. Until Jett explained everything to me."

"Nice to know I wasn't the only one in the dark."

London shakes her head. "Kayne and Jett are good at keeping secrets."

"That's part of what scares me."

"It shouldn't. I've never felt safer than I do with Jett. I really love him, Ellie. And Kayne really loves you. They're a package deal. So please can we try and be friends?" she implores me.

"I say go for it," a voice echoes through the small bathroom, and then a toilet flushes. London and I look at each other with wide eyes as an elderly woman emerges from one of the privacy stalls.

"I don't know which one of you was talking, but very sincere." A short, gray-haired woman in a printed dress walks out and nonchalantly washes her hands. "I didn't mean to eavesdrop, but you were entertaining me." She smiles kindly.

London and I just stare at her dumbfounded.

"Have a good evening." She grins, thoroughly amused, and then leaves.

Once she's gone, London and I look at each other and immediately burst out laughing.

"We would be terrible spies!" I double over as the sound of our cackles fills the room.

KAYNE

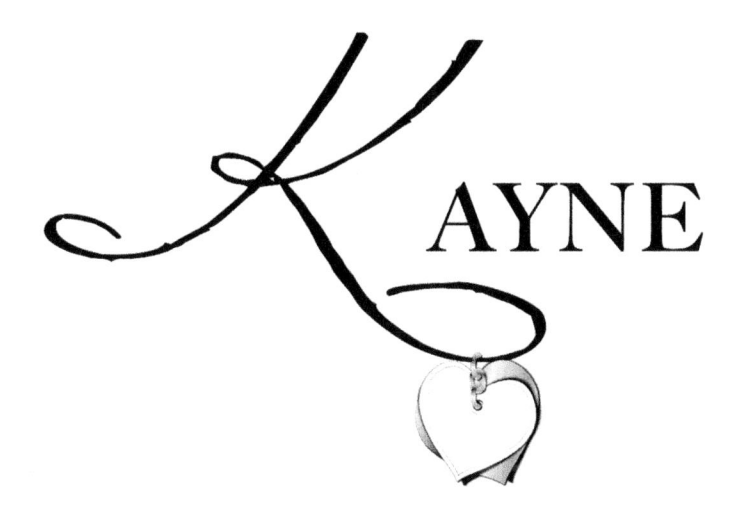

I LOST MY VIRGINITY TODAY.

Yes, I may have slept with other women, but for the first time, I didn't bind one or spank one or bring one to tears. Instead, I just poured my entire heart and soul into loving another human being. So, as far as I'm concerned, today is the day I officially lost my virginity.

I'll never regret it was with Ellie, either; even if this thing between us doesn't work out, which I pray to God that it does. She is the only one who deserves to own that part of me. She's the only one I want to own it.

"Have you heard anything else from our friend visiting the Aloha State?" I ask Jett as casually as if asking for the time.

"Quiet as a mouse. Juice has ears to the ground. If he's up to something, we'll know."

"Shit." My jaw ticks. Twelve months without an inkling of retribution and suddenly this guy surfaces out of the blue. "It doesn't feel right."

"Well, there's no sense making waves if we don't have to."

"The last thing I want is to be caught off guard." I glare at Jett sternly. "Like last time."

"No one wants that." Jett pulls on the collar of his light-blue dress shirt, scanning the restaurant. "Just let Juice and Endeavor handle it for now. You have more important things to worry about," he says as Ellie and London approach, arm in arm, falling all over each other, laughing. I shoot Jett a questioning look. He just shrugs. "That bathroom must have magic toilet paper or something," he mutters under his breath.

"Apparently." Considering Ellie was as stiff as a board when she left with London a few minutes ago, and now they look like best friends. We both stand when the girls reach the table.

"Is there an inside joke you want to let us in on?" Jett asks London, which seems to make her and Ellie giggle harder.

"Nope." She tries to compose herself by turning away. Ellie just looks up at me smiling brightly, her cheeks pink and eyes soft.

"What's that smile for?" I ask.

"No reason. Just because," she says sweetly.

I glance at Jett once more. He just smirks. Alrighty then, magic toilet paper it is.

"What do you like, Ellie? London asks fanning herself with the menu. She's finally pulled herself together.

"Everything. I eat everything," she informs her.

"Except sesame seeds," I chime in.

Ellie whips her head up at me. "How did you know I was allergic to sesame seeds?"

I shrug. "I know everything I need to know about you."

"Oh really?"

"Mmm hmm." I lean in close to her, getting a whiff of her sweet smelling perfume. "Elizabeth Anne Stevens, born August twenty-eighth to Alec and Monica Stevens. Sister Tara, three years younger. You attended Long Island City High School in Queens. You ran track, which explains why you're so damn fast." I smile from the memory of chasing Ellie down the hall at Mansion, and being surprised at how quick she was. "You also graduated with honors. Shortly after that, you were hired at Expo, a small but thriving import/export company owned and operated by Mark J. Atkins, where you quickly moved up the ranks from secretary to personal assistant. Your favorite color is purple, your blood type is O, and your favorite cupcake flavor is a toss-up between red velvet and lemon drop." I flash her a haughty grin.

Ellie's eyes are as wide as green soda bottles by the time I finish speaking.

"Kayne, that's creepy."

"It's my job to know things, Ellie."

"Still. Creepy."

"Creepy enough to scare you away?"

"No, although I am curious, Super Stalker Extraordinaire. You know I'm allergic to sesame seeds, but do you know how I found out?" Ellie asks loud enough for everyone at the table to hear.

"Um . . ."

"Yeah, do ya?" Jett repeats annoyingly.

"No," I snap at him.

Ellie giggles. "Mark."

"Mark?" London asks.

"My old boss in New York."

"And what does Mark have to do with it?" I ask.

"Well, when I started working for him, I was eighteen, right out of high school, and pretty green when it came to, well, mostly everything. Especially fancy dinners. So Mark, being Mark, wanted to broaden my horizons, starting with sushi." Ellie chuckles to herself.

"So what happened?" Jett inquires.

"He ordered some seared ahi tuna, and did nothing but rave about how much I was going to love it. I took about three bites before my face started to blow up." She uses her hands to emulate the swelling. "Mark did nothing but freak out while I went into anaphylactic shock. My throat closed, and I came close to passing out. That's when he pulled out his EpiPen from his man purse and stabbed me with it." She mocks her story by pretending to stab herself in the neck and laugh. "He even screamed like a woman when he did it."

"What kind of man screams like a woman?" London says, giggling along with Ellie's infectious energy.

This makes Ellie laugh harder. "A flaming gay one with drama written all over him," she explains. "He had a full-on panic attack right afterward because he thought he almost killed me. The waiters had to bring him a brown bag to breathe into."

The story has the table chuckling so long we don't even

notice the waiter standing over us until he clears his throat. Loudly.

After we order enough sushi to feed a small army, Ellie continues to captivate everyone at the table with her charm and spirited personality. She tells us all about her sister and parents, and what it was like growing up in New York. She recounts the story of when we first met and how she spilled hot coffee in my lap. Also, how she attended the prom with two black eyes because her track coach made her run hurdles, even though she begged him not to because she always fell.

By time we get the check, my love for Ellie has grown leaps and bounds. As if that was even possible. I memorize the way her green eyes sparkle and face lights up when she laughs. How she talks with her hands when she gets into a story and how attentive she is to everyone at the table, London included. The tension between them seems to have completely dissipated as they whisper to each other and gang up on Jett and me to do more Saki bombs.

All I keep thinking about is that picture pinned up on Ellie's old desk of her and Mark on St. Patrick's Day, and how much I wanted to know that girl. Well, tonight I think I'm finally getting my first glimpse. What did Mark call her once? Oh yeah, magic glitter in high heels. I'm starting to see why. She's enchanting.

After a memorable meal and way too many shots, Jett, London, Ellie and I end up closing down the restaurant. They were nearly kicking out our rowdy bunch.

After some quick goodbyes and promises to meet up tomorrow, we each go our separate ways. I hail a ride for us back to our bungalow as Jett and London walk off to theirs. I'm assuming. You never know with Jett, though.

"Did you have fun tonight?" I run my nose up Ellie's neck once we're in the golf cart.

"Yes." She sighs as she wraps her arms around my neck and pulls me close. We have a hard time keeping our hands and lips off each other as we're chauffeured through the resort. I hear the driver chuckle to himself as we nearly give him a show.

"Have a good evening," the young man says, highly entertained, as we climb out of the cart a hot, drunken mess.

"We will." I grin roguishly at him as Ellie and I stumble to the front door. Once inside, we nearly take a tumble as Ellie rips off her shoes and tries to kiss me all at the same time.

"Let's go skinny dipping." She pulls me through the living room, driving her tongue into my mouth.

Now what stupid man would say no to that?

By the time we make it out to the deck, we're nothing but hungry mouths, hot bodies, and frenzied hands. I turn Ellie in my arms and press her back to my front, devouring her neck and groping her breasts. I may have just had dinner, but I am still a starving man. I pull the straps of her shirt down her arms to expose her chest, clutching and massaging and stroking her nipples until they are hard little pebbles beneath my fingertips. She moans freely, rubbing herself against my now throbbing cock. It makes me crazy, makes me need her, makes me delirious with lust.

"Bend over," I order her, as we stand a few feet away from the pool. She bends, grabbing onto the metal railing that rings around the entire sundeck.

I can hardly breathe as I run my palms along the back of her smooth thighs and up over her ass. Her clingy skirt bunches around her waist as I work my hands over her two perfect little round cheeks. God, how I love Ellie's ass. The beast swings his spiked tail against the door of its cage, demanding to be set free as I press and knead her behind over the delicate lace underwear that barely covers her bottom. I ignore the snarling monster, and the overwhelming urge to spank her as I peel her panties down to her thighs.

Ellie glances back at me, her eyes hooded and lips parted, like she's just daring me to touch her. But I have other ideas. I lean over and trap her face, covering her mouth with mine. I thrust my tongue and my hips at the same time, as I subdue her against my body. Ellie kisses me back with such intensity it takes me by surprise and eggs me on all at the same time.

"Touch yourself, Ellie."

I don't know if it's the alcohol or the need or just my kinky desires that spurs the request, but I run with it, hoping I'm not pushing her too far too fast. "Touch yourself, baby, and get wet for me," I rasp in her ear. Ellie pants loudly as she slowly removes one of her hands from the railing and places it between her legs. "That's it."

She closes her eyes and nuzzles her nose against my jaw as she starts to massage herself. I hold onto her tight, digging my cock into her ass as tiny pleasured sounds begin escaping from her throat.

"Feel good?"

"Yes."

"Did you ever touch yourself when we were apart? Did you ever finger your sweet little pussy and think of me?" I ask, tightening my grip on her face.

She inhales and exhales hard.

"Did you?" I urge.

"Yes," she expels the word with a huff, still rubbing herself. "I thought about you all the time. I couldn't get you out of my head."

"Me, too." I graze my nose against hers. "I pictured you every time. I thought about the first time I made you touch yourself. How fucking hot you looked with my cock inside you rubbing your clit. Remember that?

"I could never forget," she chokes out, stroking herself harder, pressing up against my pulsing erection.

"You came so fucking hard; I can still feel how tight you squeezed me."

"You tortured me," she moans.

"You liked it," I counter. "I loved it. Will you show me again? Will you let me watch you make yourself come?"

Ellie is nearly falling apart by the time she forces out her answer. "Yes."

"Good girl." I release her and spin her around, stripping her of all her clothes in a second flat. "Show me." I pin her hips against the railing.

With deep breaths, Ellie runs her hand down her stomach until she reaches her wet folds. She spreads herself wide, exposing the engorged pink flesh of her clit, and begins to rub in slow circles as if she knows just how it's going to affect me.

"Feel good?" I can barely speak; she looks so fucking hot completely naked, touching herself under the moonlight.

"Yes, but I'm missing something." She looks up into my eyes, the blazing lust evident.

"Need me, baby?" I lift one corner of my mouth wickedly.

"Need and want." She slips one finger inside her pussy, and I become an unhinged man.

"Fuck, Ellie." I crush my lips against hers as I tear off my pants.

Once out of the way, I grab one of her thighs and hook it around mine, so her legs are wide and my view is unobstructed.

"Keep touching yourself." I sink inside her half way and am bathed in her scorching wet heat. "So good."

Ellie moans as she strokes and massages herself into a frantic state with me partly buried inside her.

"Kayne, more," she pleads, her voice elevating, her hips jerking.

"No, baby that's all of me you get. You have to make yourself come first."

She groans in agony. "Please."

"No," I deny her as her face contorts, tormented with pleasure, just tempting me to slam inside her and shatter on the spot. "Keep going."

"Oh God!" She moans loudly as her sweltering little pussy sucks on the tip of my cock vigorously. "I'm going to come." She fists her free hand in my shirt just as the tremors begin and fluid drips down my shaft.

I thrust inside her at that exact moment and fuck her straight through her orgasm as she screams out into the dark night.

"Fuck, fuck!" I fight off my own orgasm until she's depleted and limp, then I lift her right off the ground and impale her onto my throbbing cock, once, twice, three times, until I explode inside the tightest, wettest, most heavenly pussy on the face of the Earth.

Still shaky from the aftershocks, I sink to the floor with Ellie wrapped around me, the both of us sucking in air like it's going out of style.

I hold Ellie in my arms as she snuggles against me with a million stars twinkling over our heads.

"Too much too fast?" I exhale breathless, suddenly worried.

She shakes her head. "If I didn't want to, I would have said no."

I tilt her head up so I can look at her.

"You can always say no."
She kisses me lightly, "I know."
"Good."
"Can we still go skinny dipping?"
"Sure," I chuckle.
"Good." She nestles herself back up against me. "It will be nice to see you naked and wet for a change."
"Ellie." I laugh, hugging her tight.
I may never, ever let go.

I'M COLD. IT FEELS LIKE my heart has stopped pumping blood through my body. I roll over to reach for Ellie, but she's not there. I snap open my eyes and sit up. It's still dark out. I get out of bed and search the bungalow, tearing through the living room, bathroom, and sundeck like a madman. I check upstairs as well before my craziness gets the best of me, and I open the front door.

She's gone.

A streak of dread runs through me. Did she just leave? I check the closet. All her things are still exactly where I put them.

Did someone take her? Paranoia flares.

I storm into the bedroom and swipe my phone off the end table. Just as I'm about to dial Jett, I hear the front door open and shut. It feels like all the organs inside me sag in relief when Ellie walks into the bedroom.

"You're up," she says surprised, wearing tight black shorts and one of my white wife beaters.

"Yeah. Apparently, so are you," I snap sharply. "Where were you?" I don't mean to bite her head off, but she just fucking left. In the middle of the night. Without telling me. Does she have any idea how neurotic I can be?

Of course she doesn't. You haven't shown her your self-deprecating, mistrusting, shithead side yet that's wracked with mommy issues.

"I went for a walk," she wraps her arms around herself.

"In the dark?"

Ellie nods.

"By yourself?"

Ellie bites her lip. "I wasn't exactly alone."

"You were with someone?" I raise my eyebrows about to blow.

She nods again.

"London?"

She shakes her head.

"Jett?" I try again.

"Yes."

"Why?"

"I needed to talk." Her smoky-green eyes cut through me in the darkness.

"To Jett?"

"With Jett," she corrects.

"About what?"

Ellie shrugs. She's being difficult, and I don't like it.

"Stuff."

"Stuff?"

"Stuff," she repeats. Her and her fucking monosyllables.

"Wanna tell me what kind of stuff?"

"No." She fidgets with her fingers.

What!?!

"Is everything okay?" I ask, on the brink of a nervous breakdown.

"Yes."

"Did I do something to upset you?" I ask, trying not to snap the thin strand of composure keeping me together. I'm sure losing my shit won't encourage her to talk.

"No." Her face drops. "Why would you think that?"

"Because you snuck out of bed in the middle of the night to go see my best friend!"

"He's my friend, too," she asserts.

"And you needed to talk to him?"

"Yes."

"Why can't you talk to me?" I have always had this issue with Jett and Ellie. I want to be the one she talks to and confides in. The one she trusts. It's apparent I still have a lot of work to do before that happens.

Ellie takes a cautious step closer to me. "I didn't want to

wake you. And I didn't mean to upset you." She takes another step, then another.

"Well, you did wake me. It's like my body knew you weren't there. I didn't like that feeling, Ellie, and I didn't like not knowing where you were."

"I'm sorry." She's standing in front of me now looking apologetic, and sexy and utterly irresistible in my ribbed undershirt.

"You're forgiven." I pull her against me, and she fastens her arms around my neck. *Sucker.*

"You can talk to me, Ellie. You can tell me anything. I'll listen."

She hugs me tighter. "I know."

Then why did you have to turn to Jett?

"I know I'm not perfect and I'm going to make mistakes. I've never done this before," I babble nervously, as I hug her. "But I'm learning."

"We're both learning, okay?" Her words console me.

I nod silently. Crushing her to me.

"Can we go back to bed?" she asks seductively, nuzzling my neck.

"Can I feel you up once we lay down?"

"You're actually asking permission?"

"For now." I smile against her temple.

"I think there are a few places on my body that could use a good rub."

"Well, if there's one thing I know how to do, it's rub." I kiss her roughly, tangling our tongues together. She moans into mouth, jumpstarting my blood flow, sending an excess straight to the head of my cock.

When we break apart, I trap Ellie's chin between my thumb and forefinger, forcing her to look up at me.

"I love you," I whisper sternly.

"I know," she responds softly.

"Good," I reply, hoping beyond hope one day she'll love me back.

ELLIE

HOW AM I SUPPOSED TO talk to Kayne when he's the one we're talking about?

Tonight overwhelmed me to the point the aftermath woke me up out a dead sleep.

It's all coming at me so hard and so fast. I'm scared, excited, hopeful, and doubtful all at the same time. It's a dizzying state. Kayne keeps telling me he loves me. Drilling it into my head the same way he drilled his perversions into my body. I just needed to talk to someone, hear a voice of reason, and Jett has always been that for me when it comes to Kayne. I was in such disarray, I didn't know up from down or right from left. I needed to purge everything I was feeling, and I knew Jett would listen.

When I called Kayne the Kingda Ka, I meant it. He's a sharply winding trestle built for speed, and I'm not sure if I want the ride to stop or make it go faster.

KAYNE

I WAKE TO MY PHONE vibrating on the nightstand. I snatch it up then glance over at Ellie's naked form. She's fast asleep on her stomach breathing softly. The sun is just starting to rise, casting a bright orangey glow over the horizon.

I keep the phone close to my body as I read the text:

FYSA. Second insurgent identified. Threat level elevated.

What the fuck? I hit delete and slip out of bed, careful not to disturb Ellie. Tucking myself into the shadows, I dial the secure number I have memorized.

"Yo," a man answers.

"Juice." I keep my voice low.

"Loverboy. Didn't think I was going to hear from you." He sounds way too awake and chipper for my liking. But that's Juice.

"Yeah, well, when you send text messages like that, I'm inclined to call in. What second insurgent?"

"Nicky Cruz."

"Holy shit. He's one of the biggest drug runners on the West Coast."

"Yup. We don't believe it's a coincidence that two of the most high-powered drug traffickers in the U.S. are both visiting the Rainbow State at the same time just for a holiday."

My blood pressure spikes.

"A commission meeting?" I ask.

"Could be. Or maybe they're both looking for the same person." I immediately glance at Ellie. She hasn't budged an inch.

"You need to fucking find out what they're doing there," I growl menacingly.

"On it, killer," he says aloofly, unfazed by my tone. "Probably a good thing you're vapor. Watch your back."

Click.

I crush the phone against my forehead and groan. Shit. Shit. Shit. Never a dull moment.

I drop my cell back on the nightstand just as Ellie shifts with a small sigh as if searching for me while she dreams. I crawl into bed and pull her against me, locking her in my arms. Locked. That's exactly how I intend to keep her — safe, secure, and completely protected. Except for once, it's not her I'm worried about. No, that conversation meant something else entirely. It meant someone might be looking for *me*, or, even worse, coming for me.

I've expected this, even anticipated it. I wasn't lying when I told Ellie you don't bring down one of the world's most notorious drug lords without repercussions. I messed up a lot of powerful people's businesses, and criminals don't usually take kindly to people screwing with their income. But I'm ready and waiting. So, let them come.

"You're awake?" Ellie stirs.

I glance down at her. Her eyes are still closed and her face is still pressed firmly against my chest.

"How did you know?"

"I heard you thinking."

I chuckle distantly. "I'm sorry if my thoughts woke you."

"It's fine." She smiles sweetly, and I melt. Jesus, the woman can cut my balls off with one twitch of her lips. "Is something wrong?" she asks, her eyebrows furrowed.

"Nope. Not a thing." I kiss her head.

"I'll take your word at face value, but I know you're full of shit."

I exhale profoundly, half amused by Ellie, and half worried about the rest of the world. "It's just—"

"Work. I know. I get it. You have to keep different kinds of secrets now." She cracks her eyes open, and the green is so deep her irises almost look brown.

"I don't want to keep anything from you." Even though, I am.

"Then don't."

"Some things I don't have a choice about."

"I can accept that. Just don't lie to me about who you are. I want to know the real you, not who you have to be for work or who you think you have to be for me."

"I wish I knew who the real me is." I've been someone else for so long, it's hard going back to who you were. Not that I really want to be that person, either.

"We can figure it out together." She snuggles up against me, and I nearly fall apart. I think that's most comforting thing anyone has ever said to me. Maybe with Ellie in my life, the person I am isn't so bad.

"There is something I do have to tell you."

"Oh yeah, what's that?"

I brace myself for the confession. "You're not the only one living in Hawaii."

"What?" She lifts her head and pierces me with her now very awake green eyes.

"I've been living in Waikiki with Jett."

"For how long?" She sits up hastily using the sheet to cover her naked form.

"Ten months."

"What!?"

"I needed to make sure you were all right," I say quickly.

"You needed to stalk me." Ellie expresses her own interpretation.

"I prefer to call it twenty-four-hour surveillance."

"So you've been watching everything I do?"

"Not everything. I respected your privacy," I inform her. "I was just making sure there were no intrusions to your life."

"Was there anything that threatened to intrude?"

"No. Nothing that I was aware of. And I intend to keep it that way."

"So you really do know everything about me?" I nod. "Even

about—"

"Your boy toy? Yes," I interrupt her.

"He's not a boy toy," she responds affronted.

"He can't be very important if you're here naked with me."

"He's a friend," she specifies. "And I can be naked with anyone I want. I'm unattached," she reminds me harshly. I cringe inside.

"I'm hoping to change that."

"I know you are," she says sternly, but her expression is soft. Good sign.

"Forgive me?"

"For stalking me?" she asks drily.

"For watching over you," I correct her.

"No."

"Come on. Wrong thing for the right reasons." I try to argue my side.

"So, you admit it was wrong."

"Nope," I contradict myself. Us spies are good at that. "Protecting you will never be wrong, no matter how I do it."

"You're going to be a very busy man then, because I don't like to sit still."

"Don't I know it." I trap her head in my hand and graze my teeth along her neck. "You're a very busy little bee."

"There's a lot to see in this world."

"I'll show you everything if you let me."

"That could take a long time." She closes her eyes and sighs as I skim the tip of my tongue under her jaw.

"Ellie, I've got nothing but time."

"Why didn't you let me know you were there?" she asks almost sadly.

"Truthfully?" I quit caressing her with my mouth. "To give you space. Plus, I saw what you did to those cupcakes."

"You saw?"

"Baby, I have never been far away," I divulge. "If you want to get mad at me for staying close, go ahead. I told you, I'll endure it just as long as I get you in the end."

"Get me how exactly?"

"Mind, body, and soul," I tell her simply.

Ellie looks at me skeptically. What I wouldn't give to be

telepathic right now.

"What are you thinking?" I ask.

"What kind of stipulations come with those things."

"None. No strings, no expectations, no demands. I told you that before. I will take whatever you're willing to give me. And I mean it. I never go back on my word. You may not believe it now, but someday you will."

"Are you always so sure of yourself?"

"Yes. When I want something, I get it. First rule of survival, identify your surroundings, accept them, and then try to improve them. I've identified, accepted, and now I'm trying to improve."

"Sounds like a lengthy process."

"Depends on the crisis."

"Are we in a crisis?" she creases her eyebrows.

"At the moment, no. But if your boy toy becomes a problem, maybe."

Ellie stares at me silently as the sun creeps up over the water brightening the room. Then she smiles impishly. "What boy toy . . ."

Now that's what I'm talking about.

I FLOP ONTO THE BED, beat.

The last five days have been the very best of my life, hands down, undisputed. Every day with Ellie I learn something new about her and myself. Her energy and love for life is infectious. She laughs more than I thought possible for a single person; she's always smiling, always frisky, always playful. I never thought I'd say this, but she's freaking wearing me out.

"Tired, old man?" she yells from the sundeck. Ever since she found out I was a whole five years older, she has teased me about my age.

"Not a lick," I lie, waiting for my second wind. I've always been energetic, but Ellie takes stamina to the next level. She never stops, whether we're out somewhere or in between the sheets. Not only have I met my match, I've met my competition.

I check my phone. No new messages. I haven't heard from Juice in three days, so I'm taking that as a good sign. Although in the spy game, no news isn't necessarily good news.

I shoot a quick text to Jett.

Me: Hear any good gossip?

Jett: No. Stop being a busybody. Only worry about that hot little piece of ass you're hell-bent on keeping all to yourself.

Me: I was never taught to share. Fuck off.

And you wonder why I'm a possessive lunatic when it comes to Ellie. Everyone wants her, even my best friend. Not that he's stupid enough to touch her, but he'll let it be known the interest is there.

"Kayne, what are you doing!?" Ellie shouts from the sundeck. "Come outside, and let's go swimming!"

I lift my head to look at her with wide eyes as she dips her foot into the pool. "We just spent the whole day snorkeling."

"So?" She shrugs.

I can't stop the smile from cracking my face. Energizer Bunny!

We have literally done everything from off-roading to jet skiing to kiteboarding. Today we took that private tour of the island Ellie was so excited about. It's been nonstop days and marathon nights. I've never been so sleep deprived in my life, even when I was on a twenty-four-hour surveillance mission in Afghanistan.

"How about instead you come inside and sit on my cock and let me watch those hot little tits bounce in the air."

Crickets.

I drop back down and close my eyes. Guess not.

"Such the romantic," Ellie chides playfully a few moments later, crawling onto the bed like a hungry cat stalking a mouse. "Is there at least going to be a little foreplay to get me wet, or should I just get right to it and fuck you?"

My cock twitches from just her words; she's definitely not shy about being verbal anymore.

I lift my head and look straight in her smoldering emerald eyes. "You want foreplay? Sit on my face."

I grab her hand and drag her upward until I can reach her waist.

"Kayne, I'm still wearing my bathing suit!" she says as I pull her body over my chest and bury my head between her legs.

"So what? I'll chew right through them to get to your clit if I have to." I bite and suck over the material.

"Oh!" She throws her head back. "You don't need to destroy my clothes. I'll take them off." She squirms, rubbing her pussy against my mouth.

"Off." I nip at her as she quickly unties each side of the pink bikini bottoms, fumbling with the strings as I tease her with the tip of my finger, slipping it just under the clingy material and stroking her lightly.

"Oh, God." She rips off her bottoms exposing her inflamed, pink pussy an inch away from my mouth. I don't waste one second diving back between her legs and licking up the sweet taste of her arousal. It has my need roaring. Relentlessly, I swipe my tongue through her wet folds, every so often sinking it deeply into her entrance until she is writhing and shuddering and soaking my face.

"Oh fuck, you're going to make me come." She grips my hair with both hands and tugs as hard as she can, fusing her pussy directly against my lips. I stiffen my tongue as she rides my mouth, bucking, moaning, and gasping for air.

Like a shattered dam, Ellie floods when she comes, her arousal as sugary as a mouthful of candy. I lap her up and suck on her clit as she lazily comes around.

"Adequate foreplay?" I ask as I wipe my mouth against her inner thigh.

"Yes," she answers sluggishly.

"Good. Now sit that wet pussy on my cock. It feels best right after you come."

"You really need to stop with the hearts and flowers. You're going to spoil me."

"I definitely wouldn't want to do that, now would I?" I answer as Ellie slinks down my body. Hurriedly, she rips off my board shorts, moving quickly to next discard the white Ginny-t clinging to my chest. As she pulls it over my head, it snags on my arms and tangles around my wrists. I try to pull free, but she stops me, tightening the stretchy shirt around my hands as if caught in some kind of trance. Silently she gazes down at me as if asking permission and me staring back—holy fuck—grants it. I've never let a woman take control before, at least not like this. Ellie binds my wrists, tying a secure knot with the fabric. Like a perfect storm of anticipation and fear, my heart hammers, my cock throbs, and my head feels light. Ellie has no idea how much trust it's taking for me to submit. To hand myself over and give her control.

"Kayne?" she speaks softly, kissing my neck, my cheek, my lips. "Tell me if this isn't okay."

"It's fine." I grip onto the underside of the headboard and respond robotically. I understand so much at this moment. So much of what I put Ellie through. How I restrained her mind and her body. For a split second, I can't even believe this woman is with me. I can't believe she is giving me a second chance. She is, without a doubt, stronger than I will ever be.

I lift my head to kiss her, trusting her with all my insecurities and all my fears.

"I love your body." She skims her fingernails from the top of my chest, over my abdomen, all the way down to the sensitive skin right above my cock. I break out in goose bumps as she does it a second time. "I also love the way you feel when you're inside me." I watch engrossed as she straddles my hips and teases my cock with her slippery little pussy. My stomach muscles tense involuntarily as she slides her slit over my pounding erection, but denies me penetration. I moan helplessly.

"Ellie," I groan, lifting my pelvis, begging to just thrust up inside her once.

"Need me, baby?" She throws my own words back at me as she glides over my length a second, a third, and a fourth time.

"You know I do." I yank on the headboard dying to get my hands on her.

"Tell me what you want." She leans over and swirls her tongue against my neck. "Do you want me to suck you? Stroke you? Fuck you?" she whispers lasciviously in my ear.

Little temptress, she knows just what she's doing. Driving

me mad.

"I want you to take your top off so I can suck on your tits while you fuck me."

You can never say I'm not a man who doesn't know what he wants. Ellie gazes down at me hotly as she slowly unties the back of her bikini top. It loosens but doesn't expose any skin until she slips it over her head and her breasts hang free. Gradually, teasingly, she leans forward and skims one nipple over my lips. I latch onto it and suck hard, causing us both to moan. As I lick and nibble and bite the little stone her nipple has become, Ellie eagerly lines up the head of my erection with the entrance of her pussy. I can't wait; I'm beyond desperate so I thrust upward, obtaining the penetration I so desperately need. Her head snaps back and her body bows as my entire length is submerged in her completely.

"Do I feel good?" Ellie asks as she takes me, engulfing my cock entirely in her tight, wet channel.

"You know you do. Nothing feels as good as you," I groan against her breast, sucking the skin until it turns purple.

"Nothing?" She starts to rock her hips in an elongated movement, stroking my entire dick from base to tip.

"Nothing. Not one thing on the face of this Earth feels better than you," I hiss as we fuck leisurely, Ellie in complete control.

"I could say the same." She sits up straight and arches her back, giving me a bird's-eye view of her naked body. I'm close to ripping the shirt around my wrists in two. If she doesn't start moving quickly and feed my body more, my arousal is going to spark into an unstoppable fury.

"Ellie." I grind my teeth and pull on the headboard until the wood strains, "move."

"Beg me." She plants her hands on my chest and digs her nails into my skin. "Beg me to make you come."

Fuck! Little brat, she's using my own tactics against me, spurring my need to soar and the beast to howl as she purposely torments me.

"Please." I clench my jaw as she tortures me with pleasure. "Please, baby, make me come."

"Let me come," she corrects me.

I inhale hard. "*Let* me come." I stare into her eyes. I can't imagine what I look like—inside I'm a shitstorm of raging hormones, on the outside, I'm trying frantically to keep my cool. I wonder if Ellie knows which side is winning out? "Ellie, goddamn it, please," I growl as I buck beneath her, her muscles clenching my cock brutally. This submissive bullshit is for the birds. I just want to grab her hips, flip her over, and fuck her until she screams, but Ellie seems to have her own agenda. Not to mention, her own frustratingly slow pace.

She leans down and kisses me hard, driving her tongue between my lips, assailing my mouth. "Good boy," she rasps as she begins to move, riding me fast, digging her nails even deeper into my chest until she's close to drawing blood.

Watching Ellie does something to me. It affects me in ways that I never believed imaginable. Letting her take control, feeling her body move, and seeing her cheeks heat with arousal physically destroys me. "Fuck! I'm going to come." My cock sharpens and my tendons threaten to tear as my orgasm speeds through my system.

"Me, too," Ellie hisses, her face tight as she keeps up the mind-bending rhythm. A few seconds later, she moans above me as I explode beneath her. Her throbbing pussy milking my climax for everything it's worth. Once the two of us are depleted, she collapses on top of me.

"God," I tear my shirt to shreds in order to release my hands and secure Ellie in my arms with this overwhelming need to hold her.

There are so many emotions escalating through me, I can barely get my thoughts straight.

"You okay?" Ellie asks, as if she can see my instability dancing like a shadow on the wall.

I don't answer.

"Kayne?" Ellie lifts her head worried.

"I'm fine," I finally answer. "That was just . . . Was just . . . way more than watching your tits bounce in the air."

We stare at each other for a beat then erupt into laughter. For me, it's a cathartic laugh. Being with Ellie is just so goddamn easy. Every stressful moment of my life seems to fade away.

Seems to never have existed.

"You scared me for a second." She lies back down.

"You scare me every second," I admit, threading my fingers into her hair.

"Why?"

"You do things to me, Ellie."

"Like tie you up with your undershirt?"

"That would be one thing," I chuckle. "But not exactly what I mean. I've never been able to relax. I've always been anxious and on edge. But with you, I feel calm. It's new."

Ellie smiles shyly at me then kisses my chest right where her name is tattooed. She doesn't say a word because nothing needs to be said. We just lay there lazily as she nestles her face against my side while I brush my hand along her back.

"Kayne?"

"Mmmm?"

"What do you think would have happened that night if things hadn't gotten all messed up?"

I smile to myself with my eyes closed. "Exactly what I planned. I would've taken you back to my penthouse and fucked you."

"Would you have tried to tie me up?" I feel her look up at me.

"Probably. Would you have let me?" I glance down at her.

"Probably."

"Interesting to know."

ELLIE

SEVEN DAYS. I HAVE SPENT six nights and seven days with Kayne, and he has me flying high. Like, literally, ten thousand feet in the air. At the moment, I'm being strapped to his body with a skintight harness. To say I'm not shitting myself would be a lie. Skydiving was the one activity Kayne pushed for. When he saw the brochure on Matias' desk, his eyes lit up so brightly they nearly blinded us. I immediately protested, arguing that if God wanted humans to fly, he would have given us wings. Kayne contested, saying God improvised and gave us parachutes. Only after a lengthy, one-sided conversation of Kayne explaining how he's probably more experienced than a skydiving instructor, having jumped over fifty times, did he finally persuade me to give in. Which brings us to now, the two of us standing in an open doorway of a tiny plane looking down at turquoise-blue water and the small circular-shaped island of Bora Bora. I think I'm going to throw up.

Kayne is nothing like I dreamed about, but everything I could have ever wanted. Every day together just gets better and better. It's almost surreal, but definitely not perfect. There's something missing. Something he's holding back, which in turn makes me hold back. I know my late-night conversations with Jett don't help, but what he doesn't understand is that by me talking to someone else, I allow myself to open up to him. It helps me process and helps me accept. Letting go of the anger and the feeling of betrayal wasn't easy. But Jett helped me work through it.

I swear he's a shrink, a sexual connoisseur, and a fashionista all rolled into one.

And as to why we talk in the middle of the night? At first, it was because I couldn't sleep, but it quickly became because I didn't want to miss one second with Kayne while he is awake.

"Ready?" Kayne asks with his mouth close to my ear.

"No." I dig my fingernails into his thighs.

"Relax," he purrs. "I would never let anything happen to you. Trust me?"

I flash back to the last time he asked me that. I was tied up then, too. The answer is still the same; I just hope the outcome is different. A few short hours after he asked me if I trusted him the last time, the sky fell on me. Now, I'm about to fall through the sky.

"Yes," I answer faintly with my heart beating so hard it's leaving an indentation on my chest.

"On three." Kayne cradles my face against his shoulder and then criss-crosses our arms in front of my chest so I'm pressed snugly against him. "Count with me." He raises his voice over the hum of the engine.

I take a deep breath and nod with my eyes closed, hoping I find the courage to actually make it to three.

"One!" Kayne yells as we inch closer to the edge. It feels like a vacuum is trying to suck us up.

"Two!" we say together, and then suddenly we're falling nose first into a wind tunnel. A piercing scream rips from my throat as we plummet downward, cool air whipping right through our clothes. *What the fuck happened to three!?!*

I know it's only supposed to last two minutes, but the seconds suddenly feel like hours as the adrenaline pumps triple time through my body. I don't know at what altitude I finally allow myself to breathe and take it all in, but once I do, the feeling is euphoric; an entrancing split of body and mind.

"Hang on!" Kayne yells as he pulls the ripcord and the parachute deploys, jerking us back only to release us a moment later into a soft glide.

"Holy shit!" I exclaim as my pounding heart echoes in my ears.

"Not too many people can say they saw the island from this angle."

"I'm sure that's true," I reply in awe as we fall slowly, drinking in the indescribable view. From here, you can see everything—the reefs at the bottom of the turquoise lagoon, the dark-green landscape, and the top of Mt. Otemanu surrounded by a ring of white puffy clouds.

"Ellie, I'm releasing the parachute. We're going to land in shallow water. Be ready for the impact," Kayne tells me all too soon as he pulls another cord a foot or two over the water. We drop, but land easily as the water cushions our fall. Once Kayne unhooks my harness, I turn instantly and jump into his arms. The adrenaline coursing through my veins like a fast moving stream.

"That was amazing!"

"You liked it?" He laughs lifting me up.

"I loved it!" I kiss him. "Let's do it again!"

"Now?"

"Yes!"

"Like the rush, huh?"

"Yes. And it's all your fault." I plunge my tongue into his mouth and kiss him fiercely.

"I created a monster?"

"You have no idea," I growl trying to kiss him again as something dark and primitive bubbles deep down inside me.

Kayne pulls away and looks at me funny. I feel high. It's the same feeling I used to get when he would control me, when he would command me. I want to tell him I want that again, but the words fall flat and insecurity takes over. What I'm scared of, I don't know. Him taking it too far? Me letting him? I know what he's capable of and how much he gets off on pushing my limits. I also know it's his dominant side he's holding back. It's the part of him that still terrifies me and thrills me all the same; I don't think any amount of time is going to change that, but it doesn't intimidate me the way it used to. I know I have a choice now, and I choose to want it. To want him. Every side and every angle.

"Ellie?"

"Yeah?" Kayne catches me staring at his mouth. That mouth

that is so spectacular and mind-blowing it could be the eighth wonder of the world.

"You seriously want to go again?"

I look up into his eyes. They're bright blue from the glare of the sun; the brown patch a stark contrast to the light color.

"Yes," I answer confidently.

He gazes at me inquisitively. "We are still talking about skydiving, right?"

"For now," I answer darkly.

"HUNGRY?" KAYNE ASKS AS HE deposits me onto the bed. I'm beat. Skydiving takes a lot out of you, or at least a lot out of me. I nodded off in the golf cart on the way back to the bungalow. I'm pretty sure my lack of sleep isn't helping either. I've barely gotten four hours a night since I arrived.

"Starving," I tell him while he is hovering over me.

"Dine in or eat out?"

"*Eat out?*" I can't help it; I burst out laughing right in his face.

"You're a pervert," he chuckles.

"Says the man who loves whips and chains and butt plugs!" I roll over holding my side.

"And spanking," he smacks me on the ass, and I jerk. "Don't forget spanking."

"Oh!" I moan loudly and all laughter dies. It suddenly feels like a thick cloud of tension has blanketed the room.

Kayne's eyes smolder, the look so hot it could burn coal. My thighs actually clench from need. But as quickly as the excitement surfaces, it disappears. Why is he holding back? Kayne straightens and clears his throat, but his arousal is still evident. It's pitching a tent in his shorts.

"Go out or eat in?" he rephrases, adjusting himself.

"Eat in," I answer softly.

He nods pensively. "What would you like?"

"Cheeseburger and French fries."

Kayne smirks. "Done."

"What's so amusing?"

"Nothing. I just like that you like what I like."

I don't think he realizes how true his statement is.

"I'll order." He heads over to the nightstand.

"Oh and—" I roll onto my stomach to follow him.

"A bottle of champagne and a glass of mango juice." He picks up the receiver. "I know."

I smile. I had the mango Bellini the other night at dinner and now I'm addicted. While Kayne orders dinner, I get up and go outside. A few more minutes of lying around and I will be out for the count. Besides, I don't want to miss the sunset. It's my favorite time of day. I shrug out of my cover-up and slip into the pool, making myself comfortable on the seat built into the side. I bask in the warm water as the sky illuminates in a medley of blues and purples and oranges and reds. I feel Kayne swim up behind me and pull me into his arms.

"Enjoying the view?"

"It never gets old." I spin around and gaze at the angelic face capable of so many demonic things, all of which he seems to keep hidden away under lock and key. I straddle his thighs and dot kisses on his lips to distract myself from my esoteric desires. I don't know how to tell him what I want because I'm still trying to figure it out myself. How do you tell your former owner that you want him to own you all over again? It sounds crazy even to me.

"Why did you join the Army?" I ask curiously. Kayne has been forthcoming about most things, but he does dance around some subjects, like his childhood, expertly. Kayne clams up for a beat before he answers robotically. "It was three hot meals a day and a roof over my head. Not very patriotic, I know, but the truth. I didn't have many choices then, it was either keep living on the street or enlist."

"You were homeless?" This is new information.

"For a little while, yeah. Not my proudest moment, but it was better than another shitty foster home."

"Was foster care that bad?" I ask.

Kayne shudders. "Let's put it this way, I won the lottery every time for crappiest foster parents."

I frown. "What was it like?"

He looks away, and I'm convinced he's shutting down.

"When I wasn't starving to death or being used as a human punching bag?" he answers bitterly, "Hell."

"How long did you live on the street?" I scan over his beautiful face, the lines angular, his jaw clean shaven and clenched tight.

He looks back at me, his eyes devoid of all emotion, like he has to put up a wall just to talk about it.

"Six months. That last home did me in."

"How?" I frown.

Kayne expels a deep breath and closes his eyes. This is clearly difficult for him.

"We don't have to talk about it if you don't want."

It looks like he's considering my out, but he surprises me and continues talking.

"I had just turned seventeen when I went to live with the Millers. My social worker raved about them," he says detached. "Said they were the best of the best. I didn't believe a word she said. By that time, I was so broken, so raw, I didn't believe anything anyone said to me. I was always on the defensive because it was all I knew how to be. They were a pretty young couple, maybe early forties. I remember them being very welcoming. Their house was big and clean, and for the first time in my life, I had a room of my own. I pretty much holed up in it for the first month I was there. Mrs. Miller would bring me all my meals and gave me the space they told her that I needed. Both she and Mr. Miller would try to talk to me, but they quickly realized how far gone I was. It took a few long months to finally believe they weren't out to hurt me. I was always waiting for them to punish me somehow, hit me, starve me, do something I was used to. But neither of them ever laid a hand on me. They just waited patiently for me to come around. After about three months, I started eating dinner at the table with the two of them and then helping around the house after school. Mr. Miller let me hang out in the garage while he worked on his old car listening to eighties' music. Mrs. Miller taught me how to do laundry and make scrambled eggs. She was the closest thing to a mother-figure I ever had. And after about six months, I finally relaxed and believed I had found two people I could trust. That's when everything went wrong."

"Wrong how?"

"Mr. Miller would go away on business trips periodically. Not for very long, a few days at the most. Mrs. Miller, or Kim by that time, and I were cooking dinner. It had become sort of a thing for us. It was our time to talk. She was really nice, funny, and easygoing. But that night she was acting weird. Usually, she dressed pretty conservatively in sweaters and dress pants, but she had on tight jeans and a button up that wasn't exactly buttoned up. She was drinking wine and being really flirty. It was odd. And then, while I was cutting peppers, she brushed up against me and it definitely wasn't by accident. I nearly sliced my finger open. I didn't like women to begin with, and I *really* didn't like it when they invaded my personal space. I tried to move away, but she ended up stalking me into a corner, telling me how attractive she thought I was, and how much she wanted me, and how Mr. Miller, Rob, would never have to know. Ellie, I was horrified. I wanted to escape down the kitchen sink. And then she kissed me and I completely freaked. I pushed her away as hard as I could and then just ran. It was my breaking point." Kayne laughs crazily. "My first real kiss and it was with a forty-year-old woman trying to take advantage of me." He looks at me so dejectedly that my heart disintegrates right on the spot. "My trust had been shattered, again. By *another* woman. I was done. So I chose one hellhole over another."

"What was living on the street like?" I search his hollow eyes.

"Fucking cold. And lonely, and hard. But it was safe because I depended on myself, and I was the only person I could trust."

I am incapable of speaking. So many things are starting to make sense.

"I spent eight hours in the recruiter's office the eve of my eighteenth birthday just waiting until the minute I could sign. It was the best decision I ever made."

"Why?"

"Being in the Army gave me structure and stability. It redefined me. I was ready to be someone new. Then I met Jett, and my life changed in a whole other set of ways. I was a wild animal before the two; I had no discipline, no self-respect, no integrity. They built me up into more. Not that I'm saying I'm perfect. We both know that I'm not, but I'm way better off than I was. And with you in my life, I'm even better." He tangles our fingers and holds on tightly.

"Are you sure about that?"

"I've never been more sure about anything. I don't think you understand how much power you have."

"I don't think I do, either."

Kayne clenches my hand, our palms smashing together. "Ellie, you're the one person who can destroy me. You're my sin and my absolution, my indulgence and my starvation, and every right to all my wrongs."

Oh Jesus, I think I just dissolved. This man can govern me with just his words. There's no controlling the onslaught of emotion that overcomes me. Compulsively, I crush my lips against his and fight back the tears as I suck and lick and plunge my tongue deeply into his mouth.

He kisses me back with matched force until we need to come up for air. "What did you mean when you said your trust had been shattered by another woman?" I press my forehead against his, winded, with my heart beating rapidly.

Kayne looks up into my eyes and his anguished expression almost destroys me. He grabs onto my neck and closes his eyes like he's holding onto me for dear life.

"Kayne?"

"Ellie," he says my name so wounded. "I'm not sure I can."

I have no idea how to keep him talking or even if I should, but I blurt out, "In high school, my prom date tried to rape me." Kayne's eyes fly open. "He was drunk and we were at an after party at a hotel. We were in the bathroom fooling around, and when we went as far as I was comfortable with, I told him to stop and he wouldn't."

Kayne looks at me disturbed. "Ellie, are you trying to kick me while I'm down?"

"What? No. Why would you say that?" Then I realize. "Kayne, you never raped me."

"I might as well have." He drops his head back and knocks it against the pool's edge.

I force his face back up so I can look at him.

"I never told anyone about it."

"Then why are you telling me now?" His voice is guarded.

"Because you said I could talk to you about anything. And I want to be able to do that. I just don't want it to be one-sided."

"I don't want that, either, but I don't know if I can . . . about this."

"We all have things that tear us up inside, and I can tell you from experience that talking about it helps."

Kayne sighs heavily. "You've been spending way too much time with Jett."

"I'm not going to force you to tell me. But I'll listen whenever you're ready." I kiss him on the lips with an abundance of *love.* Yes, exactly that. Love.

"I'm going to go dry off for dinner." I go to pull myself up so I can get out of the pool, but Kayne latches on to my thighs and stops me dead with just his impenetrable stare. The wall just got two feet thicker and twenty feet higher.

"I only met my mother once," he says, his voice so cold it freezes the pool. "I was seven and having a really rough time with the foster family I was with. They were especially abusive." I settle back down onto Kayne's lap. "They would lock me in a dark, tiny closet and leave me there for days. I still don't know why, maybe so they didn't have to deal with me." He swallows a very large lump in his throat, and I'm suddenly having second thoughts about him taking this trip down memory lane. "They made me pee in a bowl and eat scraps of food they threw at me like a dog." He clears his throat. "One morning my social worker shows up with this woman. She was really pretty." He says it like a child as his eyes tear up. "She even sort of looked like me. Same face and eyes, even hair color. And she was sweet. Really sweet. The two of them took me out, we went to the park, and for pizza, and even got ice cream. It was probably the best day of my life." His voice cracks and so does my heart. "When they took me back to my foster home, the woman, her name was Sarah, took my hand and sat me on the curb. That's when she told me who she was."

"Your mom."

He nods. "She said she had been sick and wasn't able to take care of me for a long time, but she was better now and wanted us to be a family again. I remember asking her if she would take me to the park if we were a family. She said yes, often. That's your biggest concern as a seven-year-old, you know, if you get to play." He laughs sadly. "I hugged her so hard before she left, pleading with her to take me with her. She was my mom, I belonged with her. But she said that there were things that needed to be worked out, so I needed to stay where I was a little while longer. She promised she would be back. She looked me straight in the eyes and promised. And I believed her. I fucking believed her and I *loved* her." Kayne splashes his face with the pool water, as if trying to wash away the surge of emotion. "She never came back, Ellie. I waited for days, weeks, months, years—sometimes I think I'm still waiting." He breaks, tears spilling out of his eyes. Unable to stop myself, I throw my arms around his neck and hug him as tightly as my arms will allow. "She destroyed me with hope, the same way Mrs. Miller destroyed me with trust." He hugs me back, digging his face into the curve of my neck. "You're the first woman I have ever entrusted with those two things."

I pull back and look at him. I think I finally understand the power that I hold. His tears continue to fall, trickles of heart wrenching sadness running down his face. They compel me as much as they destroy me. With no hesitation I lick his cheek tasting the salty anguish on my own tongue.

He jerks back, stunned. "Why did you do that?"

"You always lick away my tears," I respond simply. Looking back, every tear I ever shed in his presence was never done in vain. It was his strange way of connecting, showing me he cared.

The doorbell rings, causing us both to jump.

"Room service," Kayne mutters.

"I'll get it." I kiss him firmly before hurrying out of the pool. I grab a towel to wrap around me, and let the young man in, directing him to set the food on the table outside on the deck. I follow him through the bungalow, and when we get outside, Kayne is already out of the pool and drying off. His mannerisms are stiff and his face is blank.

The young, tan waiter quickly sets up our plates and leaves unobtrusively. Kayne and I both stare down at the food, but I don't think either of us is hungry at the moment.

"I'm going to go shower," he tells me withdrawn, walking toward the sliding doors leading to our bedroom. I grab his wrist as he passes by me. "We can take one together later if you want." I look up at him naked of all reservations. This man's emotional deprivation runs deeper than I could have ever imagined.

"Of course, I want that." His voice is gruff. "Do you still want it, that's the question?"

"Why wouldn't I?"

"Because I was just acting like the biggest pussy on the face of the Earth."

He's hiding again.

"No, you weren't. You were acting human, and that's the sexiest thing on the face of the Earth." I cuddle up to him, encouraging him to take me in his arms.

"You can hurt me, Ellie," he says, stripped bare.

"I know, but that's the last thing I want to do."

"I hope so," he breathes.

"Just keep trusting me, the way I've learned to trust you."

KAYNE

ELLIE IS HOLDING ONTO MY wrist with a death grip telling me to trust her. What she doesn't realize is that I do. Completely, wholeheartedly. I'm all in—one-hundred-percent. I'm just not sure if she is. Hearing her tell me that she trusts me gives me faith in whatever it is we have, but she hasn't even hinted to me about how she really feels. It makes me wonder if she can ever really love me. If she can let go of who I was in the past and accept me for who I am now. Whomever that may be. My biggest fear is that Ellie will wake up one day and realize I'm not what she wants, that I'm too intense or controlling or broken to truly love. I know it's only been a week, but Ellie has become an unshakable part of me, my nucleus.

I can only hope that she feels it, the truth of my love, and someday gives me the truth of hers in return.

ELLIE

I KNOCK SOFTLY ON JETT'S door.

I know he's expecting me.

The door creaks open exposing a dim light and a shirtless Jett.

"Evening," he says flippantly.

"Hey."

"You know, this ritual is starting to bug London. She thinks there's something going on with us, and she's jealous she can't join in."

"I highly doubt talking about all my jumbled feelings is going to excite her."

"Sexually, no. But she likes you, Ellie. She wants things to work out with you and Kayne. I do, too. I didn't realize how much I missed having you around. I even miss dressing you up." He grins.

"And by dressing me up, you mean seeing me naked."

"Exactly." He shoots a finger and winks.

I roll my eyes.

"So? What are we chatting about tonight?" He walks outside, and we take our usual seat on the ledge of the wooden walkway right outside his bungalow.

I shrug as I gaze up at the sky. It's the middle of the night and the stars look like a blanket woven together by streaks of silver clouds.

"We went skydiving today."

"I heard. Twice. Someone is a closet adrenaline junkie." I don't think Jett realizes how true that statement is. I bite my lip nervously. "Ellie? Can I be frank?"

"Are you ever not frank?"

"You've got me there. So here I go. I feel like there is something you want to talk about. Something very deep-seated and dark. But you're holding back. Am I right?"

I stare at Jett. How the fuck does he do that?

"Kayne told me about his mother," I divert.

Jett nods. "I figured he would. He told you way sooner than he told me. Took him years."

"She really just abandoned him like that?"

"Apparently. I've tried to talk him into looking for her. See what happened and get some closure, but he doesn't want anything to with it. That wound is just too deep."

"It nearly killed me when he told me. To see him hurt that much." My heart is still stinging.

"Yeah, but being with you is definitely filling a void in him."

"You think?"

"Definitely. He actually smiles now. Like genuinely smiles. And he isn't so uptight either. I swear there were times he was so tense, I worried he was going to trigger a natural disaster."

"That sounds pretty extreme."

"Yeah, well, Kayne is pretty extreme." He swings his bare feet.

"Then I guess I haven't experienced the eye of the storm yet."

"What do you mean?"

I fiddle with my hair, running my fingers through my low ponytail manically. "You weren't wrong when you said there was something deep-seated and dark that I wanted to talk about."

"Go on." Jett is now tremendously invested in our conversation.

"I just feel like Kayne is holding back."

"Holding back? His feelings?" Jett raises his eyebrows.

"No, he's very clear about how he feels, but physically he treats me very *delicately*. That's the best way I can describe it."

"Delicately," Jett ponders. "Like, makes sweet love to you?"

"Like he's suddenly taken a liking to vanilla."

"Oh."

"And your tastes have evolved beyond vanilla."

"Way beyond." I turn red.

"You want him to dominate you?"

"I want him to *own* me. The way he used to," I admit. Is there a hole I can crawl into and die?

"Oh, you are far gone."

"I'm crazy." I put my face on my hands.

"No, you're not. You were exposed to the lifestyle, and you liked it. It's perfectly normal, and it speaks volumes about how you feel about Kayne and the bond the two of you share."

"But everything is so different now. I don't think he wants that with me anymore."

"I disagree. He's afraid he's going to scare you off."

"That's funny, because I'm scared of the same thing."

"Impossible. Short of you sprouting a dick, that man isn't going anywhere. And trust me when I tell you, even if he isn't showing it, he wants to own you just as much as you want him to."

"What do I do?" I ask anxiously.

"Sweet thing, the best advice I can give you is to put on your big girl panties and tell your man what you want. Communication is important in any relationship, but it is vital in the one you're after."

"Why is communication such a scary thing?" I bite my nail.

"I don't know. You seem to have no problem communicating with me."

"I don't sleep with you." I elbow him.

"I know, it's such a shame." Jett shakes his blond head.

"Jett," I chastise him.

"What? Kayne is stingy. I share."

"Maybe if our communicating goes well, I can persuade him."

"Sweets, if your communicating goes well, I'll never see that cute little pussy again."

"I didn't realize you wanted me." I bat my eyelashes flirtatiously. It's an empty gesture, but it's still fun to play around.

Jett leans in close to me. "Do you remember the first time we met and you asked me if Kayne and I both owned you?"

"Yes." My eyes widen.

"If it had been up to me, we would have."

"Seriously?"

"Mmm hmm." He moves in a little closer and inhales me. It actually makes me tingle. Don't get me wrong, Jett is, well, Jett. He's smooth and seductive and drop dead gorgeous, but I never considered he actually wanted me like that. Up until this moment, we've always just exchanged flirtatious banter. It was innocent at best, but at the moment he's stirring something very deep inside me. Something surprising. Don't misunderstand, I'd never be unfaithful to Kayne — unless he gave me his permission. "I think it's time for you to go, Ellie," Jett says like I'm in danger. Like he's a vampire catching a whiff of forbidden blood.

"I think you're right." We both stand up hastily.

"I also think this is our last late-night conversation. You know what you want and how you feel. You don't need me anymore. Just be the strong girl we all know you are and take it slow." He tucks a strand of hair behind my ear and smiles. "You need a haircut."

"I know," I laugh. "Kayne likes it long."

"You're beautiful either way."

"Thanks."

"Now go make my best friend a happy man." Jett spanks me. "He deserves it, and so do you," he whispers then kisses me on the cheek. It feels like he just cut the last string of the past, and I'm perfectly okay with that.

More okay than I have been in twelve months.

I CLOSE THE DOOR TO the bedroom as quietly as I can. The room is darker than usual, the shades to the sliding glass doors are pulled, and all the window treatments are drawn. Strange.

"You and Jett have a nice chat?" Kayne's voice startles the hell out of me in the darkness.

"Jesus." I jump as he flicks on a small light. I turn to find him standing behind me, leaning against the wall, shirtless, with his arms and legs crossed and his eyes a harrowing black. "What are you doing up?"

"I could ask the same, but I already know." His voice is as cold as his stare.

"Why is it so dark in here?"

"Complements my mood."

"What's wrong?"

"Oh, I don't know." He stalks across the room toward me. "Maybe it's the fact you sneak out of bed every night to see my best friend."

"Just to talk," I respond automatically.

"Yeah, talk. Talking is important. I talk to you, Ellie. I tell you my deepest darkest secrets. I slice myself open and let my emotions pour out and what do you do? You leave. Not one night do you have the decency to stay with me. So tell me, little girl, is there something going on between you and Jett?" He crowds me, forcing me to step backward. "Do you want him, Ellie? Do you want him now that you know all about poor, pathetic Kayne and his fucked-up issues?"

"No." I bump up against the wall. "It isn't like that."

"Then what is it like? Tell me."

"We're just friends," I scramble. Pissed off Kayne is a scary thing. "He was there; he's the only one who knows what happened between us. Who else am I supposed to talk to?" Tears cloud my vision.

"Who else?" Kayne seethes. *"Me!"*

I jump. "How am I supposed to talk to you about you?"

"You can talk to me about anything. I have been trying, Ellie, really trying to be everything you want, everything you need. But it's just not enough. I will never ever be enough." He hits his chest with a closed fist.

"That's not true. You're everything."

"Then why run to Jett?"

"Because I was confused!"

"About what?"

"How I felt."

"About me?"

"Yes, at first and then . . . then . . ."

"Then?" He hangs on my last word.

"What I wanted."

"Wanted!? You don't want me, Ellie?"

"No . . ." I shake my head flustered. "Yes! Of course I want you. It's just . . ." My lip quivers, this is not how I pictured this conversation going.

"Just? Dammit, Ellie, tell me!" Kayne erupts.

I start to breathe heavily as the tears roll down my cheeks. I hate that I'm being such a girl, but this hard for me, wanting something so taboo. More than wanting . . . dying for.

"I want you," I profess.

"You have me."

"Only part of you," I contest.

Kayne looks at me like he's staring at one of those crazy 3D pictures.

"What are you trying to tell me?" He steps forward and takes my face in his hands, wiping away my tears with his thumbs.

"Being with you changed me." I look up at him. Now that he's a little calmer, it's easier for me to talk. "You made me want things. Things I could never want with anyone else."

"Things?" There's surprise in his voice.

I nod, pressing my cheek into his palm.

He stares silently for several long moments. "Are you telling me what I think you're telling me?" Fire ignites in his eyes and burns straight through to my core.

I nod again.

"Ellie," he breathes my name, and it sounds excruciating. "I don't know."

"Please."

"If I open Pandora's Box, I don't think I'll be able to close it again."

"You won't have to."

"I'm not sure I want to take that chance. I swore to myself I wouldn't hurt you. I wouldn't give you another reason to leave me. I don't know if I could survive losing you again. You mean too much."

"You won't lose me. I want it as much as you do."

He shakes his head, clearly torn.

"Guarantee me," he demands. "Guarantee me that if we do this you will still be here, you'll still want me."

"I promise. I need you." I swallow the lump in my throat. "I need you to own me."

"Why?" He searches my face intensely. I shrug.

"Maybe you're not the only one with a beast inside you."

"Shit, baby, that could be a dangerous thing."

"I know, and I don't care."

I'm being reckless, I'm fully aware, but Kayne is my drug of choice and I can't wait to get high. He looks me in the eye, hesitant to act.

"I told you, I want all of you. All your sides." I try to reassure him. Coax him. I thought he would jump at this opportunity, but his reluctance only makes me want him more, care about him more. It tells me how precious I really am to him. How he really meant those words he spoke back in that room, my luxury prison.

"Beg me."

I smile. "Please, please." I lean in and try to kiss him, but he stops me, trapping my head with his hands that are still clutching my face.

"I didn't give you permission to move," he growls, and I shiver. That voice. That stern, commanding, all-encompassing voice that makes my insides flip-flop.

"Yes, Kayne," I reply obediently, and that seems to stir something inside him.

"Fuck," he mutters to himself like he knows he's in trouble. Like he just gave in. "Kneel. Now."

I drop in front of him, surrendering complete control, pressing my forehead to the wood floor attempting to get as low as possible.

"Good kitten." At the use of my pet name, I literally liquefy. My panties drench with want and my pussy pulsates with need.

"Stay," he orders, and then I hear his heavy footsteps move around the room. I'm shaking; I'm so anxious, nervous, and excited.

A few moments later, he returns to me. "Ellie, look up."

I raise the upper half of my body but remain on my knees. Kayne lovingly runs one finger under my jawbone while he stares down. There are so many emotions playing across his face—worry, elation, fascination, and fear. I'm so entrapped by him; I don't notice what he's holding in his left hand until he moves to wrap it around my neck. The light in the room is dim, but I can still make out the leather belt with the double holes along its entire length. Kayne fastens it, leaving just enough room for me to breathe, yet tight enough to keep me in line. He yanks on the end forcing me to my feet.

He's panting as hard as I am as he backs me up against the wall. "Ellie, what's your safe word?"

Safe word? He's never let me have one of those before. Things really are different.

"Cupcake," I exhale.

"Good." He places his thumb on my lower lip and drags it down. "I want you to know what's going to happen next. I'm going to beat you, then fuck you, and I expect you to thank me when it's all over. Understand?"

I nod, dry mouthed.

"I'm very upset with you, kitten. You left me. You walked away and didn't look back and now you need to be punished. To be reminded of who owns you." He tugs hard on the belt, jerking my head. "What do you say?"

"Yes, Kayne," I reply immediately, surprised I can even use my voice.

"Good girl." He steps back with an hysterical look in his eyes. I know that look—it's manic, lust-fueled desire. It's Kayne's point of no return. "I want you to run, Ellie. I want you to run so I can remind you what happens when even the thought of leaving me crosses your mind." He snaps another leather belt in front of my face making me jump sky high. Holy shit.

The last time I ran from Kayne, my ass hurt for days, and I definitely remembered who I belonged to. He steps back, giving me some much-needed space.

"Go!" He snaps the belt again, and I take off, tearing out of the bedroom into the living room with Kayne right behind me. I dart and dash, jumping over the couch and knocking over a lamp in an attempt to get away. I scream as Kayne grabs one of my ankles and takes me down. My knees hit the floor hard, but I dig my nails into the wood and attempt crawl away from him. That's when he hits me the first time. Crack! Right across my backside. I see stars and shriek at the top of my lungs. I'm suddenly caught up in fight or flight, not wanting to suffer another hit. I kick and flail until Kayne loses his grip on my ankle. I hear him chuckle a little; he loves this game. Me, I'm not so sure. I run through the bungalow heaving for air with Kayne still hot on my tail.

"All around the mulberry bush the monkey chased the weasel," he taunts as he chases me. It's disturbing. I catch sight of the stairs. We haven't been up there before, but in a rash decision, I think now is as good a time as any to explore. With my heart jackhammering in my chest, I book it two stairs at a time while Kayne sings behind me, "A penny for a spool of thread. A penny for a needle." I make it to the top step, and he catches my ankle again. "That's the way the monkey goes." He pulls my leg out from underneath me causing me to fall face down on my stomach. "Pop goes the weasel." Crack! He hits me once more, and I let out a scream.

"Kayne," I cry as I crawl across the floor away from him. The second floor is an all open space. There is a massage table in front of us, wide-open windows, and a large sundeck with Jacuzzi and lounge chairs. The door to the sauna is all the way in the back.

"Am I making an impression, kitten? Is this what you wanted?" He hauls me up by my shirt, the spandex material ripping slightly. I don't answer. I just suck in the oxygen my lungs so desperately need.

"I asked you a question, Ellie." He slams me face first onto the massage table and pins me there with his forearm. Then he hits me again. Whack! Harder than the two times before. Oh shit, my poor ass.

"Is this what you wanted?!" he asks again.

"No, maybe. I don't know!" Tears stream down my face.

"Do you want me to stop?" he pants.

"Do you want to stop?"

"No, I want to peel your pants down to your thighs, spank you until your ass turns red, then fuck you until you beg me to stop."

"Then do it! You never gave me the choice before!" I'm not sure what's driving me here. Residual anger? Overpowering lust? I'm goading him for a reason. I need to know if this is what I truly want. I've dreamed about it, obsessed about it, and now

I'm facing the moment of truth.

Kayne doesn't respond. Not verbally anyway, I feel him rip my yoga shorts down to my knees, exposing my bare behind. Oh shit, oh shit, the belt really hurts!

Whack! The first bare blow knocks the wind right out of me. I try to push myself up, but Kayne's strength overpowers mine.

"You're not going anywhere."

Whack!

"Understand?"

Whack!

"Answer!"

Whack!

"Yes, Kayne!" I sob.

"Ever, Ellie. I'm never going to let you go. Ever!"

Whack!

"Ah!" I screech.

"I'll kill you before I let that happen again."

WHACK! He hits me again, and I wail like I never have before. My body is strung so tight it feels like my muscles may rip. I whine feebly as I hear the creak of the leather and prepare for another blow, but it doesn't come. Only the feel of his erection pressing into my ass. The contact is brutal; my backside feels like he lit my skin on fire.

"I'm going to fuck you now. Are you wet for me, baby?" He slides one finger easily into my pussy. Shamefully, I am. I want this man so badly I endured brutality just so he'd fuck me freely, with no reservations, and nothing holding him back.

I nod zealously.

He grabs hold of the end of the belt around my neck and pulls it tautly, forcing my head to snap back. He's going to ride me like an animal. Like his pet. I grab onto the edge of the table for dear life and brace myself. Good thing, too, because he slams into me violently, the dual sensation of his stabbing cock and stiff hips colliding with my abused ass makes everything inside me constrict to the point of almost painful. *"Ohh,"* I grate. Kayne said he was going to fuck me and that's exactly what he does, beating into me over and over, pulling on the belt hard while my body bucks forward. I'm completely helpless, rendered his.

I claw at the table as his cock thickens inside me. Hitting me harder and deeper each time. My body tenses, as an all-consuming orgasm booms like thunder in my core.

When I moan, Kayne moans, when I gasp, Kayne gasps — like we're in sync. He feels what I feel.

"Come, Ellie," he grits out as his thrusts become erratic. "Come all over my cock and show me how much you need me."

My head is twisting with conflicting thoughts, but my body, my body is reveling in the tyrannical way he takes me, the way he commands me. He feels so fucking good, I freely give into the sensations storming inside me, give into Kayne and to my fucked-up desires. I push my throbbing ass back against him and let go, screaming, crying, and moaning as my orgasm unleashes. Then, without any warning, Kayne snaps the belt against my ass cheek just at the height of my pleasure, and I let out a hoarse howl as my climax ratchets up several more notches, sending me flying. The world vaporizes as I get lost in the elongated seconds of extreme ecstasy; Kayne hammering away at me as I drench both of us with my uncontainable arousal.

"So good," he chants, "so fucking good." He slams into me one last time, his fingertips piercing into my hips as a sound so powerful and male escapes from him it shakes just a few more drops of pleasure out of me.

The two of us collapse forward, moaning feebly in the aftermath. Kayne's large, hard body covering mine. After a few long wit-collecting moments, he begins kissing my shoulders; sweet, soft kisses that tickle my skin.

"Ellie?"

"Mmm?" I answer absently, still reveling in the lingering bliss.

"You know I would never kill you right?"

"I hoped you weren't being serious." I smirk.

"No." He tightens his arms around me. "If you decide to leave, I'll kill myself."

My eyes pop open. "Kayne, don't talk like that. No one is killing anyone, and I'm not going anywhere." I crane my neck to look at him. His eyes are so raw. "I promise."

We stare vehemently at each other before he wraps his hand around my throat and pulls me against him, crushing his mouth to mine. The kiss is awkward yet passion-filled all at the same time. Kayne is still buried inside me, and I feel him growing hard again. I moan freely, so ready for round two.

"I love you." He pulls away and digs his face into my neck. "I love you, I love you."

I smile. "I know. I lo—"

We're suddenly interrupted by someone banging on the front door.

"Monsieur! Monsieur!"

Kayne and I both freeze. "The night concierge," he tells me. "I'll handle it."

Kayne withdraws from me, and my body frowns. It misses him already. I watch over my shoulder as he pulls on his shorts and hurries down the stairs. I suppose I should do the same, but my body is so sore, and the thought of pulling my pants over my battered ass is distressing. I'm not going to be able to sit down tomorrow, I'm sure of it. Probably not the next day, either, so I just lie there spent.

I listen to the faint voices of Kayne and a very upset concierge. Then I hear something that shocks me. Kayne speaking French. Like fluent, beautiful French. It's totally arousing. He's full of so many surprises. And I love surprises.

"Ellie?" I hear Kayne jog up the stairs.

"Mmm hmm?" I answer still draped over the massage table.

Kayne chuckles as he pulls me up. I groan miserably.

"Everything okay?" I ask him.

"Yes, crisis averted." He kneels in front of me and removes my pants so I'm left standing in just my ripped pink tank top and belt around my neck.

Scratch that, he just pulled off my top. "We scared the neighbors."

"Us? Preposterous," I snort.

Kayne laughs, tugging me by the makeshift collar into a quick kiss. "Yes, I had to assure him it was just a bout of rough sex."

"In French?" I look up at him.

"Yes, speaking his native tongue helped." He smiles.

"I didn't know you spoke French."

"Yup." Kayne nods. "And Spanish and Arabic and Mandarin."

"No Italian?" I joke. "Such an underachiever."

"Tell me about it," he jokes. "Maybe I can learn a few choice words just for you."

"Mmm. Maybe." I lean against him seductively and kiss him right where my name is tattooed on his skin. His chest is warm and smells so good, like sex and sweat and body wash.

"Come on, siren," he moans. "Let's take care of that bottom before we go another round."

"I'm all for another round."

"In bed," he promises darkly, then takes the end of the belt and leads me back downstairs. It's so hot, him toting me around the bungalow, I almost want to purr.

"Lay down," Kayne commands once we're back in the bedroom. I slide forward on the bed and stretch my body out like a lazy cat. Kayne's lazy kitten. He groans appreciatively behind me.

"Relax." He rubs my back starting from the tip of my tailbone and circling upward. I just sigh, sated, until I feel the tickle of his warm breath against my cheek.

"I'll be right back."

"Where are you going?" I protest.

"To get something to rub on your ass. I didn't exactly come prepared for this."

"For what?" I question.

"Kink."

"I think you're doing a bang-up job so far."

He glances at me fiendishly then walks out of the room.

"The only thing I could find was Vaseline," he says as he climbs onto the bed and straddles my thighs. "This might hurt a little." He rubs the sticky substance over my welts.

I whimper in return. It does hurt. Like a son of a bitch.

"Kitten, are you okay?" Kayne almost sounds worried. I crack my eyes open and look at him over my shoulder. "I'm fine." I smile. "Better than fine." I blush.

"I wasn't expecting that," he confesses as he wipes his hands with the towel he also brought from the bathroom.

"Neither was I."

Kayne stares at me quizzically. "I don't understand."

"What's to understand? Being with you changed me. Or

awoke something in me." I try to rationalize.

"You like it when I dominate you?"

I shrug demurely. "Apparently. I like it when you're rough."

Kayne palms my sore ass, and I hiss. "You like getting punished?"

I nod silently.

"You like being reminded who you belong to?" He grins like the Cheshire cat.

"Yes. To a point." I wince as he rubs.

"What happened to you hating being conditioned?"

I touch my chin to my shoulder flirtatiously. "I guess it's not so bad when it's my choice."

"Ellie." Kayne breathes my name like I'm a deity he worships, burying his face into my neck. "You are so mine."

Agreed.

KAYNE

I RUB MY TEMPLES AS I stare out over the water. My head feels like it's going to explode.

I unleashed myself last night. I let the beast out of its cage and handed over control. To say I didn't like it would be lying. I loved it, every second of it. From the moment I wrapped that belt around Ellie's neck, I was a goner. I keep playing it over and over, the way she ran from me, the way she fought me, the tears she shed, the reddening of her smooth white ass and the plush feel of her soaking wet pussy. All reason and rationale flew out the window as soon as she knelt at my feet. She was so turned on. It was more than I could have ever asked for—to have my kitten back for just one night—but it is also the one thing that feeds my fear. It's a serpent-like creature that burrows itself into the recesses of my subconscious. A gnawing worry that makes me regret last night ever happened. Because, in that dark black cavity, my one true terror lives—that Ellie is going to wake up and realize it was all a mistake. That she's going to wash her hands of whatever it is we have and leave. I keep telling myself she isn't my mother, but the nagging little voice in the background keeps reminding me that she left me once, she could do it again.

The thought nearly demolishes me. She really is the one

person who can destroy me. She may kneel at my feet, but she holds all the power. I'm the slave. I always have been. I stare out into the blue-green abyss trying to picture my life without Ellie. It's nearly impossible. I wasn't living before her, and I could never live after her. My chest feels like it's going to cave in. Why do I do this to myself? I let the worry and anxiety win. *"I'm not going anywhere."* I replay her words over and over trying to reassure myself.

"I'm not going anywhere."

"I'm not going anywhere."

She's not going anywhere.

I suddenly feel a nudge against my leg, and it yanks me away from my worrisome thoughts. When I look down, I nearly fall back in my chair because Ellie is kneeling on the ground, wearing nothing but a collar and one of my white Ginny-tees.

"ELLIE, WHAT-WHAT ARE YOU DOING?" I can barely speak.

She looks up at me with just her eyes, the green extra vibrant from the bright island sun.

"I wasn't snooping, I swear." She crawls up my legs to sit on my lap. "I wanted to wear one of your shirts, and I accidentally kicked over your suitcase. When it fell open, the tag caught my eye," she says coiling into herself, a little insecure and a whole lot sexy.

"I didn't bring it with any expectations," I blurt out. "It just made me feel close to you." I run my finger over the leather. It's not exactly the same collar she wore when she was with me at Mansion—that one was snapped in two—but this one is close. Thick black leather with large rhinestones adjacent to three D-rings and a light pink satin interior. Just feminine enough with a bit of bondage edge.

"It makes me feel close to you, too."

"You don't have to wear it." Although, now that she has it on, I never want her to take it off.

"I want to wear it."

"Why?"

She shrugs shyly. "Do you really have to ask?"

I search Ellie's face for any kind of reluctance or inkling of uncertainty. But there's none, only sincere eyes and a sultry expression.

"Say it." *Say the words I have been dying to hear.*

Ellie leans forward and slides her hands up the back of my neck and into my hair. "I love you. I have always loved you. Even when I hated you, I loved you. And I love you even more now."

My chest feels like it's going to explode. Those three words unlock something deep inside me.

"Say it again." I grab onto Ellie's bare ass. She's naked under my shirt.

"I love you," she says again, and I slam my lips against hers. Of all the emotions Ellie's made me feel—this moment, right now, is the most potent. I'm aerating with so much happiness I almost feel stoned, like I smoked straight elation.

"Don't stop saying it," I mumble against her mouth as I shoot up, Ellie wrapping her legs around my waist for support. "I want to hear you say it while I make you come." I walk straight into the bedroom while driving my tongue deep into her mouth. She moans loudly and my erection hardens into a stiff peak. I flip Ellie onto the mattress, and she lands on her back with a firm bounce. I shrug off my basketball shorts and climb onto the bed. "Lift your shirt up," I order as I crawl over her. With wide eyes, she immediately pulls the soft white material up to her chin exposing her completely naked form to me. My cock pulses with anticipation. It already knows how good she feels, how soft, warm and wet, and all for me.

"Open your legs, wide," I direct as I grab her wrists and pin her down. Panting heavily, she obeys, dropping her knees as far as they can go.

Good girl.

"Say it, Ellie." I rub my throbbing cock against her entrance.

"I love you," she breathes, her eyes fixated on mine.

"Again."

"I love you."

I thrust into her as deeply as I can. *"Oh!"* She closes her eyes and strains.

"That's not what I want to hear." I pull back and drive in deeply again.

"Look at me, Ellie. Look at me and say it," I snap.

Ellie's eyes fly open, and then with clipped breaths, she repeats the words. "I love you, I love you, I love you, I love you." Her voice elevates, and her face tightens as I keep a painfully slow tempo with my hips, brushing my pelvis over her swollen clit until she's struggling beneath me.

"Kayne, please," she begs as her pussy clamps down around me. "Faster, harder. Please," she expels.

Ellie begging does it to me every time.

"Tell me again, baby. Tell me while I make you come." My voice is unrecognizable as my body unleashes. I no longer have control as I pound into her, her breasts bouncing and tag jingling on her collar. Fuck, she really is completely mine.

"Oh God, I love you!" she cries out trying to fight against me, trying to find an outlet for her orgasm, only to realize it's being forced between her legs. Her fists clench in my hands and her body quakes as her climax rockets through her.

The hot rush of her arousal washes over me like lava and I come without any warning and absolutely no control. It's pure instinct, primal and primitive. Our hips fasten together as I bury my cock as deep inside her as it can possibly go, as if my body wants to become one with hers.

Once the sensations subside, the only thing that's left of us is labored breathing and warm fluids.

I look down at Ellie and for the first time, I see my life with clarity, in bright shining color. "Marry me." The words just fall straight from my lips, and I mean them with everything I am, everything I have.

"What?" Ellie's eyes pop open.

With a quick tug, I pull her up and place her on my lap. "Marry me," I say again. I never planned to propose, at least not this soon, so her shock is as genuine as mine. "Stay with me, Ellie. Wear my ring and my collar. Become my family, make me whole."

Ellie stares at me speechless, and I wonder if I've pushed her too far. Her silence is deafening. I prepare for a 'no,' for 'it's too soon' or 'I need to think about it.' My manhood shrivels. Stupid idiot.

"Yes," she finally speaks.

"What?" My eyes widen to the point my eyelids nearly rip off.

"Yes, I'll marry you," she repeats, for my sake I'm sure. "I'll wear your ring and your collar. I'll make you whole."

It may not have been a perfect proposal, but that was definitely the perfect response.

I lay Ellie on the bed and nestle myself between her legs. "It's my turn to tell you how much I love you." I nudge my semierect cock against her slick entrance.

She smiles up at me. "You can tell me as many times as you want." She rocks her hips, inviting me inside her.

"That could take a lifetime." I slide easily into her.

Ellie wraps her arms and legs around me. "We have an entire one to share."

I love the sound of that.

ELLIE

"ELLIE, WAKE UP." I FEEL something cold run over my lips, and I flinch. "Kitten, wake up, I can't watch you sleep anymore." The cold wetness drips over one of my nipples, and my eyes fly open.

"Morning," Kayne smiles hedonistically as he massages the ice cube against my clit. I suck in a sharp breath from the freezing sensation.

"How long have I been sleeping?" I rub my legs together and glance out the door. The sun is already setting.

"A while." Kayne pops the ice cube into his mouth and stares down at me with ravenous blue eyes. It's a gaze I recognize immediately.

"You're wearing me out." I smirk.

"I haven't even begun to wear you out. Up." He pulls me by my hands, and my body willingly goes. "Go to the bathroom and then come right back." There's authority in his voice. The kind that reduces me to just sensitive nerve endings.

I hurry up and do my business—my butt still so sore from last night—and immediately return to the bedroom. Once standing in front of him, Kayne runs his fingers reverently up my neck, over my collar, and then threads them into my hair. Controlling my head with a firm grip, he tilts my face up and spears his tongue into my mouth. I melt against him as the kiss consumes me.

"Kitten," he says once he pulls away. It isn't a question; it's a statement, a fact. Part of our foundation. "Do you still want to marry me?" he asks so vulnerably.

"Of course, I do. Nothing will ever change that. I'm yours," I reassure him.

"Good." He drops a chaste kiss on my lips. "Because I'm dying to play." His eyes burn bright and so does my core. This is what I've been missing, what I've been craving. Kayne in complete control—control of my mind, control of my body, control of my pain, and my pleasure. Am I crazy? Maybe. But isn't that what love is? Insane. I wasn't lying when I said I wasn't snooping. I found the collar exactly the way I said I did, by accident. As soon as I saw that little silver heart, I knew it was mine. The first time Kayne fastened a collar around my neck, I hated it—I hated him. But after a while, things changed. I changed. And once I held it in my hand again, felt the leather under my fingertips and read the inscriptions on the tag—one side Kayne's Kitten, the other side, Loved, Collared, and Owned by Him—I couldn't resist. It was like I found a missing part of me.

I never knew that second inscription existed. Maybe if I had, things might have ended differently. Regardless of past outcomes, it's the truth of the present that's important now.

And the truth is Kayne has always owned me, since day one. I'm pretty sure I would have done anything he asked whether I was wearing a collar or not. That's the claim he has on me—the power, the authority, the domination. And I wouldn't want it any other way. I love every part of him—the Dom, the thrill-seeker, and even the broken man—I couldn't stop myself even if I tried.

I breathe heavily with anticipation. He hasn't even touched me yet and I'm already coming undone. Kayne pushes me back until I'm crushed between his hard body and one of the bedposts. "Put your hands up and hold on."

I raise my arms and grasp the square post with both hands. Kayne steps back and looks greedily at my scantily covered form. I'm dressed in only his soft white undershirt and black collar, my nipples sharp as nails under the cotton material.

"Stay," he commands, and then leaves the room. I wait anxiously as I grip the bedpost trying not to combust.

Kayne returns with a small bundle of zip ties of various sizes and a silk tie. I look at him curiously, but don't say a word.

"Some things you just don't leave home without," he says haughtily as he pulls out several plastic ties. My heart rate speeds up as I watch Kayne fasten one zip tie around the top beam of the canopy bed directly above me. Then he connects another to that, and so on, until he's constructed a plastic chain link. Finally, he takes the maroon silk tie and wraps it around my wrists. "So it won't leave any marks." He winks as he binds my hands with a zip tie, tightening it so my wrists crush together. Once secure, he pulls my arms up until I'm forced to stand on my toes, and attaches my bound wrists to the hanging zip ties.

"Perfect." He admires his handiwork. Me, hung like a fish on a hook, helpless and gasping for air.

Kayne takes advantage of my defenseless state, cupping my pussy and groping my breasts until he has me moaning.

"Don't get too wound up, kitten. No more orgasms for you."

I frown.

"At least for a little while." I swallow hard, trying to keep my balance on my tippy toes. "Baby, I want you to understand. I'm going to punish you, tease you, and fuck you so hard . . ." Kayne outlines my lips with the tip of his thumb. "But I'm going to love you even harder." He then shoves his thumb into my mouth forcing me to suck on it energetically. I moan, unhinged.

"Good girl." He removes his finger from my mouth then grabs my chin. "Now hang out and think about what it means to be a good little kitten. I'll be back."

With that, he leaves the room and me dangling.

Anticipation is always what gets me. The waiting, the solitude, and the fear of the unknown are the worst kind of mind games and the most powerful kind of arousal. Kayne playing me perfectly each time.

After way too much time alone with my thoughts, Kayne returns wearing only a pair of white linen pants that hang loosely on his hips. No shirt, no shoes, but definitely ready to be serviced. I can't help but stare at my demonic angel who's capable of being as bad as he is good. I shiver from just the thought of what he can do.

"Still hanging around, kitten?" He stands in front of me holding a rocks glass with bourbon in it. I know this because I recognize the smell. It's Kayne's drink of choice.

"You haven't given me much of an option," I respond.

Kayne arches his eyebrow at me with the glass close to his lips. "Getting sassy are we?"

"No. Just stating a fact." I wriggle in my restraints. My body is starting to ache from its overstretched position.

"How disappointing." Kayne takes a sip of his drink then places it on the end table next to the bed. He then opens the drawer and pulls out what looks like a pocketknife. I jump as he flips it open and holds the blade up in front of my face. "Something else I never leave home without," he says as he runs the tip of the knife down my neck. Holy shit. I know Kayne likes pain, but I'm not sure I'm prepared for this. I hold my breath as he continues to run the tip over my collarbone and down to the center of my chest right above the line of my shirt. He presses lightly, digging the blade into my skin until it pinches. I whimper as my heart completely stops.

"Trust me?" he asks.

I nod unsurely because, up till this moment, I have trusted him, but now I'm not so sure.

"Good." With a quick flick of his wrist, he slices my shirt open, the fabric ripping right down the middle. I nearly pass out.

"Relax, Ellie. I'm not really into knife play unless I'm stabbing it into the heart of someone who deserves it."

"Good to know," I swallow hard, breathing heavily.

"I do, however, like to inflict a little pain." Kayne reaches into his pocket and pulls out three little black *things*. It takes me a second to realize what they are.

"Binder clips?"

"Second rule of survival. Utilize your surroundings. I told you I didn't come prepared for kink so I had to use my imagination." He pinches one of the clips with his fingers. I think I go pale. "I found these in the workstation desk. I'm getting my money's worth at this resort." He smiles. I don't see the humor, only little chomping metal clips with a death grip.

"You look worried, Ellie. Don't think you can handle it?"

I shake my head.

"I think you can." Kayne begins stretching the clips, testing them on the tip of his finger several times before he's satisfied.

"That should do. Now be a good kitten and stand still."

Like I have any other choice!

Kayne leans down and sucks my left nipple into his mouth, pulling on it hard with his teeth until it stiffens into a firm pebble. I can't contain the moan from the feel of his mouth and how he can make my insides spiral. Then, without warning, he clamps my engorged nipple. "Oh, God!" My whole body goes rigid.

Kayne tsks me. "Didn't we have this conversation? Oh, Kayne," he reminds me. "I'm your maker now, Ellie."

I'll never forget that conversation or that situation. Strapped to a table while Kayne clamped my nipples, very much like he's doing now. I'll also never forget the orgasm he gave me. I still feel it in my dreams. Even sometimes when I'm awake. "I think we need a refresher course." He sucks my other nipple into his mouth, repeating the process. The second clamp is just as severe as the first. I'm panting heavily trying to channel the pulsating pain.

"Kayne," I protest.

"I love that sound." He leans in close to my ear. "That tortured plea."

I look down to see him adjust himself, the head of his erection peeking out the top of his pants. "I've barely touched you, and I already want to fuck your brains out." He circles my clit with the tip of his finger.

"Yes, please," I mewl feebly, my head dropping back.

"Much better, kitten. You're starting to remember your manners." Kayne drops to his knees. "But this isn't about pleasure. At least not yours. Not yet anyway." He runs his tongue between my folds, lashing at my clit before he sucks it into his mouth. I groan noisily as my body tightens and a knot begins to grow in my stomach.

"Kayne, please." My nipples throb, my arms strain, and my pussy clenches.

"Sorry, kitten," he says as he clamps my inflamed clit, and I cry out. Holy shit!

"Perfect." He tugs on the binder clip, and I nearly see stars. By the time he stands, I'm gasping for air, my whole body is on fire, and there is an ache growing inside me faster than the speed of sound. "Now let's review.

Who owns you, Ellie?" He yanks on one clamped nipple.

"You do," I draw in a sharp breath.

"When I tell you to kneel, what do you say?"

"Yes, Kayne," I grate as he pulls on the other binder clip. The sensation shooting through my breast like a bolt of lightning.

"When I tell you to lie down and open your legs, what do you say?"

"Yes, Kayne." I sag in my restraints.

"When I tell you go bend over so I can spank you, what do you say?"

"Yes, Kayne."

"What do I want from you, Ellie?"

I look straight into his eyes. "My obedience."

"And?" He lightly twists the clamp on my clit.

"My submission," my voice pitches.

"And?" He does it again and every one of my muscle fibers constrict.

"My body."

"Do I have those things?"

"Yes," I pant.

"What about your heart? Do I have your heart?"

"Yes, Kayne. It's yours," I say exhausted.

"Good. No one will ever protect it better than me."

"I know." I smile weakly as he steps back and takes a long sip of his drink sitting on the nightstand.

He swirls the brown liquid while he gazes at me with piercing eyes, starving with desire and glowing like bright-blue orbs.

"I never had the chance to appreciate you, Ellie. To really take you in like I would have if things had been different." He finishes the last bit of his bourbon, and places the glass aside. He then proceeds to just stare, absorbing every single clamped, tethered inch of me. It's oppressive, uncomfortable, and highly erotic as he begins to stroke himself while looking at me.

"Fuck, Ellie." He steps closer so our bodies are touching. I can feel the stroke of his hand against my abdomen as he jerks himself off. "See what your body does to me? All I need to do is look and you make me want to come." He yanks himself harder, grabbing one of my tender breasts forcing a loud, torturous moan out of me as the clamp bites my nipple. True to his word, he loves my agonizing sounds, squeezing my breast again and again, using my strain, struggle and torment to get himself off.

"I'm going to come," he heaves in my ear. "You're going to make me fucking come." A moment later, a warm blast of semen coats my stomach as Kayne lets go. I can't do anything but hang there as he marks me, my arousal turning up a notch as I watch him explode.

With a few deep breaths, he composes himself, wiping off the ejaculation on his palm across my thigh like I'm a hand towel as he nuzzles my neck right above my collar.

"Time to get clean, kitten. But first."

He leans in and kisses me, swiping his tongue roughly against mine as he simultaneously unclamps my nipples. I whimper and kiss him harder as all the blood rushes to the surface causing the sensitive skin to thump with returned feeling. He then unclamps my clit, and I bite down on his lip as it pounds and throbs with a dull pain.

"Easy." He rubs between my legs gently, easing away the discomfort.

"Please don't stop," I sigh desperately as I drop my forehead to his chest, an orgasm so achingly close.

"Sorry, Ellie." He removes his hand, and I nearly weep. "Only when I say."

I slump in my restraints. Kayne gives me a few minutes to decompress—or so he thinks, my orgasm nowhere near tapering off—before he picks up the switchblade from the bed and cuts me loose, catching me before I hit the floor. My body is completely limp from dangling so long. He unties my wrists, then lifts my dead weight into his arms and carries me into the bathroom. He doesn't put me in the shower or run a bath; he merely places me in the tub and turns on the water.

"Hands and knees," he says as he sits on the edge. I frown at him.

"Aren't you going to take a bath with me?" I ask.

"Nope. I'm cleaning my dirty kitten. That's all. Now get on your hands and knees."

I do as he says with a sulk. Kayne chuckles. He knows exactly what he's doing. I do, too. He's re-establishing roles. Master and slave. I suppose it has to be done for the order of things. It doesn't mean I have to like it any more now than I did then, but he's the only one who can give me what I want, what I need. And he's making damn sure it's clear I understand that.

Kayne lathers me up, not missing one single spot on my quivering body. His touch feels good and so does the warm water. He washes my back and my front as I stay situated on my hands and knees like I'm a dog at the groomer.

Kayne works his sudsy hands over my ass and I tense. Not because it's still sore, which it is, but because he presses the tip of his thumb against my back entrance.

"I can't wait to fuck you here, Ellie." He pushes in and penetrates the tight ring of muscle.

"Oh," I moan over the running water. It doesn't exactly hurt, but it doesn't exactly feel good, either. Not until he fingers my ass several times do my muscles relax and then tense up again in a completely different way.

"Mmm." I push back into his hand as my orgasm starts to rapidly grow.

"You like that?" he asks as he slides his middle finger into my pussy and simultaneously fucks both holes. "It feel good?"

"God yes, please don't stop." I'm so fucking close to the explosion I desperately need I can practically taste it.

"That's all you get, kitten." He withdraws his fingers, and my body deflates.

"Kayne!" I whine. I need to fucking come!

He slaps me hard on the ass, and I yelp.

"Are you complaining, kitten?" he chastises me. I don't have a chance to respond because he goes on. "You're wearing my collar. And that means you do as I say. And I say when you come, understand?"

I shrink, "Yes, Kayne."

"Good girl." He spanks me again, and I clench my jaw. My backside is still overly tender. "Next time you talk back, I'm using the belt. And my dick won't be in you when I'm done."

"Yes, Kayne," I answer softly as he rinses me off. I know I should feel embarrassed or put off that he scolded me, but it just makes me want him more. Want to please him more. I don't understand it, and I don't think I ever will. All I know is that I have an erotic compulsion to obey him. To make him happy.

Kayne rinses me, then turns off the water. The ends of my hair are wet and so is the rest of my body, except for my face and neck. He didn't wash me there because he never removed my collar.

He helps me to stand, and once I'm out of the tub, Kayne dries me off, still feeling like a windup toy ready to race.

"There. All clean." He drops the towel into the hamper. "But I'm not sure for how long." He smiles wickedly.

I stare up at him, trying not to give away how needy I am. It's his fault, by the way. He created the insatiable monster.

"Now stay." He grabs my chin and lifts my face, dropping a small kiss on my lips, then walks out of the bathroom, with me completely naked and a soft breeze from the wide-open window caressing my skin. I have a feeling clothes are a thing of the past, at least for the time being. Kayne returns holding a leash, a thin chain with a light pink satin ribbon braided through it that matches the color on the inside of my collar.

"I told you I had no premeditated intention when I bought these, but since we're embracing the moment, I figure I'll use it." He hooks the leash to the front ring of my collar. "No locks, okay? No locks ever again." He runs his hand down the chain and I nod.

"You always have a choice, Ellie," he reminds me.

"Always?" My lip twitches.

"Yes."

"Then I choose for you to fuck me."

Kayne laughs. "I love when you talk dirty, but that's not how it works. You chose to wear that collar, you choose to obey me. House rules. I tell you what to do, you say, yes, Kayne. You will please me. End of story."

I just had a bout of déjà vu.

"So, are we doing this?" He yanks the chain.

"Yes, Kayne," I answer taunting him. Bring it on.

"Good girl. Now get on your knees and crawl. No standing unless I give you permission."

I sink to the floor, never taking my eyes off Kayne's. His gaze morphs into a perverse approval. My arousal spikes as my hands touch the smooth wood. Jesus, this man makes me so hot my insides just sizzled to dust.

"Come, kitten. I want to pet you." He jingles my leash, and then leads me out of the bathroom and into the living room. He picks up the back cushion of the chair and drops it onto the floor in front of the couch.

"Kneel there." I climb onto the light cream pillow and kneel as I remember, with my feet tucked underneath me and my head bowed.

"Your refresher course in obedience training seems to be working well."

I don't know why, but I smile to myself. I like the praise in his voice.

I hear Kayne pour a drink, but I never lift my eyes to look at him. I just wait. Once he's finished, he sits on the couch, making sure I'm situated right between his knees.

"Closer, Ellie." He motions with his hand, and I immediately scoot closer, placing my head on his lap. Kayne smirks as he runs his fingers through my hair, massaging my scalp as he sips on his drink. In some weird way, I feel closer to him like this than I do when we're kissing or fucking or even making love.

"My kitten?" he asks as the sun sets, casting shadows around the room.

I nod as he lulls me. "You're the only one who can make me purr."

***

"HUNGRY, KITTEN?" KAYNE ASKS AS I crawl behind him out onto the sundeck.

"Yes," I answer, but not for food.

"I figured. You had a long night," he says with some amusement. Long is an understatement. I've been playing consensual sex slave for over thirty-six hours, and in that time, Kayne has licked, fingered, and fucked me, chained me to the bed and spanked me, and used my body as a canvas to paint with his cum, all the while denying me an orgasm. I'm about as fragile as a thin piece of blown glass. I need release so badly, I could shatter with slightest kiss of an island breeze.

And Kayne fucking knows it.

The table outside is set up with breakfast; room service is a miraculous thing. It's how we've sustained nutrition the last day and a half.

I kneel, naked except for my collar and chain, on the pillow he put down for me next to his chair. It's another perfect morning, the sun shining brightly, the temperature warm, and the water sparkling. But it's Kayne's eyes that have my full attention. They've been on fire ever since I slipped my neck jewelry back on. It's that look—that acute, heated gaze that's so hot it could set the Society Islands on fire. That's the look I live for, lust for, endure for. Because I know for as much punishment he inflicts, he'll match it with an equal amount of pleasure, possibly even more. What this man makes me feel is above and beyond just physical. He reaches further inside me than anyone else, stroking my mind and caressing my soul; consuming me to the point that all I'm aware of is him. The outside world ceases to exist; I've become his willing captive, and I love every second of it.

I watch transfixed as Kayne picks up a piece of fruit from his plate, an orange cube of cantaloupe. He brings it to my mouth and rims it around my lips. I go to bite it, but he pulls it away.

He shakes his head, moving his hand down my naked breast to massage my nipple with the cold piece of fruit; it hardens to a painful point. I'm over-stimulated, moaning inwardly as I try to control the ravenous need flaring inside me.

Kayne pops the melon into his mouth then feeds me a piece. He repeats the teasing and massaging on each of my breasts until all of the cantaloupe is gone, and I am a panting mess.

"Please," I beg. I've had enough. I've reached my breaking point; I don't even care what I sound like, what I look like. I just need to come. "Kayne, please." The tone of my voice is pathetic, broken down and desperate. He smiles because he has me exactly where he wants me. Which is dependent on him. And I am. His reconditional training worked. I'm enslaved, his bonded servant, trained to obey.

"Okay, kitten. You've been a very good girl, time for a treat." He picks up a large strawberry from his plate. I stare half mentally removed as he brings it to his mouth and licks it with his tongue the exact same way he licked cream cheese frosting off a red velvet cupcake. *Holy fucking shit.* "Hmm, sweet," he muses then reaches down between my legs. I gasp as the chilled strawberry tip grazes my sensitive clit.

"I want you to come, kitten." He rubs the strawberry firmly against me and my need ruptures.

"Oh, God." I sink my nails into my thighs as everything below my navel tightens. "Kayne," I whimper as he rubs in a circular motion, making me crazy. I start to rock my hips as my orgasm takes on a life of its own, commanding me to climax.

"Who owns your pleasure, Ellie?"

"You do." I suck in a ragged breath.

"Who owns your body?" he asks as he slips the strawberry into my pussy and fucks me with it.

"You do," I moan deep in my throat.

"Who owns your heart?"

"You do!" I come so fucking hard and loud I'm pretty sure the neighbors hear as every ounce of pent-up frustration gushes out of me onto the strawberry and Kayne's hand. Oh God, I'm destroyed. My body feels like Jell-O and I can't hold up my head, but I stay kneeling until Kayne instructs me to move.

"Mmm," I hear Kayne moan. I crack open my eyes just as he bites the last bit of the dark-red fruit. "You're sweeter than whipped cream." He licks his fingers, then plucks me up from the ground and straddles me on his lap. "Feel better?" He nudges my cheek with his nose and grinds his erection between my legs.

"Honestly? No," I laugh. "I could use ten more of those."

"Good." Kayne slams both of his hands on my bare ass and I jump like a spooked cat. I'm still unbearably sensitive. "Because I'm not done with you yet." He kisses me hard, spearing his tongue into my mouth and my arousal begins a countdown to launch.

"Go—" He starts to order me, but we're interrupted by someone banging on the front door. Oh no, not again.

"Kayne!" We hear Jett's voice. "Kayne, come on, man! Open up!"

"Shit," Kayne mutters. "Next time, I'm taking you to a private island with no neighbors, no doors, and no interruptions."

I giggle. "I'm in."

"You don't have a choice." He yanks on my chain.

"Kayne!" Jett bangs again.

"Coming!" he barks so loud, I jolt. Jeez, he can be scary in so many different ways.

"Sorry." He kisses me softly. "Go inside and clean up, then wait for me bent over the side of the bed." He threads his fingers into the underside of my hair and grips tightly. "I want your ass, Ellie." Then he kisses me again, deep and hard, and my body responds without delay.

"KAYNE!" Jett's voice breaks us from our kiss.

"Go." He spanks me with blatant irritation. I slide off him quickly and scurry into the bedroom. "Jett, this better be important or I'm going to rearrange your face." I hear Kayne yell from somewhere inside the bungalow.

I quickly wipe off the cum dripping down the inside of my leg with a damp washcloth, then position myself exactly the way Kayne wants me—bent over with my ass in the air and my hands placed firmly on the mattress. I shake, still wanton with need and slightly distressed. I know what's coming, and it's going to hurt just as much as it's going to be pleasurable.

"Fine," I hear Kayne say loudly, and Jett laughs.

I can't imagine what they're talking about. A minute later, Kayne walks into the bedroom. I'm facing the headboard so I have to look slightly over my shoulder to see him.

"Damn." He slows his pace as he walks over to me.

"Everything okay?" I ask.

"Fine," Kayne answers oblivious, solely fixated on my bare, wide open ass.

"What did he want?"

"Nothing." He caresses my left butt cheek. "We can talk about it later." He squeezes, and I wince.

"Jesus, Ellie. You don't know how many times I dreamed about you just like this." He runs his finger along my ass crack, putting slight pressure against my hole. I hold my breath.

"Ellie, I love you." It's a statement, like a reassurance.

"I know." I peer at him.

"Good. Because this is going to be intense. It's going to hurt, and I'm going to like it." He stares at me with manic lust.

Oh, shit.

"What's your safe word?"

"Cupcake," I automatically answer.

"Good girl. Stay." He walks into the bathroom, and a few seconds later, returns with what I recognize as a very tiny bottle of lubricant. In that small fraction of time my anxiety has spiked through the roof.

"Another thing you never leave home without?" I ask shakily.

I hear the top pop. "When you're in a committed relationship with your hand for a year, yes." He drizzles the sticky substance over my tiny little hole. I glance back to see Kayne naked and fully erect, rubbing his length down with the lube as well.

"I'm going to stretch you with only my cock, Ellie. No fingers. We'll go slow."

He lines up behind me, and I feel the head of his erection poking against my tight little rose bud. I haven't had anal sex in over a year, and it's only ever been with Kayne. He penetrates me with the tip of his cock, the lube helping to ease it in, and the pain is immediate. I lunge forward, but he grips my hips and pulls me back.

"Don't. Take it." He pushes harder, and I whimper as he slowly rips me open. I claw at crumpled sheets, the bed a messy sea of white from last night.

Kayne relentlessly works himself into my behind, every inch a battle, every tear a victory. I heave air as he rocks in and out, the pain gripping me like a vice. I moan in agony as my body tries to reject the foreign object plunging its way into me.

"Let it out," he grunts with a firm thrust, and my eyes spill over with tears. I press my face into the mattress and sob with his cock halfway inside me. When he pulls out, it only gives me one second of relief before he's pushing back in, deeper than before. When he bends over me and grabs my collar, I know I'm done for. There's no more reprieve, no more withdrawing, only a straight shot of hard cock directly into my ass. Kayne yanks at my collar as he thrusts, using it almost as leverage to bury himself to the hilt, reducing me to nothing but saggy bones and uncontrollable sobs. He takes over my body exactly the way he wanted—he invaded, enslaved, and then conquered it.

"I love your tears, Ellie." His voice is rough, and his hips are relentless as I cry helplessly on the bed, letting the tears fall freely because I know that's what he likes, what gets him off. I remember all too well, Kayne's favorite things are pleasure, pain, and pushing me to my limit. Seeing how far he can take me before I finally crack.

"Fuck, I missed this," he strains. "I missed getting strangled by your tight little ass." His thrusts become jerky and erratic. "Touch yourself, Ellie. Touch yourself now." He slams into me, and I cry out. With my face still planted on the mattress, I slide my shaky hands between my legs and do as he says, massaging my clit until my pussy relaxes.

"That's it, baby." He moves freely now, my burning ass completely stretched to accommodate his long length and wide girth.

"I wish you could see it," he groans as he fluidly slides all the way in and then pulls all the way out like he was always made to fit me. "How you swallow me whole." He sinks himself inside me again. "And fuck, it's so good." He slaps my ass so that my muscles clench around him. "Finger yourself. I want you to come. I want you to come with me." He starts to pump fast, and I have to bite my lip to absorb the discomfort, the tears a steady, constant flow. But even with all he's put me through, the need for release is still as strong as ever. I need him to fuck me; I want him to fuck me. I sink my middle and ring fingers inside my now soaking wet pussy and press my palm to my clit. I rub and finger myself all while Kayne uses my body for his wicked pleasure, the three acts swirling together to become the perfect storm of desire. My orgasm comes on like a high-speed turbine, all pressure and velocity, intensely working its way through my system until I can't contain it anymore.

"Please, may I come?" I scream out at the very last second before I seize, my muscles grinding like steel brakes as my insides splinter.

Kayne doesn't respond, he just repeats 'mine, mine, mine, mine' like a broken record as he's sucked down with me, stabbing into my ass so deep I swear I can feel my heart beating against the head of his cock.

He pins me against the mattress as we both collapse to our knees, breathing harder than I think we've ever breathed before. When he withdraws, I feel like an overused rag doll who has been taken off her stick. I am sore, battered, and I think half dead. I cry some more. I'm not even sure why, I think just for some cathartic relief. The past day and a half has been the most taxing of my life. Being denied orgasm after orgasm and then broken open like a coconut has depleted my mind and my body.

Kayne wraps his arms around me and licks my face the same way he has all the other times I've cried in his presence.

"Your body and your tears are the closest to heaven I will ever get." He burrows his face between my shoulder blades. "You're the purest thing in my life."

"There's nothing pure about me, anymore," I giggle and sniffle all at the same time.

"Your love is pure."

I glance at Kayne out of the corner of my eye. The ferocity of his gaze is what makes me love him so much. It's always drawn me to him. His presence is all empowering. That stare tells me I'm his entire fucking world, and he would do anything to protect it. To protect me.

How do you walk away from something like that?

Someone like that?

The answer is simple. You don't.

KAYNE PLACES ME IN A steaming hot tub, and my muscles whistle like a kettle. Oh, that feels so good.

He climbs in right after me, situating himself underneath me. The tub is quite large and looks out over the lagoon. There isn't one lousy view from any room. Kayne massages my back, rubbing firm, hard circles over my spine as our bodies slip and slide together from the bubbles.

"You feeling okay?" he asks as he kisses my neck and holds me close.

"There's a pain in my ass," I reply drily.

"And I bet you love it." He nips at me.

"Maybe just a little." I rub up against him, the water sloshing, and slip my tongue between his lips. I suddenly break our kiss. "Oh! What did Jett want?"

Kayne frowns. "You're kissing me passionately and thinking

about Jett?"

That does kind of look bad.

"Not in the sexual, *I want you to own me, rule over me, spank me kind of way.*" I flutter my eyelashes at him.

"Well, thank God for that." Kayne rolls his eyes, the brown lightning bolt prominent in bright sunlight.

I kiss him again. Hard, but playfully. He tickles me, sending more water over the edge of the tub.

"Hey!" I squeak.

"That's what you get."

"For asking about Jett?" I laugh and squirm as his fingers dig into my side.

"For asking about Jett while you're naked and wet!"

"I'm sorry!" I screech. "It just happened! Kayne!" I try to claw my way out of the tub, but he pulls me back and kisses me, wrapping one leg around mine.

"Forgiven. Don't do it again." He spanks me, but the hit is broken by the water so I barely feel it."

"Yes, Kayne," I purr anyway.

"Good kitten," he patronizes.

"So really, what did he want?" I ask again.

Kayne sinks deeper into the tub, locking his arm around my lower back crushing me to him. "He wanted to make sure we were both alive."

"What?"

Kayne nods. "Since he couldn't get ahold of me all day yesterday, he wanted to check in. I think he was more concerned about you than me."

"Me? Why?"

Kayne shrugs. "You were one of his girls once. For Jett, that doesn't just go away. You were as important as any of them. Even more so."

"Oh. Does that bother you?"

"No. I'm glad he cares. He's the only other man I would ever trust you with."

"I sort of got that impression." I smile and hook my arm around his neck. The man did wax me, bathe me, and dress me up like his doll. "Kayne? Speaking of being someone's girl." I bite my lip. "How come you never made me call you Master?"

"What?" He eyes me surprised.

"Well, in the books I read and the research I did, most submissives call their Dom Master or Sir. You never made me do that. Not even now."

"You did research?" He raises his eyebrows.

"I was curious. Being with you made me curious." I blush.

"I guess that's understandable. I did expose you to a lot of things in a short amount of time." That's putting it mildly. "Why didn't I make you call me Master?" he considers. "To be honest, it felt too impersonal. I wanted us to have a connection, even if I couldn't tell you that. I thought letting you call me by my name would somehow humanize me, even if I wasn't acting very human." He brushes his hand lovingly down my back. "And as for why I don't make you do it now? It still feels too impersonal. I like hearing you say my name. It's reassuring, and I need that," he says apprehensively.

If there's one thing I've learned in the very short time I've been with Kayne, it's that he hates his vulnerability as much as he realizes it's what makes him human. "I understand."

"Does it bother you that I call you kitten?"

"No," I answer honestly. "I like it. It makes me feel sexy."

"You are sexy. And smart and funny and loved. You are so fucking loved, Ellie." Kayne kisses me feverishly as if trying to personify his affection, but he doesn't need to bring it to life, I can already feel its warmth and fluttering heartbeat.

AFTER A VERY LONG SOAK in the tub, until our fingers pruned and our muscles unfurled, Kayne and I lounged around the bungalow. It was a nice afternoon. Relaxing and stress-free.

Now, I'm just about finished with my makeup, swiping blackest black mascara over my eyelashes. I'm starting to get the hang of this, I think, as I inspect myself in the mirror.

Apparently, Kayne's word wasn't good enough for Jett because he insisted that he produce me at dinner tonight. If you ask me, I just think he and London miss us.

I catch Kayne leaning against the doorway staring at me through the mirror. He's wearing a light-brown button-up shirt, tan dress pants, and a scorching hot expression, like he wants to devour me right where I stand.

"See something you like?" I ask him as I close the mascara and place it back in my makeup bag.

"Maybe." He strolls up behind me. "These are a bit short." He tugs on the hem of my white shorts.

"So?"

"You know how I feel about you showing your body off to anyone but me."

I turn to look at him, placing my hands on his chest. The material of his shirt so incredibly soft.

"I think we need to establish something," I flirt. "The only place you get to tell me what I can and cannot wear is in the bedroom. Outside those doors, I'm my own woman."

Kayne's eyes flash with something I've never seen before, nothing angry, but excited, perverted almost. "Oh, yeah? That's good to know because I do want to dress you up. I want you to really be my kitten. I want to slide a pair of ears on your head and plug a tail in your ass and fuck you while you purr," he says groping my behind. My jaw drops from the vivid image.

"I didn't realize you were into fetish," I reply breathlessly as he kisses and tickles my neck with his warm breath.

"I never really was, but being with you makes me want to . . . *explore*." He looks at me with ravenous lust in his striking blue eyes.

I'm trapped in place, my knees about to buckle. This man is going to be the death of me.

"So, is that a yes, Ellie?" He rasps in my ear while unbuttoning my pants and dropping them to the floor.

"Yes," I gasp as he slips his hand into my panties and starts to finger me. "Oh God, yes." My eyes roll into the back of my head. "If it will turn you on, I'll do it." He caresses me slowly, allowing me to feel every microscopic touch as he massages the walls of my pussy.

"Good girl. Shit, you're wet. Looks like I'm not the only one the idea of fetish excites." He presses his rock solid erection against my thigh.

"No," I answer mindlessly, flinching as my orgasm flares like a wildfire. "Are you trying to make me come?" I breathe harshly.

"Maybe." He fingers me faster. "Maybe not." He withdraws from me completely, and I nearly topple over.

"Kayne," I whine miserably.

"Sorry, kitten." He slides his middle finger into his mouth and sucks off my remnants. I just watch with wide, transfixed eyes.

"Definitely sweeter than whipped cream." He hums then fishes his hand into his pocket. He retrieves his switchblade and pops it open right next to my head. I jump.

"I would also like to establish something." He runs the switchblade all the way down my body stopping at my hips. "I will always have some kind of say in what you wear." There's a loud tear as he slices through the spandex and lace of my underwear. "No panties tonight." He repeats the motion on the other side, leaving me stunned. He picks up my mutilated underwear and discards it in the trash.

"Now what do you have to say about that?"

"Yes, Kayne," I answer automatically like I'm conditioned to do.

"Good, kitten. Now hurry up and fix yourself, I don't want to be late." He makes for the door, his erection uncensored in his pants.

"God forbid," I snark.

He leers at me while he adjusts then disappears into the bedroom.

Tease!

Pulling myself together like instructed, I blot between my legs with some toilet paper and pull up my shorts. I look in the mirror. I'm flushed and feel achy, and it's all Kayne's fault. I huff, throwing some of my hair over one shoulder as I leave the bathroom. He really is going to be the death of me.

Kayne opens the front door for me once I emerge from the bedroom.

"Our ride will be here any second." We walk outside into the pleasant evening air fragrant with something sweet. Island flowers, maybe.

We see Matias driving a six-seater golf cart down the boardwalk, his white shirt and dark hair rippling in the wind.

He stops in front of us with a wide smile, and we climb onto the cart. I'm starting to get spoiled being chauffeured around like this. He takes off and stops at the large bungalow right next to ours where another couple is waiting. They're a bit older and very well dressed, late forties I would say. When they see us, their looks are ones of curiosity, and I think disdain. I cuddle next to Kayne as they sit behind us, suddenly uncomfortable. He puts his arm around me and glances back at them. I'm certain he also feels the quiet hostility. The ride up to the main part of the resort is silent and quite uncomfortable, even with Matias' best attempt at casual conversation. I've never been so happy to see a lobby in my life.

Kayne gets off the golf cart hastily, extending his hand to help. As he does, the woman comments offhandedly, "Women deserve to be treated with respect."

Kayne and I both freeze as she pins us with her cold blue stare. If I was suspicious before, I'm confident now that these are the neighbors who called the concierge on us the other night.

Kayne smiles, without showing any teeth, but it's contradictory to the vicious look in his eyes.

"I couldn't agree more," he responds evenly. "They also deserve to be fucked. Maybe you should let your husband try it sometime. Right in your opinionated mouth."

The woman gasps in horror.

"Kayne!" I chastise as I jump out of the cart.

"Young man!" The woman's husband stands up outraged.

"Let's go." I push him away before there is a brawl right before my very eyes. He steps backward, unable to remove his crazed stare from the couple.

"What the hell was that about? You should have just ignored her," I say once we're safely inside the lobby.

"I'm not going to let anyone accuse me of not respecting you. I respect you more than any other man ever will. What we do in our bedroom is our business. I won't let anyone ruin that."

"It's going to take more than one ignorant comment to ruin what we have." I try to placate him, realizing something very important. Kayne will become aggressive when he feels threatened despite where we are or who we're with.

"I'm not going to let anyone take you away from me, Ellie." Determination dripping from his tone.

"No one is going to take me away, and I know you respect me."

"Good. You're the most resilient person I have ever met." He swipes his thumb across my cheek.

"And you're the scariest." I laugh.

"It's part of my conditioning. I don't take shit."

"Clearly. But you can't just pop off on people like that."

"I can and I will," he argues with me.

"Kayne," I sigh.

"Ellie. This one you'll never win. I'll never roll over and play dead where you or we are concerned," he says with an unyielding look in his eye.

"You're crazy."

"Yup. Mostly about you." He presses a kiss on my lips. "Now come on." He takes my hand. "We have to make a stop before we go to the restaurant."

"Stop?" I repeat confused as he drags me down a white marbled hallway clustered with stores and enters the jewelry store.

"What are we doing in here?" I ask.

"Good evening." A bright-eyed salesman in a dark gray suit greets us.

"Engagement rings?" Kayne asks, and I nearly fall over my feet.

"What?"

"Last case in the back." The man motions fluidly with his hand.

"Thank you." We reach the case with Kayne still clutching my hand. "I asked you to marry me, and you said yes. You need a ring. I may not know much, but I do know that. So, go ahead. Pick whichever one you like. I want you to be happy."

"What?" I repeat again an octave higher than before.

"Ellie." Kayne laughs at me as the salesman steps in front of us. His name is James, according to his tag.

"What can I show you?"

I look down into the glass at the shimmering diamonds and truly feel like a cat mesmerized by the light.

"Let's see a variety," Kayne answers for me, and the nice looking man with salt and pepper hair immediately pulls out several different rings. Some with round diamonds, some with square, one with an emerald cut. If someone told me when I got on that plane a week and a half ago that I'd be shopping for an engagement ring, I'd have laughed in their face—like cackled loudly. Yet here I am, staring down at some of the most beautiful jewelry I have ever seen, and it becomes a sobering reality.

"Hmm." Kayne doesn't seem impressed with any of them. "See anything you like?"

I'm overwhelmed. "Maybe you should just pick for me."

"You deserve an opinion. You're the one who has to wear it."

"If I may," James cuts in politely. "Not to offend you, but can you tell me your price cap?"

"We don't have one," Kayne tells him matter-of-factly. The salesman's eyes glitter just as brightly as the diamonds in front of us.

"In that case," he pulls out a ring from the far side of the case and places it in front of me, "you two seem unique. I can tell these things. I see many couples walk through that door, and I can usually read them pretty well."

I glance at Kayne and blush scarlet. Are we that obvious?

"You should wear a ring that reflects your personality. Two-carat cushion-cut diamond with a half carat of pink sapphires haloing around the center stone," he explains.

I immediately fall in love.

"What do you think, Ellie?" Kayne inquires.

I'm speechless.

He chuckles, taking the ring from the James's hand, "I think she likes it," and places it on my ring finger. "Will you marry me?" he asks softly, and my breath catches. I look at the perfect ring and then at the perfect man with tears forming in my eyes. *Is this really happening?* I reflect. First, Kayne was the man of my dreams, then he was a monster, and now he's . . . *everything*.

"Yes," I answer and know beyond a shadow of a doubt that regardless of what happened in the past, it's the future that's important now.

"We'll take it," he tells the salesman, then bends down to

kiss me on the cheek, whispering, "Cupcake," in my ear.

"There is also a matching wedding band. It's a set if you're interested?"

"Fine, yes, we'll take that, too," Kayne says still looking at me.

"And what about you, sir?"

"Me?" Kayne looks over at him confused.

"Yes. You'll need a ring eventually. Would you like to take a look while you're here?"

I cock an eyebrow. This guy has balls. He's going to squeeze every dime out of Kayne he can, and Kayne totally knows it, too.

"I'll take a look," he says shrewdly.

"You look like a titanium man." James pulls out a flat velvet board with a number of rings impressed in it.

Kayne looks them over and then shrugs at me.

"That one." I point to a silver band with an extremely thin row of black diamonds.

"Ah. Very nice choice," James comments with dollar signs in his eyes as Kayne slips the ring on and makes a fist several times, trying to get used to the feel.

"Make you anxious?" I tease him.

"Makes me excited." His eyes flash with something sinful.

I bite my lip, knowing full well that look means trouble. A delicious kind of trouble.

"Done." He slips the ring off and hands it back to the deliriously happy man in the gray suit. I can't even imagine how much money he just spent, and frankly, I don't want to know. Kayne is wealthy. That's obviously no secret. He has been since I met him. I'm just not exactly used to him spending large amounts of money on me. I guess that's something I'm going to have to get used to.

"I can have the two rings wrapped up and sent to your room if you'd like," James says. "It looks like you're going out."

"That's fine." Kayne starts to peruse some other glass cases while I admire my new ring. This *is* really happening.

A few moments later, I hear Kayne ask James to see something at the far end of the store, near the front.

"Ellie," he calls me over. "Stand here," he says once I reach him, both of us positioned in front of a mirror. "Pull your hair back, please."

I move my long, sun-kissed hair to the side. I blew it out straight and braided the front like a headband. Kayne drops something in front of my face, a necklace, and fastens it around my neck.

"Now you can always be collared," he murmurs in my ear as the salesman watches us.

"The heart is Tiffany," James informs us as I admire the sparkly pave charm attached to a black silk choker in the mirror. "We can change it up if you like. Maybe put the heart on a platinum chain?"

"No," Kayne snaps mildly. "It's perfect."

I keep my mouth shut. This purchase is much more for him than it is for me. I secretly love it, and I'll show him how much later.

"Very good, sir. I'll add it to the bill."

"Thank you."

I glare at him over my shoulder. "This was your diabolical plan the whole time," I accuse him playfully.

He shrugs. "A man always has to have a plan." He tickles the heart on my 'necklace.' A prideful gleam of ownership shining in his eyes.

I barely remember the walk to the restaurant, and I'm pretty sure if Kayne wasn't leading me by the hand, I would have walked straight into a wall.

This *is* really happening.

"Ellie? Earth to Ellie?" Jett waves his hand in front of my face.

"Huh?" I blink.

"I said congratulations." His big aqua eyes sparkle.

Where the heck did I go?

I think the enormity of the last week and a half—hell, the last year of jumbled feelings, the love, the hate, and the confusion—is finally hitting me like a ton of bricks.

"Thank you," I smile brightly because, for the first time in so long, I am truly happy.

Kayne pulls out my chair at the table and the four of us sit.

"You okay?" he asks quietly, concerned.

"Yes," I reply in my most confident voice, because I am.

"A bottle of your best Prosecco, please." I hear Jett order and see the waiter hurry off.

"Let me see again!" London grabs my hand and moves it so my engagement ring catches the light. "I love the pink! It's perfect for you, Ellie." She leans over and kisses my cheek.

"Thank you." I feel like that's all I've been saying for the last ten minutes.

The waiter returns with four champagne glasses and the chilled bottle of Prosecco. I suppose if you're going to drink Italian champagne, the best place to do it is at a high-end Italian restaurant.

When our glasses are full, we raise them for a toast.

"I'd like to say something," Jett announces.

"Oh shit," I hear Kayne mutter.

"Shut up, idiot," Jett snaps. "I just wanted to say that I'm elated this story has a happy ending. God knows we all needed it, not just you two."

"Cheers," Kayne says hastily.

"No," Jett pulls his glass back. "Quit ruining my moment," he spits.

"Fine." Kayne drops his head and huffs.

"I want to relay something someone very wise once told me. A man's most precious possession is the woman who walks by his side. And I don't think you could have found a more perfect woman." Jett clinks Kayne's glass. Kayne stares at him idly with a glint in his eye and ghost of a smile playing on his lips.

"I couldn't have said it better myself."

"You couldn't have said it at all. You suck at heartfelt speeches." Jett gulps his Prosecco.

"I'm not so sure about that," I grin behind my glass right before I take a sip. The champagne is delectably sweet, clean, and crisp. Delicious.

Dinner moves swiftly as we dine on flaky bread, fennel and aged pecorino salad, filet mignon with a balsamic glaze, and indulge in several more bottles of expensive Prosecco. By the time dessert rolls around, not only am I stuffed, but feeling no pain as well.

"You know what I think you guys should do," London says as she drains the last drops of champagne from her glass, "and it may sound crazy, but I think you two should do it while you're here."

All three of us look at her strangely.

"Not that. I know you do that." She sticks her tongue out and laughs. "I mean get married. You should totally find a deserted beach at sunset and get married."

"I'm sure Ellie would want her family there," Jett says.

I nod, glancing at Kayne. He's staring at London stoically. A little tingle of worry runs down my spine. Did she just spook him? Is he coming to realize we're moving too fast? Is he suddenly having second thoughts?

"Probably." London drops her head into her hand dreamily. "It would be romantic, though."

"We can always have a sunset ceremony. On Maui maybe?" I look at Kayne apprehensively.

"We can have anything you want." He smiles, but it's a distant expression.

I internally panic, but I'm not going to dwell. If there's something to be worried about, I'll find out soon enough.

Once the bill is paid, we move outside to the patio where oversized couches surround a large brick fireplace; dark-red lanterns hang overhead and sweet smelling cigar smoke lingers in the air. London and I park on a couch while Kayne and Jett stand by the bar and cut new cigars. I never found it appealing—a man smoking a cigar—until now. Until I watch Kayne wrap his lips around the thick brown Churchill and elegantly puff one O out after another.

"You happy, Ellie?" London asks as she lazily twirls a piece of my hair around her finger.

"Yes. Are you?" I ask surprised.

She smiles, her eyes glassy from all the alcohol. "Deliriously. Even if Jett and I never get married, he could make me happy for the rest of my life."

"Well, that's good to know. I'd hate for you to spend it with a man who makes you miserable," I laugh.

She laughs, too, her head resting comfortably against the thick maroon cushion. "You're funny," she says as she gazes at me, the fire illuminating her dark-red hair and crystal-blue eyes. "And really beautiful, you know that?"

"You think?" I tuck some hair behind my ear shyly. It's one thing to get compliments from a man, but a woman, a woman who you've had sexual relations with, is a whole other story.

"Can I tell you a secret?" She sits up and scoots closer to me so our bare legs are touching. I nod, having to keep my knees together to keep from being tickled by the nighttime breeze as it brushes up under my shorts and pets my unclad privates.

"Sure," I shift.

She leans over to whisper in my ear. "Sometimes, when Jett makes me touch myself, I think about you."

"What?" My eyes fly to hers.

"I've had a lot of sexual experiences, but that night with you was one of the best." She looks down at my lips, and my heart skips like a scratched record.

"Do you think . . ." She runs one soft finger up the inside of my thigh, "you'd want to give Kayne an engagement present?"

I'm momentarily stunned. One, because she's hitting on me; two, because the memories of that night are uncontrollably flooding my mind, and three, because suddenly I really want her to kiss me.

Same sex is an acquired taste," I hear Jett say, and he's right. That night was one of the hottest, if not the hottest, of my life. I glance over at Jett and Kayne as my mouth and London's hover closely together. Vance Joy singing about riptides and dark sides softly in the background. They're both watching us closely, like two lions spying on a gazelle.

"I think he'd like that," I tell her summoning my courage and stroking my excitement all at the same time. London brushes her lips against mine, and I inhale a sharp breath. She smells good, like some kind of spicy perfume, but feels even better. When our tongues graze, a million little tingles race all over my skin. For a second, I forget where I am, solely concentrating on the feel of London's mouth and the smooth caress of her hand on my naked thigh.

Someone suddenly clears their throat very loudly, breaking the spell the two of us are under.

I look up to see Jett standing over us, with Kayne behind him, arms crossed.

"Time to go," Jett informs us. "You two are drawing a little too much attention," he says with a wicked gleam.

I glance around to see most, if not everyone, on the patio staring at us. Oops. Jett extends his hand to London and pulls her to her feet. Then Kayne does the same to me. I look up at him a little guilty. Should we have asked permission first? How does this work?

"Yes. You're in trouble." Fire dances in his unique, spellbinding eyes. I gulp.

"You told me I could fuck as many women as I want."

His gaze darkens. I don't think I'm helping myself here.

"I remember. I also told you I would be the only man who ever touches you. So don't get any ideas."

"Ideas?" I say as he pulls me in the direction of London and Jett. In no time at all, the four of us are crunched in the back of a golf cart.

"Bungalow forty-six," Jett tells the driver, and he steps on the pedal. "Please." He then turns to London and me. We're practically sitting on top of each other. "Feel free to pick up where you left off."

London doesn't miss a beat, she dives her tongue back into my mouth and kisses me without any hesitation. I'm suddenly trapped, my back pinned to Kayne while she freely explores my body, her hand brushing down my neck, over my breasts, and around to my ass.

The golf cart suddenly jolts to a stop and I realize we have reached bungalow forty-six.

The four of us pile out, London yanking me eagerly behind her. I see Jett pull out a wad of cash and smack some into the driver's hand. "Bet you don't get tips like that every day," he says to the wide-eyed boy. I giggle to myself; he so wasn't talking about money.

The inside of London and Jett's bungalow doesn't look much different from ours; it's just on a smaller scale.

"How come you aren't staying in a big bungalow like ours?" I ask Jett as he turns on a light.

"I'm not ostentatious. Besides, this is enough."

"All we really need is a beach and bedroom," London says impishly. "The bedroom is this way," she tugs me. I glance back at Kayne as I follow her. He's been threateningly quiet, despite his howling presence. Images of him from the first night London and I spent together turn over in my thoughts, the way he touched himself as he watched us, the way he instructed us, the way he fucked me while I made her come. It was barely human.

Once inside the bedroom I stop, slipping my hand out of London's. What was I saying about their bungalow not being much different than ours?

I was dead wrong.

There are shackles attached to each post of the canopy bed and a thick black collar dangling by a chain on the headboard. The nightstand is covered with an array of sex toys, a ball gag, lubricants, and wax candles. But it's the long rope on the floor that has me looking at Jett strangely. He just shrugs. "I'm into Kinbaku."

I draw in my eyebrows. "What?"

"Rope bondage."

"Oh." I stare at him blankly.

"It's a very beautiful art form," he tries to explain, almost like he's defending it.

"Okay." He doesn't need to sell me. I willingly walked through the looking glass. *This time.*

"I'm a kinky bastard. What can I say?"

He brushes past me to the opposite side of the room, opens the sliding glass door and pulls in two chairs from the sundeck.

"It takes one to know one?" I jest.

Jett smiles entertained as he sits in one chair and Kayne sits in the other, suddenly making me feel like the main attraction in a private XXX show.

"London, come," Jett says, and she immediately drops to all fours and crawls to him. Once she reaches him, she kneels submissively between his legs. I automatically look at Kayne.

He just lifts his hand off his knee slightly as if signaling me to stay.

Jett lifts London's face so she's looking directly into his incandescent eyes.

"You're a bad girl," he admonishes her, "and I love it. Now stand up and take your clothes off."

"Yes, Jett," she hums, and for some reason I shiver with excitement.

London rises to her feet and slowly starts peeling off her navy tube dress that's clinging to her body. I can only see her back from my angle, but Kayne and Jett seem quite invested in her little strip show. Once she's left standing in just a black thong and high heels, Kayne looks over at me and smiles like the demon he is.

"Good robin. Now take Ellie's off," Jett instructs her.

"Hold it." Kayne suddenly stops her in her tracks, and all three of us pause to look at him. I'm suddenly nervous. God only knows what's going to flow out of his mouth. With all the apparatuses in the room, I could end up being fucked upside down while hanging from the ceiling. "Ground rules." He glares at Jett. "London can touch Ellie all she wants, but you keep your hands off my fiancée."

Jett grimaces, "You're such a party pooper."

"Tough shit, I don't share."

"I'm calling sexism. You're discriminating against me just because I have a cock."

"Exactly, and it's not getting anywhere near *her*. Call it whatever you want. Accuse me of being prejudice, of being a chauvinist, whatever. You still can't touch her or I'll break your hands."

Jett bristles. "I'll still be able to use my cock." He sticks his tongue out at Kayne.

"I could always break that, too," Kayne informs him menacingly.

I know I probably shouldn't, but I laugh.

"Do you find my jealous, overbearing side funny, Ellie?" Kayne asks, without looking at me.

"No. Kayne." I clear my throat and find my composure. That's his 'do not fuck with me' tone. London and I may have started it, but it's clear Kayne and Jett are going to finish it.

"Good. Now, London, go undress my kitten."

"Slow your roll," Jett interjects. "I'm giving the orders. You've already driven one of these."

Kayne rolls his eyes. "Fine. Be my guest."

"London, go undress Kayne's kitten," he instructs with mirth.

These two.

London turns to me, displaying her mostly naked body. I

almost forgot how perfect she is—tall, toned, and curvaceous. I felt a little inadequate then with my petite frame and small breasts, and I still feel inadequate now. But it's a little too late for insecurities because London drops to the floor and crawls across the room to me. I feel, rather than hear, the collective intake of breath as she approaches me swathed in seductiveness, servile and obedient. I nearly come on the spot. I now understand the appeal, the feeling of power and domination, as one person freely hands themselves over to another. I also understand that in this position I would never want to hurt or take advantage of that person's trust or safekeeping. It makes me see the relationship I have with Kayne from a completely different angle.

Once London reaches me, she rises to her knees. I gaze down at her and run my hands earnestly through her thick red hair, hoping she understands my subtle gesture of respect. I find it amazing that I can be just as sexually attracted to a woman as I can to a man.

London kisses my navel as she unbuttons my shorts, taking her time with her mouth as she lowers the zipper. She pulls the white material down my thighs and follows the path with her tongue until she realizes I'm not wearing any underwear. She moans softly, eagerly, but stops kissing me as she slides my pants the rest of the way off. She pushes up my shirt but can't reach past my breasts, so I end up yanking the top over my head for her. I'm not wearing a bra, either, because of the tunic's open back. As soon as my nipples hit the air, they harden, sending a ripple of excitement straight through to my core.

With her cheek pressed against my abdomen, London and I look over at Jett and Kayne now that we're just as they want us. Both men appear composed, but if you look hard, you can see the quick compressions of their chests and the tightening of their forearms. Not to mention the carnivorous lust in their light eyes.

"Do you want to touch Ellie, London?" Jett asks.
"Yes, Jett," she hums.
"Where?"
"Everywhere."
"With what?"
"My tongue."
"You've wanted to do that for a long time, huh?"

"Yes." She glances up at me.

"Ellie, do you want her to lick you?"

"Yes."

"Where?"

"Everywhere."

"So go ahead, bird. Show Ellie how much you want to taste her."

London wets her lips before she presses her mouth to my pussy and tongues my clit.

"Oh." The pleasure is immediate as she applies pressure and explores my slit, stroking and sucking rhythmically until my legs start to shake.

"She feel good, Ellie?" Kayne asks.

"Yes," I strain, trying to absorb the dizzying sensation of London lapping me up.

"She making you want to come?"

"Yes." My voice is engulfed by a panting whisper. My body feels so heavy, and I want so much more of London's mouth, so without even thinking I sit on the edge of the bed, lean back and spread my legs wider.

Both men groan as London buries her head between my thighs, sinking her tongue deeply into my entrance. I gasp loudly, grabbing her head as she nearly eats me alive. Just as I begin to undulate against her mouth, Jett snaps, "Enough." Within half a second London pulls away, leaving me a winded mess on the bed. "No one is coming yet."

I grumble silently, my body feels like it's being put through a wringer.

"Come. Both of you," he commands.

London crawls over to Jett and I follow suit to Kayne. Sitting on our knees, we wait for one of them to instruct us.

"You like my little bird eating you up, Ellie?" Jett asks as he pets her reverently. I glance up at Kayne before I answer. It feels like his stare is going to drill a hole right through my chest.

"Yes," I tell him truthfully.

"She is one of a kind." He tilts London's face up with one finger. It's clear how much he adores her. I've seen many expressions on Jett's face, but it's the first time I've seen this one. It's a mix of what looks like admiration, loyalty, and possibly a hint of fear, as if he's terrified of losing her.

"Will you make her feel good, Ellie? I know how much she wants you to make her come," he says.

I nod, stumbling into the intensity of Jett's aqua eyes once he turns his head to look at me. I have no idea how London and Jett came to be, but something tells me it wasn't just some casual thing. I recognize that gaze, that desperate love, because Kayne looks at me exactly the same way.

"Go sit on the bed," Kayne finally speaks. I restrain myself from running my hands over his thighs and climbing into his lap. As much as I want London to touch me, I want Kayne to touch me, too. "Go." He tickles the heart dangling from my throat, one of his new symbols of ownership over me.

I sit on the end of the bed like directed.

"Stand in front of her, London," Jett orders as both he and Kayne get up and walk to each side of the four-poster bed. London positions herself between my legs. "Take her panties off," he says from behind me. I move to slide the dainty lace thong off London's hips and down her long legs. Once removed, I sit back further on the mattress. That's when I feel it dip behind me and Kayne swiftly fasten a blindfold over my eyes. I inhale harshly from surprise.

"Relax, Ellie. Trust me." He kisses my neck and whispers in my ear.

"You've never blindfolded me before." I touch the lace-like material.

"First time for everything," I hear Jett comment.

"It won't be the last time. There are so many things I'm going to do to you, Ellie." It's a promise. "Now lay back." He pushes me down. "Enough playing around. London, sit on her face."

I nearly combust with need as I feel London crawl up my body and straddle my head, the fragrance of her arousal potent and heady.

"Lick her, Ellie. Slowly. London, don't come," Kayne instructs.

I flatten my tongue against London's pussy, eager to please. The sound that escapes from her is pure delight. Although I can't see, my sense of smell, hearing, taste, and touch amplifies, making me hyper-aware of everything around me.

As I lick between London's folds leisurely, I feel someone grab one of my ankles. I flinch, but the hand grips me tighter.

"Easy." Kayne placates me like he's talking to a spooked horse. I relax momentarily until I feel him strap a restraint around my ankle.

"Don't stop, Ellie," Jett encourages me as the mattress dips above my head. I try to breathe steadily, concentrating on London, as Kayne fastens my other ankle.

"Does she feel good?" I hear Jett ask London between kisses, the bed teetering slightly from their entwining bodies.

"Yes," she whimpers. "Oh God, yes."

I reflexively stab my tongue into her entrance when Kayne tickles the inside of my thighs.

"Ellie!" she gasps, grabbing my hair.

I pull my tongue back and take a breath, giving us both a second's reprieve. I squirm in the restraints, my knees slightly bent and my legs spread wide open.

Then I hear the distinct sound of a zipper and the rustling of clothes.

A moment later, I feel a light touch trace my lips. Jett? Then a finger is slipped into my mouth. "I want you to make my little bird come." He pumps his finger in and out, coercing me to suck. It's the most erotic gesture Jett and I have ever shared. I hold onto the moment as long as I can, picturing his face as I swallow his finger, wishing secretly that for just one second Kayne would share.

Jett grunts as he withdraws his hand, leaving me wanton.

"Put your mouth on me," I hear him say, and London leans forward, situating her clit at an even more accessible angle to my face. "I want to feel everything she makes you feel." There's more shifting over my head, and then a loud moan from Jett. Just listening to him is arousing as hell. "Make her come, Ellie."

The room almost feels like a pressure cooker of elicit desire as I begin to lick London, sliding my tongue in and out of her slick folds and circling it around her clit. I'm completely lost in her soft feel and the carnal sounds of Jett's panting breaths when Kayne brushes something up the inside of my leg. His fingers? His nose, maybe his lips, I'm not sure. But the added sensation makes me jerk on my restraints and apply more pressure to

London's pussy. When Kayne sinks his tongue deep inside me, I spasm, spurring a chain reaction — me to lick faster, London to suck harder, Jett to moan louder.

"Shit! London!" Jett hisses as she lets out a jagged, muffled cry, suddenly coming uncontrollably. I writhe beneath her, yanking at the leg restraints as she floods my mouth, while Kayne at the same time dangles me right over a razor-sharp edge. I fruitlessly kick and squirm as my own orgasm converges in the dead center of my thighs.

"Fuck. I'm coming," Jett groans while the sweet taste of London's arousal stains my lips, the bed dipping rapidly over my head, as he fucks her mouth.

"Please, please, please!" I hear myself beg as London is suddenly pulled off me and replaced by the brute force of Kayne on top of me. I recognize the fresh smell of his cologne and feel of his skin as he breathes wildly in my ear, slams into me savagely, pulls my hair, and sinks his teeth into my neck like a blood-starved vampire.

There's no time for even a sound as I follow Kayne into the light. My clit aches and my pussy throbs as my orgasm tears me apart, limb from quivering limb.

The last thing I remember is hearing Kayne's jagged lungful of air, seeing shadows move on the ceiling, and then darkness sucking me under.

I WAKE UP IN A tangle of bodies.

"Ellie," Kayne whispers, nudging me with his nose.

"Hmm?" I respond lazily, realizing I'm sandwiched between him and London.

"Come on, baby. Let's go," he speaks softly.

"Go where?" I open one eye.

Early dawn is just peeking over the horizon. It's still mostly dark, but a crack of light is allowing me to see.

Kayne slides out of bed first and shrugs on his pants. I reluctantly follow, as he moves me away from London and drags me up into a sitting position. I then follow suit by sleepily searching for my shorts and top as London and Jett lay soundlessly in bed. Her hair is a mess of red against the white sheets, his hand over her stomach almost protectively.

"Oh." I put my hand on my head once I stand up straight. "I think I'm hung over."

Kayne laughs quietly. "That's what happens when you drink three bottles of Prosecco yourself," Kayne whispers.

"We were celebrating."

"That we were," he says happily, picking up my shoes.

"Did you like your engagement present?" I ask, knowing I look like a hot mess.

He nearly burns a hole straight through me with a blistering glaze. "What do you think?"

"I think I need medical attention because someone tried to gnaw through my neck." I touch the sore spot right above my necklace, where I'm sure I have a bruise.

"It was a love bite." He takes my hand and leads me out of the bedroom, through the living room, and into the warm morning air.

"A love bite by a crazed man with a loaded erection."

"That's what happens when you feed my addiction." He puts his arm around me and draws me tightly into his side as we walk back to our bungalow.

"I like to feed the beast," I tell him lasciviously.

"So I've noticed." He kisses the top of my head firmly and cuddles me tightly. "Brat."

"It's all your fault." I giggle accusingly.

We continue to walk while the sun comes up. It's a showy display of golden rays over the aquamarine water and clouds colored different shades of orange and blue.

"Ellie?" Kayne says tentatively. "I've sort of been thinking."

"Yeah, about what?" I reply dreamily, a mixture of exhaustion and happiness.

"What if we did it?"

"Did what?"

"Got married while we're here. Just the two of us."

I stop walking. "What?" I stare up at him, and he stares back. I open my mouth to say something then close it again.

"You're being serious?" I finally muster.

He nods like he's holding his breath.

"Kayne," I sigh.

"That's a no, I take it." He sounds disappointed and starts walking again.

"No, it's not a no," I scramble, grabbing his arm. "It's an '*I don't know.*' I mean, it's one thing to get engaged, but it's a whole other thing to rush into an actual marriage."

"You think we're rushing?"

"You don't?" I actually laugh.

"No. I want to be with you, you want to be with me. I don't see what's so complicated."

"It's not complicated, it's just—"

"Just what?" he asks anxiously.

"We haven't really talked about anything."

"What's there to talk about?"

"I don't know? Kids," I blurt out.

"Kids?" he replies incredulously.

"Yes, like, do you want them?"

"I don't know." At least he's being honest. "I never really thought about it. I never thought I would get married. Do you want them?"

"Yes, I think. Eventually."

Kayne ponders this. "Okay, so we'll have them. Eventually."

"Just like that?"

"If it's what you want, Ellie. If it will make you happy."

"Will it make *you* happy?" I counter. "It'll never work if it's all give and no take."

He looks at me strangely. Like he's seriously considering my words. "I think I take plenty." He grins.

I snort. "I don't mean take like that."

"I know. I think kids would make me happy, especially if they're half of you. I sort of like the idea of giving someone a childhood I never had."

I frown immediately. I never took into consideration Kayne's past when I brought up the subject of kids.

"Oh . . . I'm sorry . . . I wasn't thinking," I stumble over my sentences.

"It's fine." He smiles. "You've got me looking forward to first words and bedtime stories." Although those are two very happy thoughts, the sound of his voice tells me he thinks differently.

"Did anyone ever read you bedtime stories?" I ask carefully.

His expression turns grim. "Yes. Once. I was about nine. There was this older girl in one of my foster homes, she was about fifteen or sixteen. She would read *Peter Pan* to me and the two other boys who lived there. She read it mostly every night before our foster father would come home drunk and rape her."

I look at him horrified, and suddenly can't help but wonder if all his childhood memories are laced with such atrocities.

"Kayne – "

"It's all right, Ellie. It's in the past."

My heart literally breaks for him.

"Okay, let's do it," I announce hastily.

"Excuse me?"

"Let's do it. We can get married under one condition."

"What's that?" The corners of his mouth curve up.

"We can have another wedding when we get home. One with our friends and family."

My parents and sister have to attend at least one ceremony. Even if it is a second one.

Will they be upset when I tell them I ran off and got married to a man they never met? Probably, but not surprised. If anything they would expect it. I have always been somewhat impulsive.

"That's fair. And I kind of like that idea," he agrees.

"Okay, good." I nestle up against him and stand on my tippy toes for a kiss.

Kayne's face feels warm and soft, despite the little bit of stubble growing on his cheeks.

"Sealed with a kiss," he says.

"I have a feeling we're going to be doing a lot of kissing Mr ... *Rivers?* Is that your real last name? Would we have to use an alias?"

"Ellie. Shhh." He pulls me close. "Yes, it's Rivers," he whispers, "and I don't know. We can use that for now."

Ellie Rivers. I can live with that.

"Okay." I yawn. "Good talk."

"Tired, kitten?" Kayne chuckles.

"Yes. I've had a very trying night. Prosecco, foursomes, weddings. I'm pooped."

"So let's go get some sleep. We have a few more days before I have to share with you with the rest of the world. I plan to take full advantage."

"I bet you do," I purr as our two-story bungalow comes into view. Looking at it now, it does seem a bit ostentatious compared to all the rest.

I fall back and melt into the mattress once inside. I lift my hand in front of my face and inspect my engagement ring, noticing how the white and pink stones glimmer even in dim light. I've barely had a chance to admire it with everything that went on last night.

"It's perfect." Kayne lies down next to me. "It's just like you—unique, brilliant, and strong enough to cut glass."

I snuggle up next to him, realizing I will be sharing a bed with this man for the rest of my life.

Crazy.

Our original bond was one built with bricks of deception and lies. The bond we share now is fused by love. A single strand of twine, woven together with trust, and stronger than steel.

"I love you," I sigh sleepily.

Kayne moans in appreciation. "You have no idea what those words do to me. No idea how much I need to hear them. How much I need you." He tickles kisses across my cheek.

"You have me. Till death do us part."

Kayne clutches me protectively, and for a split second I think I've said something wrong.

"Go to sleep, Ellie. We can talk nuptials later." He embraces me firmly, yet tenderly, banishing everything else in my life except him.

"Yes, Kayne," I murmur against his lips and let slumber have me.

KAYNE

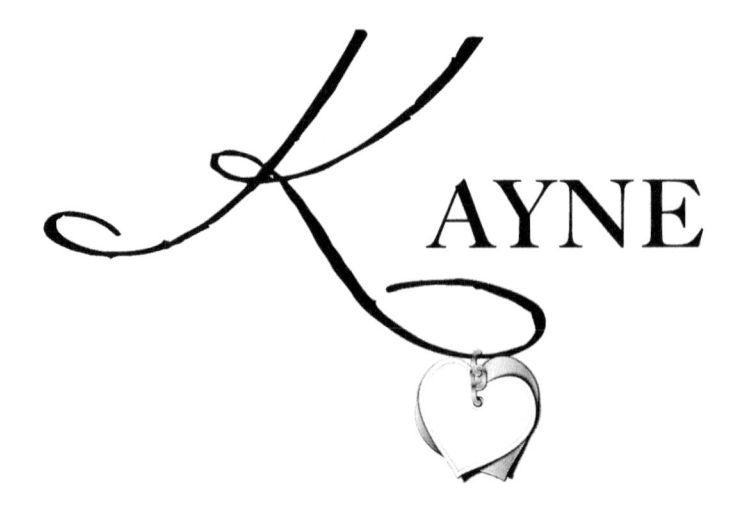

I DON'T THINK ELLIE AND I have been laying down for more than five minutes when I hear my cell phone beep. Three distinct chimes that communicate a problem.

"Kayne? What is that?" Ellie stirs.

The chimes sound again as I grab my pants off the floor and fish my phone out of the pocket.

"Nothing. Go to back to sleep," I say urgently, but when I turn to look at her, she's sitting up, bright-eyed and bushy-tailed. Sleep doesn't seem like much of an option at the moment.

I stand up and dial a secure number, waiting impatiently to be connected. "Sundial enterprises," a woman's robotic voice answers.

"Seven AM on the eastern shore," I reply.

"Pin, please."

"007263."

"Codename."

"Havok with a K."

"Password?"

I glance back at Ellie. "Elizabeth Ann."

"Confirmed. Hold for patch."

"Kayne?" Juice's voice comes through.

"What's up?"

"We have a security breach."

"What kind?"

"Someone's hacked Endeavor's classified server."

"What does that mean?"

"The identities of all operatives, handlers, informants, and analysts have been compromised."

"Jesus."

"Yeah. The bosses are on a rampage. They're calling in everyone that they can. They want them secure, which means your fun in the sun is over."

"Shit." My heart beats riotously.

"Sorry, man."

"Yeah, me too."

"Be in the air within an hour. I'll check back then."

"Roger."

The call ends.

"Everything okay?" The voice that can cut through my darkest nightmares fills the room.

"No. Get up. We have to go."

"Now?" She clutches the sheet to her chest.

"Yes. Grab only what you need. Everything else will be packed and shipped later."

A moment later my phone rings again.

"Yeah," I snap.

"I've called ahead. The plane will be ready," Jett informs me. There are no formalities now, only protocol and procedure.

"We'll meet you at the boat. Ten."

"Roger."

Click.

I rush Ellie around the room. She changes into a sundress and comfortable shoes. I throw on shorts, a hat, and a t-shirt and set up a ride to the lobby with Matias.

Making sure we both have all the essentials, we vacate the bungalow and our private escape.

"Kayne?" Ellie asks worried as we walk outside. I know she's scared and confused and wants answers, but I just can't give her any at the moment.

"Not now, okay?" I squeeze her hand. "We'll talk about everything later."

She nods as we climb into the golf cart.

"Book it. We have a plane to catch," I tell Matias, and he takes off, flooring the cart as fast as it can go. I think the thing only tops out at fifteen miles per hour.

Almost exactly ten minutes later to the second, we pull up to the lobby and the long dock housing multiple white boats. I spot Jett readying one near the end.

"I'm sorry your stay had to end so abruptly," Matias says to us once we're out of the cart.

"Yes. It is disappointing." I quickly pull out a wad of cash. "Your service was impeccable." I hand it to him.

"Thank you, Monsieur."

"De rien."

You're welcome.

I glance around us as I lead Ellie to the boat. She hasn't stopped crushing my hand since we left.

The speedboat looks to be a thirty-footer with a dark-blue canopy. It's nothing flashy but will fit the four of us comfortably.

I help Ellie onto the boat then jump in after her, still keeping a sharp eye on our surroundings.

"Ready?" Jett turns on the ignition and the engine purrs.

"Yup." I untie the two ropes anchoring us to the dock and push off.

"Hang on. This is going to be a quick ride," Jett says as we get out into open water. Then he pulls the throttle and the boat speeds through the glassy water, throwing Ellie and London back in their chairs and jolting me on my feet.

I hear a groan and look over to see London with her head on Ellie's lap.

"What's wrong with you?" I ask as Ellie strokes her hair.

"She's hung over. Hasn't stopped puking all morning," Jett informs me.

That sucks.

"There's ginger ale on the plane," I tell her, like that's supposed to help.

She makes a face. "I don't think I can even keep liquids down. I am never drinking again."

"I think I've heard you say that three times on this trip." Jett laughs behind the wheel. He's wearing a baseball cap, mirrored sunglasses and looks like he's a born captain in boat shoes and chino shorts.

"That's because I've been sick almost every morning that I've been here. You're trying to kill me," she accuses him.

"Oh, that's right, blame me." Jett laughs. "I was the one pouring martinis down your throat."

"I hate you sometimes." She snuggles closer to Ellie.

"I love you all the time," he replies.

Ellie and I smirk at each other during London and Jett's little exchange. Of all the women I've seen Jett with—and it's been *a lot*—he's never had a rapport with any of them like he does with London.

We dock the boat and hurry the girls along.

"Ellie, this way," I tug on her hand when she veers toward the main entrance of Motu Mute airport. We enter through a side service door in order to lay low, and then walk straight out onto the runway.

"Don't we need tickets?" she asks confused.

"Not this time, baby." Our private jet is already waiting with the doors open.

"This yours?"

"Mine and Jett's. It's smaller than our old one but it gets the job done."

"Old one?" She raises her eyebrows.

I nod. "Liquidated."

"Oh." She then understands. We had to get rid of everything that tied us to our undercover op, including the G600 I loved.

"Mr. Andrews. Mr. Collins," the captain greets us once were safely inside.

"Henry." He's an older man with gray hair and a crisp white uniform. He's also an ex-fighter pilot and employed by Endeavor.

"Please sit down and buckle up. The runway is clear, I plan to have us in the air in ten minutes."

"Sounds good." Jett and I both shake his hand.

"Also, comms are set up in the back."

"Very good." We take our seats. I strap Ellie in next to me. Jett does the same to a sickly looking London. I wonder idly if she's going to throw up during takeoff.

I watch a curious Ellie inspect the interior of the plane decorated in a cool beige and glossy wooden accents.

Without delay, the jet roars to life and the interior lights flash.

"Stand by for taxi." Henry's voice comes on over the loudspeaker.

Ellie grabs my hand. "Are you afraid of flying?" I ask her.

"Only when under duress."

"It'll be fine." I try to assure her. "The safest place is in the air."

"If you say so." The plane begins to roll.

After we are at thirty thousand feet, Jett and I leave the girls up front and head to the back of the plane where a laptop is all set up for use.

With one hit of a button, we're connected to Juice.

"Yo." His face pops up on the screen.

"Yo, yourself. Any updates?" Jett asks him.

"Nada. Endeavor is working to find out who the hacker is, but nothing yet."

"Do you think this has any connection with our visitors on Oahu?" I question.

"There has been no identifiable connection." He swivels in his chair, "But I don't think they're ruling anything out."

"Fuckin' great." I run my hand through my hair. I glance up and see Ellie and London sitting together. London's head resting on Ellie's shoulder; it seems they've become quite comfortable with each other.

"I'll check in if anything changes. For now, just sit back, relax, and enjoy the friendly skies," Juice says, tossing a small basketball up over his head like he's pretending to shoot.

"Roger that." I snap the laptop closed and suck in a breath. *Relax?* Yeah, right. It feels like the universe is out to get me. Not one hiccup in twelve months, then BAM—this happens. Just when my life feels like it's finally coming together.

"I'm going to check on London. I'll send Ellie back." Jett taps my shoulder as he stands.

I nod, sliding down a black hole of despair.

"Kayne?" I hear Ellie's concerned voice and look up. "Where were you?"

I just shake my head. "Someplace you don't need to worry

about." I put my hand out to her. She takes it and slips onto my lap, curling up like the kitten she is.

"You're tense," she says concerned.

"I call it more alert," I clarify.

"Do you know what's going on?"

"No, not entirely. Not yet."

"Will you have to go away once you do?" She looks up at me with troubled green eyes.

I want to tell her no, that I'll never leave her side, but I can't guarantee that. At the moment, I can't guarantee anything, and it sucks.

"I don't know, Ellie."

She hugs me securely. "All that time I was with you, do you know when I was most scared?"

"No."

"When Javier had that gun to your head. I just remember thinking this man is going to take you away and destroy me right on the spot."

"Ellie, stop—"

"I know this is your job," she keeps speaking despite my protest, "and that you're proud of what you do. I just want you to know I'm proud of you, too. No matter what happens. I'm proud to love you."

"Ellie," my voice wavers, and my chest aches.

"I just wanted you to know." She rubs her nose against my chin. "I wouldn't change one second of our past. It helped shape who we are. And I really love *us*."

"I really love *us*, too." I bury my face in her neck and crush her against me.

I hold Ellie in my arms until her eyes close and she's breathing heavily. It's no wonder she crashed hard. The last forty-eight hours have been *demanding,* so to speak. Yet, in true Ellie fashion, she surprises me with her fearlessness, her resilience, and her buoyancy. Now more than ever, I'm convinced this woman was made specifically for me.

She's my sanity, and my reason, and my glue. I'm seven broken pieces of a fucked up man, held together solely because of her.

"Sleep, baby." I kiss her forehead, preparing for whatever

danger may come my way.

"WHERE ARE WE GOING?" ELLIE asks as we drive down Kalakaua Avenue in Waikiki. The day, like always, is perfect. Tourists fill the streets, the beach is crowded with sunbathers, and the water active with surfers.

"Home. As soon as possible." A disgusted—not to mention shirtless—Jett answers.

"I said I was sorry," London grumbles in the fetal position next to him. "The landing was bumpy."

"The landing wasn't that bumpy. And I know you're sorry. It's not your fault." Jett pets her head.

I feel sorry for London; she's miserable. But I wish I had a camera when she threw up on Jett. His face was priceless. I would have blown it up and stuck it on a billboard.

"Where is home, anyway?" Ellie asks with a raised eyebrow.

I lean over her and point out the window to a high rise. "The tallest one."

"Why does that not surprise me?" she quips.

I grin duplicitously. "Part appearance, part necessity, part selfish desire."

Ellie rolls her eyes at me. "Is that your excuse for everything?"

"I find it covers all bases," I reply as we pull onto a side road, and then into an underground garage.

"Good thing we live someplace tropical," Jett comments as he helps London out of the limousine.

The air is cooler in the garage, but still comfortable enough to get away with limited clothing.

The four of us step into the marble elevator, and I hit the code for PH36. We're then whooshed up thirty-six floors to the penthouse Jett and I share.

The doors open to a large foyer with colored orchids etched on the mirrors and a light wooden floor. Jett exits with London first and unlocks the front door.

Ellie and I follow close behind.

"Oh." Ellie does a slow pirouette as we walk through the apartment. "This is . . ." she seems to be at a loss for words.

"Nice?" I answer for her.

"Very."

The condominium is a split-level with an open floor plan and one hundred, eighty-degree views of Diamond Head, Koolau Mountains, and the Pacific Ocean. Cherry wood frames the two-story French windows encasing the ultra-modern decor. Clean lines and dark accents make it a vast contradiction to the mansion we lived in on the East Coast.

"Come on. I'll show you the rest of the house later. We need to check in first." I take her hand and lead her through the kitchen.

"Bye, Ellie," London croaks behind us.

"Feel better," Ellie replies as Jett helps London climb miserably up the stairs.

"I'll be right there," Jett tells me.

"I really feel bad for her," Ellie pouts. "Maybe she has food poisoning?"

"Maybe? I'm sure if she doesn't start feeling better, Jett will take her to the doctor. He isn't one to make a woman suffer. At least not in the sickly way." I wink.

"Seriously, the two of you."

"The two of us, what?" I ask defensively.

"Are terrible."

"So terrible both you and London are madly in love with us?"

"Brainwashed is more like it." She teases.

I shrug. "Whatever works." I drop a kiss on her lips then place all five of my fingertips on a mirror hanging on the back wall of the condo. A moment later a pair of pocket doors slide open.

Ellie's gasp is all I need to hear to know I've made an impression.

"You have an arsenal in your apartment," she says as we walk into the secret room. Every wall is decorated with some kind of specialized firearm—submachine guns, assault rifles, breaching shotguns, sniper rifles.

"We like to call it the Toy Box." Juice spins in his chair and stands up. "Welcome home," he shakes my hand.

"Thanks. Wish it was under different circumstances."

"You? I know you." Ellie interrupts us, examining Juice closely.

"Ma'am," he says with a smile, which sparks her recognition.

"The driver?" She looks up at me.

"Well, I couldn't just send anyone to pick up my precious cargo."

"You work for him?" she asks Juice.

He laughs boastfully. "I work *with* him," he corrects her. "And I'm CJ, by the way." He puts his hand out.

Ellie takes it graciously. "It's nice to formally meet you."

"You, too."

A moment later the door opens and Jett appears. "Did I miss anything?" He walks in donning a new shirt.

"Just introductions," I tell him.

"How is London feeling?" Ellie asks him.

"Still not great, but she's resting."

"Good."

"Maybe you can go keep her company," I suggest, glancing at Jett, "while we work."

Ellie catches on immediately. "Oh. Yes. Of course. I need to charge my phone anyway. I have a bunch of calls to make." She starts backing up.

"Who do you have to call?" I follow her, opening the door so she can get back into the apartment.

"My mom. My sister. Mark. Michael."

"Michael?" I step out after her, possessiveness flaring.

"Yeah. I just picked up and left. I sort of owe him an explanation."

"You don't owe him jack shit, Ellie," I snap.

"Kayne. Don't be ridiculous. He's my friend."

"He's a guy you were fucking," I snarl.

"Keep your voice down!" she hisses, her stare glacial. "We had a relationship, yes. But that's over now. I at least have to tell him why."

"And what exactly are you going to tell him?" I ask warily.

"As much of the truth as possible."

"Which is?"

"You want me to recite what I'm going to say?" she asks confounded.

"Yes."

"Fine. I haven't really thought about it, but it will probably go something like this. I dated this guy. He was a total douchebag. I thought it was over, but apparently it's not."

Douchebag?

"Does he know anything about said douchebag?" I ask irritably, my hand twitching. She's going to get so punished for calling me that.

"No. I never said anything. I never even uttered your name. I was told I could land in jail if anyone found out about you or the operation," she says bitterly.

As much as it kills me to hear her say that, I'm relieved.

"Now if you'll excuse me, I have to go break up with my boy toy." She starts to storm off and then stops. "Where the fuck am I going?" she huffs annoyed.

"My room is upstairs. Last door on the left."

She doesn't even turn to look at me, just stomps away.

Shit.

I walk back into the Toy Box nearly pulling out my hair.

"Trouble in paradise?" Jett asks. I want to punch him in his sarcastic mouth.

"Just a hiccup." I plop down in one of the black leather rolling chairs.

"Women, like cheap wine, can give you a headache," Jett offers his two cents.

"They also, like cheap wine, can make you drunk and horny," Juice adds.

I rub my temples. These two are not helping.

The thought of Ellie even talking to that guy has me wanting to put my fist through a window.

"Relax. Ellie isn't doing anything to hurt you. If anything, she's cutting ties so nothing is stopping the two of you from being together. She's a very well brought up girl. She has morals and family values. You're going to have to step up your game,"

Jett says entertained. He's eating this up; me and my domestic issues.

I just glare at him. "How would you feel if London was conversing with one of her exes?"

"Me? I'd gut him with a fishhook. But we're not talking about me."

"Five minutes in your presence and I'm reminded why I elect to stay single." Juice laughs, tossing that stupid basketball in the air. I stand up and grab it, then squash it with my bare hands. It screams while it dies. I feel much better.

Juice gasps. "You just killed Wilson. He was my only friend."

"You need to get out more." I toss the flat basketball back at him.

He catches it. "I would, but the two of you keep me chained to this desk like a slave."

I freeze, and Jett blanches. "Don't ever fucking say that around Ellie," I bark, about to rip his throat out. "Even if it is a joke."

"Okay." Juice puts his hands up. "I think we need to take a step back. Everyone's tensions are running a little high."

I take a deep breath. I haven't kicked the crap out of anything or anyone in nearly two weeks. I thought sex would sate me, but apparently that's not the case. I need to make someone bleed.

I didn't realize how difficult it was going to be sharing Ellie with the people in her life. I think I might be totally screwed.

Like I've said before, I've never really been good at sharing.

"Why don't you brief us on any updates," Jett suggests.

Juice shakes his head. "There aren't any. It's been nothing but radio silence. We just have to lay low and wait for word."

Wonderful.

"I'm going to check on Ellie then." I push out my chair.

"Go smooth things over?" Juice digs.

"Shut up or I'm going to smooth cement over your face while you're still breathing."

"So hostile." He heckles me.

"Isn't he?" Jett agrees.

"Fuck you both." I storm out of the room. I need to either fuck, run, or slam the shit out of a punching bag real soon.

I climb the stairs quickly and quietly, silently making my way down the hall. The door to my room is slightly ajar and when I peek in, I see Ellie sitting on the floor, looking out the wall of windows with the phone to her ear.

"The Starbucks on the corner in an hour? . . . Yes, I'll explain everything. That's why I want to see you . . . I know, I'm sorry I up and left like that, but I needed to . . . Okay . . . yeah, okay, bye."

I watch her for several long seconds before I push the door open. "Going somewhere?" My voice vibrates and Ellie jumps.

"Were you listening to my conversation?" she asks annoyed.

"Yes." I lean against the doorframe and cross my arms.

"That's rude."

"I was never taught manners."

"I find that hard to believe." She stands up. "You just pick and choose when to use them."

I try, but fail miserably, to stop an evil smile from spreading across my lips. "You're mad at me."

"You're acting like a jealous asshole."

"I am a jealous asshole." I walk into the room.

"There's nothing to be jealous of," she responds steadfastly as she watches me approach her. "You're the one I want. You're the one I'm marrying." She holds up her hand and shows me the ring.

"I know." I take her hand in mine. "That doesn't mean I don't feel threatened. It doesn't mean I won't always worry about some guy trying to steal you away. Or you getting tired or frustrated or fed up with me. I told you I wasn't perfect, that I'd make mistakes. I always knew I'd have to share you at some point, I just wasn't prepared for it to happen so fast."

"You don't have to share me. I'm yours."

"That's not true. You have a life and friends and goals and dreams. I have four walls, a dangerous job, and you. That's it. That's my entire world. Three entities."

"What about Jett? He's part of your life."

"For how long? He has London. He wants to get out. I can't lean on him forever."

"You don't have to, you have me." She grabs my shirt and looks up at me.

"Prove that's true and don't go. Blow him off."

She shakes her head. "I have to go. I have to do this. For my peace of mind. I won't be able to live with the guilt. Michael has been a good friend to me. He was there when I needed someone."

"I would have been there for you."

"I know. But I was so mad at you, it wouldn't have helped."

"I could always lock you in my room and force you to stay."

"You could, but I don't think that would be very healthy for our new relationship, do you?"

"No. But it would be fun." I slide my hands down her back and grab both of her butt cheeks. "Mine."

"Yes, yours, and nothing's going to change that. I'm ruined."

I snap my head back and look at her. "Ruined?"

"Yes. You ruined me."

"Ruined you how?" I ask in a panic.

"You ruined me for all other men. So you can scratch someone stealing me away off your list."

I breathe a sigh of relief. I've always worried that Ellie's time as my captive did ruin her somehow. That *I* ruined her somehow. But if the worst side effect was ruining her for other men, I can definitely live with that.

"Don't go," I press her again.

"I'll be two blocks away and gone for an hour."

I bite my tongue and refrain from demanding her to stay. Refrain from tying her up and gagging her while she's locked up tight behind closed doors.

"You know I have other ways to persuade you to stay." I press her up against the window and slip my hand under her dress.

"Yes." She goes up on her toes as I caress her clit over her soft cotton underwear. "*Kayne.*"

"What?" I rasp.

"Don't." She grabs my wrist.

"Are you saying no to me, Ellie?"

I slide my middle finger under the fabric and straight into her pussy.

"Yes," she moans, "I'm saying no."

"You can't."

"What?" she gasps as I finger her.

"As long as that necklace is wrapped around your throat, I own you. Wherever, whenever. You're mine. And I want you right here, right now."

"No."

"Are you disobeying me, Ellie?"

"Yes."

"Do I have to show you what happens to bad kittens who disobey?"

"Yes." Her eyes smolder with defiance.

"Tell me to stop," I dare her.

"Stop," she says sternly.

As soon as the word leaves her lips I pull her across the room and slam her on top of the red wooden dresser.

"Beg me. Beg me to stop."

She squirms beneath me, trying to kick and punch, but I force her legs open and grind my erection right between her thighs. "That's going to be inside of you in two seconds whether you want it or not," I snarl in her ear as all the pent-up aggression of the morning brews like a hurricane inside me.

"No!" she screams, but I can smell her arousal like perfume in the air. She wants it.

"Fight me all you want. I'm still going to fuck you." I wrap one hand around her neck and pin her against the large square mirror behind her. A small, scared whimper escapes from her, doing nothing but urging me on. I swiftly pull down my shorts, springing my throbbing erection free with Ellie still flailing, but her fight is diminishing. She wants me. Wants this. Wants me to take her, possess her, rule over her. I can see the carnal desire flashing in her bright green eyes. With my free hand, I slide her panties over and thrust into her in one rapid blow. She nearly climbs the wall as she cries out.

"I know that's good, baby. I know you love it." I push her skirt up and pull the top of her dress down so she's as exposed as possible. "Watch me fuck you. Watch me fuck you so you never forget who owns this pussy," I slam into her again, jerking her back, "or this mouth," I swipe my thumb across her lower lip then place it back over her jugular. "Or this body." I grab her breast until she moans in pain.

"Watch." I clasp her neck a little tighter. Gasping, she lowers her eyes as I feed my cock into her starving little cunt, over and over.

"I know you like that. I know you love to watch. I remember how wet it makes you."

She whimpers as I relentlessly slide in and out of her, making sure she feels the entire length of my erection. From this angle, I can see how much bigger I truly am compared to her. From my height to my muscle mass to the way my cock stretches her to the max. She has to strain just to take me all in.

"Kayne," she mewls as her pussy tightens, begging for it. I have her exactly where I want her. Legs high and wide, upper body subdued, airway compressed. She's fundamentally the twisted little sex toy she agreed to be.

Ellie's breathing quickens and her knuckles turn white from gripping the edge of the dresser as she frenziedly saturates my cock with her arousal.

"Please," she fights to speak.

"Please what?" I continue my assault on her body, the dresser shaking violently.

"Please may I come?"

"Why the fuck are you asking me? You clearly do whatever you want."

I thrust into her again, finally shattering her to pieces. She expels a strangled scream as she comes, my cock glistening, greased by her arousal.

"Fuck," I grind out as my dick swells to the point the buildup is almost unbearable. Right before I blow a load, I lean over and hiss in her ear, "I may not have you locked away, but you're still my slave, still my possession, and one thing will never change. Everywhere I touch you, inside and out, will always be mine." I pound into her one last time still clutching her neck and fucking explode, a river of ecstasy flowing over my bones.

The moments after are fuzzy as I float down from the ceiling like a piece of burning ember. I open my eyes to find Ellie limp and wheezing beneath me.

I have no words or explanation for what just happened. So I just haul her up and take her into my arms. Languidly, she hugs me back.

"Ellie?" I whisper worriedly.

"Yup," she answers drily. "Definitely ruined."

I actually chuckle and then steal a glance at her face. Her eyes are closed and her cheek is resting on my shoulder.

"You okay?" My heart is beating uncontrollably in my chest from a mix of physical exertion and fear. I'll never stop worrying that one day I'll take it too far. Push her over the edge and drive her away.

She nods. "Yes. And I'm still going."

Now I full-out laugh. "I know."

"Good. That was fucking amazing," she says lethargically.

"I was worried I was pushing too hard."

"No such thing," she giggles.

"I love you." I can't help but say the words.

"I love you, too." She squeezes me. "Too much for my own good."

"No such thing," I repeat.

She nestles herself against me. "I need a shower."

"Not a chance in hell. You're going with my scent and sweat and cum inside of you."

"Fine," she relents. I really just think she's too spent to argue. "See, we can compromise."

"I have a feeling we're going to be doing a lot of *compromising*." I shift so I can look down at her.

Ellie nods eagerly in agreement. "And I can't wait."

"You're a little minx, you know that?" I kiss her nose.

"I'd be boring if I wasn't."

"True. I also have a feeling you're going to make me go prematurely gray."

"Ooo. I love older men."

I pick her up and whack her ass as she wraps her legs around my waist. "I'm not that much older."

"Says you. You're in your *late* twenties."

"Ugh." I groan as I lay us on the bed and cuddle Ellie in my arms. "I'm going to spank the shit out of you later for saying that. And for calling me a douchebag."

"I'll make sure to be extra bad, then," she purrs.

I have created a monster.

"When I get back, I think we should go shopping online,"

she says.

"For what?"

"Ears and a tail." She looks up at me with just her eyes like she's a little embarrassed and a lot excited by the idea. "So I can prove to you how much I love you and how much you own me."

"Fuck, baby, you better be careful about what you say." I grab my now rapidly growing cock. "There might be round two."

The picture of Ellie naked, wearing ears, a tail, and a collar has just relaunched my arousal.

"Save it for later."

"Are you telling me what to do?" I challenge her.

"No, Kayne," she hums.

"I didn't think so." I smack her ass.

ELLIE AND I DON'T GET much downtime. Before I know it, she's out of bed, fixing her clothes and re-braiding her hair.

"Do you have a toothbrush I can use?" she asks.

"Why? Plan on kissing someone?" I ask petulantly.

"Eventually," she taunts. I know she's talking about me, but still, she's spending the next hour with another man. It's bothering me. "I'm going out in public. I care about my personal hygiene."

"Bathroom." I point behind me to the door.

Ellie skips past me and my annoyance grows. Does she have to be so damn cheerful?

I drag myself out of bed and change my clothes as Ellie attends to her personal hygiene concerns. At least she agreed not to shower. I'll bathe her later, and spank her, and fuck her, all over again.

I walk out of my closet to find Ellie checking herself in the mirror one last time. I step behind her and put one hand on her hip. In the reflection, we look like any ordinary, run of the mill couple. She, dressed casually in a light-blue sundress and sneakers, me in my favorite pair of worn jeans and black t-shirt. But appearances can be deceiving. I know that better than anyone.

We aren't ordinary, and we aren't run of the mill. We're . . . *us*. Just like Ellie said. I never thought I'd be part of an *us*. I now understand why I was so easily provoked. The thought of losing *us* strangles me with fear.

Ellie and I walk hand in hand down the stairs. I don't know if it's my paranoia or my possessive side, but something in me just doesn't want her to go.

I try to ignore it. I tell myself I'm being overprotective and irrational. Ellie is a big girl, and big girls do what they want. Unfortunately for me.

"Can you give me the key to your apartment? I want to start having some of your things brought over," I ask her as we reach the last stair.

"Things?"

"Yeah, things. Like clothes and whatever."

"Am I moving in?" she asks.

"Yes."

"Really?"

"Yes, Ellie. You're my fiancée, and I'm not going to spend another night without you for as long as I live." I put my hand out for the key.

"Don't you think you should ask Jett if it's okay? He lives here, too, right?" She digs through her purse and pulls out a key ring.

I look at her *like don't be ridiculous*. "Jett would never say no. He'll probably want to have a pajama party tonight."

Ellie laughs. "You mean there'd actually be pajamas?"

"Yes, and I'm sure they'd be highly inappropriate." Ellie hands me the key. "Is there anything in particular you want?" I place it in my pocket.

"My toothbrush." She smiles.

"I'll buy you a case so you never run out."

"You spoil me." She lifts onto her toes to kiss me.

"You have no idea." I back her up against the wall. I *really* don't want her to go.

"I'll be back in an hour," she breathes heavily.

"Exactly sixty minutes," I stipulate, "or I'm coming down there and dragging you home myself."

"I might like that."

"Ellie." I bite her lip. "Behave."

"Yes, Kayne."

The way she says that sends tingles down my spine and blood pumping straight to my cock. I once dreamed of hearing Ellie say that of her own free will. Of belonging to me—not because she was forced, but because she wanted me. It was the first time I ever let myself wish for anything. She was the first thing I ever wanted in my entire life, and I finally have her. I imagine this feeling is similar to winning the lottery. Amazement, bewilderment, joy. Joy. Such a foreign concept for me, yet so easily accepted when I'm with her.

"I'll see you in an hour." She kisses me one last time, but before she turns the knob, I stop her.

"Wait," I put my hand on the door. "Just wait right here."

I leave her standing in the foyer and head back into the Toy Box where Jett and Juice are still hanging out.

"Do we have any Jimmies?" I ask Juice. "Like really small ones?"

"In the cabinet," he points to the right, "second drawer."

"What do you need that for?" Jett asks as I pull out what looks like a dark slate business card.

"You'll see." I hand it to Juice. "Activate it. I'll tell you when to turn it on."

Juice takes the card, punches a few numbers and letters into his computer, and hands it back. I pop out the tiny little chip from the cardboard and peel off the paper from the back. It's so small you can barely decipher what it is on the tip of my finger.

I walk back out to Ellie, who is pacing the foyer. "Is everything okay?" she asks restlessly.

"As okay as it can be." I tickle the heart dangling from her throat.

"Did I hurt you upstairs?"

"No. It was intense. A little scary. But fucking amazing. I know you'd never intentionally hurt me." She smiles coyly. "No matter how mad I make you."

"I warned you I was going to fuck you hard. But baby, I meant it when I said I would love you harder." I trap her face with one hand.

"I know." She melts against me as I lean down and kiss her.

Her lips are warm and her breath is minty.

"Now go." I land a hard blow on her behind. "When you get back, I'm chaining you to the bed and eating you for dinner."

"Oh God," she says, flustered with desire. "I'm going."

"Just give the doorman your name when you get back," I tell Ellie as she steps on the elevator. "You'll be on the list."

She grins and does a little sexy wave to acknowledge me just as the doors close. Then she's gone.

And I'm completely miserable.

I head back into the Toy Box and plop down into a seat. Both Jett and Juice stare at me.

"What?" I ask defensively.

"Whatcha doing?" Jett asks.

"What does it look like I'm doing? Sitting down."

"Where's Ellie?"

"She went out."

"To do what?" His eyebrows crease.

"Break up with her boy toy."

"And you let her?" His tone elevates.

"Yeah. What do you think the jimmy was for?"

"You bugged your fiancée?"

"Well, I had to keep an eye, or ear, in this case, on her somehow. I know I couldn't force her to stay." *Unfortunately.*

"Don't you think that's a little . . . stalkerish?" Juice asks.

I glare at both of them. "There is an unidentified threat out there, and although it doesn't seem to involve Ellie, I decided to play it safe anyway."

"Translation," Jett arbitrates, "I am insecure about my fiancée hanging out with another man, so I took it upon myself to eavesdrop."

"Fuck you," I spit. "If the two of you have such a problem with my moral turpitude, you can leave."

Jett and Juice glance at each other decisively.

"I'll get the popcorn." Juice jumps up.

That's what I thought.

Once gone, Jett swivels his chair so he's looking directly at me. "You've come far, Grasshopper."

I raise my eyebrows at him. Condescending cocksucker. "You do know I'm going to throw knives at your head while you're sleeping tonight, right?"

"Good." He runs his hand through his blond hair. "Take a little off the top. I'm due for a trim."

"Ass—" Loud popping noises like gunshots suddenly echo from inside the apartment.

"Juice!?" We both yell as we jump up and grab the closest firearm in reaching distance. We hear more pops and then the smell of popcorn fills the air.

We glance at each other hesitantly, waiting a few moments before Juice reappears with a big bowl in one hand a bottle of soda in the other.

"Should I put my hands up?" he asks as he stares down the barrel of two semi-automatic handguns.

Jett and I both exhale.

"When you said popcorn, I thought you meant you were going to rip open a bag."

"No way." He sits back down in his captain's chair. "This is first-class entertainment. It warrants the real stuff." He pops a kernel into his mouth.

"Just turn the fucking thing on." I uncock the gun, and then grab a handful of popcorn for myself.

A few seconds later, the sound of cars passing and Ellie humming plays through the room.

"Good acoustics," Juice mouths.

I roll my eyes; idiot loves his gadgets.

She has to be close to the coffee house by now, if not there already.

There's a low ringing noise, and then a muffled voice I recognize.

"You've reached Mark at Expo Shipping and Receiving. I'm sorry I missed your call but please leave a message and I'll get back to you as soon as possible."

Beep!

"Mark, you going to be really sorry you missed this call! I'll only forgive you if you're doing something really important, like Pretty Pete. Call me! I have to ask you something. Bye."

Ask him something?

"Pretty Pete?" Juice asks with wide brown eyes.

I shrug. "He's gay. It's her old boss."

"Ah." He acknowledges, then goes back to munching on his popcorn.

A few moments after she hangs up, tires screech, there's a sharp intake of breath, and then what sounds like a scuffle. I fly out of my seat when I hear Ellie scream *'no!'* and a car door slam.

"Ellie!"

The sound of tires peeling out tears through the room, and then there's just silence.

I barely remember making it down to the street — there's just a faint recollection of Jett ordering me into the elevator because the stairs would take too long. We retrace Ellie's steps with my mind in a panic. Someone took her. Someone took her *again*. I can't think, I can't see, as pedestrians and tourists knock me around. I feel like I'm caught in a wind tunnel.

"Kayne!" Jett calls a few yards away from me. He's crouching by the curb on the corner. I walk over to him dazed. He stands up, holding Ellie's necklace. "They grabbed her here."

Those words slice through me like I've just been cut with a burning blade.

"And look." He points to several spots. "Traffic cameras and ATM machines. Maybe they caught something."

"They better fucking have."

I'm shaking with rage by the time we get back to the Toy Box. Juice's fingers are already flying as he hacks into every camera in the area.

"Anything?" I growl.

"Not yet. Give me a second."

"Juice, fucking find something," I snap.

"You yelling at me isn't going to make the process go faster, so back the fuck off." He concentrates on the screen.

"Kayne." Jett pulls me back and I begin pacing like a lunatic. Who am I kidding, I am a lunatic. SOMEONE TOOK ELLIE! This is all my fault. I knew I shouldn't have let her leave. I should have listened to my fucking gut. It's the one thing that's kept me alive the past twenty-eight years. I just gambled with, and lost, the most important thing in my life and these two want me stay fucking calm.

"Okay." There are lots of different things popping up on Juice's screen. "Look there," he points to a few mismatched images lined up in a row. "Here she's walking." He points to her back. "Then here." A car pulls up right in front of her just as she reaches the corner. It only takes a second, the picture is blurry, but there's definitely two of them—one driving an old model sedan and the one who grabbed her. It literally took a split second to get her in the car and drive away.

My brain feels like it's expanding in my skull from stress.

"Can we get a better picture of the car? Maybe a shot of the license plate?" Jett asks.

"Yup, found that." Juice bangs on the keys. "It's only a partial, but you can see the make, too. That's huge."

The letters FHK and MALIBU display across the big screen on the wall.

"I'm cross-referencing both identifiers in the DMV database and searching to see if there are any police reports about a stolen Malibu."

The whole process feels like it takes forever. I know every second that ticks by is one more second our chance of finding Ellie diminishes.

"Okay," Juice finally announces. "There are three potential hits on the car with that make and license plate letters. No reports of stolen vehicles."

"Three?"

"Yeah, two in Honolulu and one in Ma'ili. I would try that one first." He scribbles on a piece of paper and hands it to Jett.

"Why do you say that?" he asks.

"Ms. Kalani has a brother who was released from prison three months ago. Drug trafficking." He cocks an eyebrow. "Her address is listed as his last known."

I look at Jett. "Let's go."

THE ADDRESS JUICE GAVE US is a small farmhouse in the middle of nowhere. I think you can literally only fit a couch and a television in the rundown structure.

There are chickens and goats roaming the property, and the grounds are completely overgrown. If I was a douchebag drug smuggler, this is exactly where I would live.

I yank on the black leather gloves covering my hands, the ones with the brass knuckles sewn right into them.

"Ready?" Jett asks as he opens the car door.

"To break someone's face? Hell yeah."

"Hey," he puts a hand on my chest. "Don't kill him before he talks."

"I wouldn't dream of it."

"We're going to get her back." I know what Jett is trying to do. He's trying to appease me so I can focus, but I've never been more focused in my life.

"In what condition?" I mutter rhetorically. I've run through every horrific scenario possible. Beaten, raped, drugged, sold, killed. There isn't one thing I've left out.

"You knock on the front door. I'll go around back. Maybe we can snuff him out."

"I know the drill."

"Glad to hear. Now get the fuck out of the car."

I walk up the front path overgrown with weeds as Jett makes his way to the side of the house. He clucks to get my attention right before I knock on the door.

"Car," he mouths. It must be hidden in the back.

I nod, then bang on the door. "Anyone home?" I yell. "I seem to be lost. And my GPS isn't working out here." I try to sound like a tourist. "Hello?" I bang again.

A second later the door jerks open to a very large Hawaiian woman in a Muu Muu dress and flower in her hair. She takes one look at me in my skintight black shirt, cargo pants, and gun holster and knows I'm no tourist. She tries to slam the door in my face, but I stop her with my hand.

"Where's Pilipo?"

"Never heard of him."

"Bullshit."

"Kayne!" I hear Jett yell. "Coming around!"

I turn my head just in time to see someone disappearing into the woods. Perfect, a chase. It's exactly what I need. My heart starts to punch through my chest as I book it across the front lawn and into the thick greenery. I can see his shaved head and tattooed arms fighting against the dense branches as I track him like an animal. *I'm going to tear you apart* is all I can think as adrenaline courses through my veins.

Just as I come up behind Pilipo, Jett barrels into him from the left side. They both hit the ground hard, rolling down a small hill. The medium-sized man ends up on top giving him the upper hand. He lands a hard blow across Jett's face, causing him to spit blood.

A second later, I yank the piece of shit up and return the favor, smashing his nose.

"Where is she?" I bark.

"Who?" he screams back wiping blood from his face.

"The girl you took this morning." I knee him in the stomach.

He keels over. "I don't know nothing about any girl." He looks up at me, and I immediately know he's lying.

"Wanna try that answer again?" I kick him in the face, and he hits the ground hard.

"I don't know shit." He splutters, his mouth foaming with saliva and blood.

I glance at Jett. He's standing on the opposite side of Pilipo. "I think he needs some incentive to talk."

He looks up at me with blood stained teeth. "I couldn't agree more." Jett hauls Pilipo up and locks him in a full nelson. Arms subdued over his head.

Pilipo is sucking in air, and although he isn't acting scared, I'm about to make him shit.

"I'm going to make this easy. I ask, you answer. Nod if you understand."

He spits on me. I wipe my shirt. This job is so glamorous sometimes. "Okay, then. I'll take that as a yes." I pull a picture out of the side pocket on my leg. "Recognize her?"

Pilipo turns white as a ghost.

"That's your daughter, yeah?"

He doesn't say a word.

"She's cute. Just turned four?" I taunt him.

He glares at me.

"Want someone to take her away?" I ask waving the picture of the little dark-haired girl blowing out her birthday candles.

His breathing becomes more erratic and his stare hostile.

"Tell me where you took her," I lean in closer, "or I'm going to take *her*. We know a lot of the same people, brother, and what they're capable of."

He doesn't utter a word, just snarls at me. I wait him out, but he doesn't budge.

"Fine. Let him go," I instruct Jett. "You just signed your daughter's death sentence." Jett drops him to the ground. "And I'll make sure you never find her body."

"Wait!" Pilipo punches the dirt. "Fuck. Swear you won't touch her!"

"Give me the information I want and I'll think about it," I sneer.

He glowers at me on all fours. "An estate. In Kailua."

"Who hired you to take her?" I grab his face.

"I don't know his name! All I know is he calls himself Protégé and is trying to take over the cartel I used to run for."

"Who's cartel?" I demand.

"El Rey's."

I look at Jett.

Shit.

WE LEFT PILIPO LYING IN a pool of his own blood.

I'm just ripping off my bloody glove when my phone rings. It's Juice.

I put it on speaker as Jett drives down a muddy road back to the highway.

"What's up?"

"Got news. We know who hacked Endeavor."

"Who?" we ask.

"Simon."

"Simon? Like the Gatekeeper, Simon?" Jett questions.

"One and the same." Juice confirms.

"Isn't he supposed be the one protecting our classified information?"

"Yes, but he also doubles as a hacker. Turns out he's been working an undercover mission of his own."

"And no one knew about it?"

"Adams did."

"Of course, he did," I state aggravated. Commander Adams knows everything that goes on with Endeavor, he's the fucking man behind the curtain. "He didn't think to clue anyone else in?"

"Too dangerous. They wanted this guy. Bad."

"Bad enough to let him think he was hacking one of the most powerful security agencies in the world?" Jett asks.

"So it seems. Simon had to lay low until all the information was transferred. Well, all the wrong information anyway."

"So, no identities have been compromised?" I ask.

"None but the guy who hired Simon to hack us."

"And that would be who exactly?" I inquire on the edge of my seat.

"That's what I'm calling about. Kayne, you're not going to like this. I'm sending a pic."

A new message pops up on my screen.

"His name is Eduardo Sanchez or, as he's known on the street, Protégé."

"Protégé?" Jett and I repeat in unison as I open the text.

"Holy fucking shit."

"What?" Jett glances tensely between me and the road as he drives. "What is it?"

I hold up my phone so he can see, all the blood draining from my body.

"It's Michael."

ELLIE

"I CAN'T BREATHE!" I SCREAM as I kick and flail, being hauled around with a hood over my head.

I'm suddenly dropped on the floor, hard.

Ouch!

I don't know what happened. One minute I was walking down the street minding my own business, and the next I was being forced into the backseat of a car where I was tied up, gagged, and then shrouded in darkness. I'm now lying helplessly on my side with my hands bound behind my back and my heart on the verge of giving out. It's been beating triple time since I was grabbed.

"Well, look who finally decided to come home," a male voice says. The hood is removed, and I look up into a pair of dark chocolate-brown eyes. Michael's eyes. I glance around erratically. I'm in a bedroom. A very fancy bedroom that has a beautiful view of the Pacific, white décor, and a polished wood floor. The smell of fresh flowers is as potent as air freshener.

"You look hot as hell like that, Ellie," he says as I stare at him angry, confused, and unable to speak.

He props me up so I'm sitting on my butt and removes the gag. I work my jaw quickly, trying to get the feeling back.

"Is this some kind of joke?" I demand.

Michael laughs at me. "Have fun on your trip?" He lifts my chin and regards the large bite mark on my neck.

I refuse to answer.

"Looks to me like you did. You never let me give you hickeys."

"You never tried."

"I was holding back."

"Why?"

"So I didn't kill you," he says matter-of-factly.

"What?"

"Ellie, Ellie, Ellie. Little gullible Ellie," he recites.

I stare at him like he's deranged. "What the fuck is going on?"

"Let me tell you a story." Michael diverts, avoiding my question. "There was this boy who had a father whom he loved dearly. A man he looked up to and idolized. A man who wanted him to go to college and live a straight-laced life. But the boy wanted to be just like his father. Wanted money and power and women. So the father took the boy under his wing and groomed him. And when the boy was just old enough, and had proven himself just enough," his voice elevates, "his father is killed in cold blood and his kingdom is destroyed. Do you know what that does to a child?"

I shake my head.

"It makes him want revenge." His eyes widen rabidly.

"Revenge on who?"

"The man who killed my father. The man who is your Master."

"I don't have a Master," I contest.

"Don't lie to me, Ellie. I saw it with my own eyes. I was there that night. I watched as he toted you around like he owned you and the world. I fucked right in front of the two of you."

My eyes widen as images of that night, the night of the party, flash in front of my eyes. Jett dressing me up. Kayne leading me around. The roped off section of the room where we watched one of his girls get taken on the same kind of table that was in my room. Taken by Michael?

"Why were you there?" I ask dubiously.

"It was a party. I was invited." He shrugs.

"I don't understand." I shake my head.

Michael sighs and crouches down so we're eye level.

"You know, I was actually jealous of him. You were so

beautiful and raw and intoxicating. I wanted what he had. I wanted you."

He leans forward and for a second I think he's going to kiss me. I pull away.

"Skittish all of a sudden?" He unties my hands, and I rub my wrists once they're free. "You always used to like it when I kissed you."

"Tell me what the hell is going on."

"I'm getting my revenge on the man who killed my father and the organization who destroyed my birthright."

"Who is your father?" I erupt.

Michael grabs my hair and yanks my head back. My scalp stings. He looks down directly into my eyes, and any warmth or feeling is completely gone. Just void. It's like I don't even know this person in front of me.

"EL REY!" he screams, and I flinch, his grip still tight on my hair.

"I don't know who that is!" I cry from the pain.

Michael looks at me like I'm insane. "I would honestly believe he has you brainwashed. You are an excellent actress." I still don't understand. "I saw him speak to you that night, Ellie. He yanked on your slave chain."

Recognition suddenly sparks. The man with Javier. The one who wanted to buy me. I see the resemblance now, straight nose, prominent cheekbones, and dark-brown eyes. They look much more like his father's at the moment. Cold and calculating, capable of anything.

"Kayne didn't kill your father!" I blurt out.

"Of course, you would say that. You're protecting him." He painfully shakes my head around with his firm hold.

I wince helplessly. "I'm not lying, I was there." I grab his hand like that's somehow going to loosen his grip. "Javier killed him. He shot him in the head right in front of us!"

"Liar!" he snaps. "Javier was my father's most loyal disciple. He would never turn on him."

"He did," I scream as Michael pulls harder. My scalp feels like it's going to rip right off my skull. "I remember his words right before he shot him. He said," I pant loudly, "'hostile takeover.'"

Michael breathes raggedly as he searches my eyes. I almost think he believes me. I pray silently that he believes me.

"You would say anything to protect him."

I have no response for that because it's the truth.

"He didn't kill him. I swear," I whisper desperately.

"Even if he didn't kill him, which he did, the organization he works for took everything from me. It's reason enough to destroy them both."

"Michael, no," I beg.

I can't believe this is the same person I've spent the last three months with. The man who would buy me shaved ice as we walked along the beach, who would listen to me ramble about nonsense and make me laugh with stupid jokes. A man who was so warm and sweet and caring.

"I don't understand. You cozied up to me all that time for what?"

"To get to Kayne, of course. I figured find you, find him. But it didn't exactly work that way." He lets go of my hair and climbs on top of me, forcing me back onto my elbows. "He was nowhere to be found. Not even a whisper in your life. I began to think that maybe you weren't as important to him as I originally thought." He's directly on top of me now. "It was your pussy that kept me coming back. You gave it up so easily. You really are a whore."

Tears well in my eyes. "I thought you were nice."

"I think you were just looking for someone to buy time with until your Master came for you." He presses his body flush against mine. An erection growing in his pants. My stomach turns. I try to wriggle away, but he wraps his hand around my throat and squeezes tightly. "I knew the minute I pulled up to your house that day it was him you were going to see. The minute I saw the car and the driver." He unbuttons his jeans and slides down his fly as I frantically squirm beneath him, clawing at his forearm.

"I love it when you fight, Ellie. This might be the most exciting sex we've ever had."

"Michael, no!" I strain, as he crushes my windpipe with one hand and rips my panties off with the other.

"Michael!" Tears flow like a river down my cheeks as I try

to fight him.

"Did you miss saying my name?" He thrusts into me, and it feels like someone just sliced me open with a serrated knife.

"Stop!" My voice is barely audible as he chokes me, while at the same time violating me over and over again.

I cry harder with every passing second he wrecks me, the pain becoming unbearable, my legs spasming, my fingernails wet with blood from stabbing them into his skin.

"Michael!" I whimper one last time before my vision fades and my spirit breaks.

"Your pussy saves you every time."

It's the last thing I hear before I pass out.

I SWEAR I WAS DEAD.

I come around to Michael zipping his pants while I lay ruined on the floor. Every inch of my body is throbbing.

"I missed you, Ellie. Never thought I'd say that."

I glare at him. "You're a monster. Just like your father."

Michael's eyes flash as he crouches down and clutches my face painfully. "Don't speak unkindly of the dead. Now go clean yourself up." He says it like he loathes me. "We have a plane to catch."

"We?"

"Yes, Ellie. You're mine now."

I look at him dismayed. "What else could you possibly want from me?"

"My cock in your mouth next time." He lifts me off the floor. "Once a whore always a whore."

Tears threaten once more. I can't live as someone's slave again. Especially Michael's. I'd rather kill myself.

"What about Kayne? You going to kill him?"

"Yes, eventually. A very long time from now. My father taught me if you really want to destroy a man, destroy what's most important to him. First, I'm going to destroy his organization, then I'm going to destroy you. And when I'm finished, I'll return you to your owner a shell of a human being."

I nearly throw up from his words. I now explicitly understand. I understand why Kayne did what he did—why he went to such extreme measures to protect me. To save from heinous creatures like this.

"You really are a monster." I seethe.

Michael's lips curl cruelly. "We're all monsters in our own way. You have ten minutes." He turns and then stops.

"One more thing," he snaps, spinning to face me again. "You won't need this anymore." He lifts my hand and pulls off my engagement ring, tossing it over his head. I gasp as I hear it ding on the wooden floor, and then watch as it rolls and bounces into a corner. "While you two were off picking out china patterns, I was assembling my army and appointing new captains. My father ruled a kingdom, I'm going to rule an empire." He glances at the ring. "Pick it up and I'll cut off your hand. Understand?"

I look at him with tear-soaked eyes. I despise this man.

"Ellie?" he grabs my chin.

I nod.

"If you want to be mad at someone, be mad at Kayne."

With that, he leaves, and all I can think about is how wrong he is. The person I should be mad at is myself.

My concentration is hazy as I clean the blood from between my legs. It literally feels like I have been hacked wide open with a meat cleaver. I cry silently, not wanting anyone to hear. What are the odds a person is kidnapped twice in their lifetime to be used as a sex slave? I must be one fucking lucky woman, I think bitterly as I throw away the white towel stained with red.

I have ten minutes to figure a way out of this. I pace the bedroom. I have a feeling this is going to be the last bit of luxury I see if Michael forces me to leave with him.

I hurry and pull on the French doors that lead to the lani. Locked. Shit. I try some windows, but they're built right into the wall, like an all-natural picture frame. I search them all, hoping beyond hope that just one has a latch. The last ones I try are at the back of the room on either side of the bed. It opens! I look down to see a slanted roof below me and a trellis just adjacent to it. There's nothing but green land all around the house, and the ocean and mountains in the distance. I remember telling Kayne that I'd rather be lost in the wilderness than be his slave. Those words were never truer. Just as I'm about to push open the window, I hear the door unlock and see Michael walk in.

"Let's go." He orders.

I just stand there.

"Didn't hear me the first time? It's time to go," he says annoyed.

I say something quietly in response.

"What?"

I say it again, no louder.

"What are you saying?" He stomps over to me enraged and grabs my arm.

"I said," I look him dead in the eye, "I'd rather die than live as someone's slave again." With that, I swiftly knee him in the balls as hard as I can. As he falls to the floor, I escape out the window with my heart battering the inside of my chest.

"Bitch!" I hear him yell as I shuffle sideways across the slanted roof until I reach the trellis and swing down. Then I run like hell, past the pool and soft lit gazebo, toward the setting sun and lush green mountains.

KAYNE

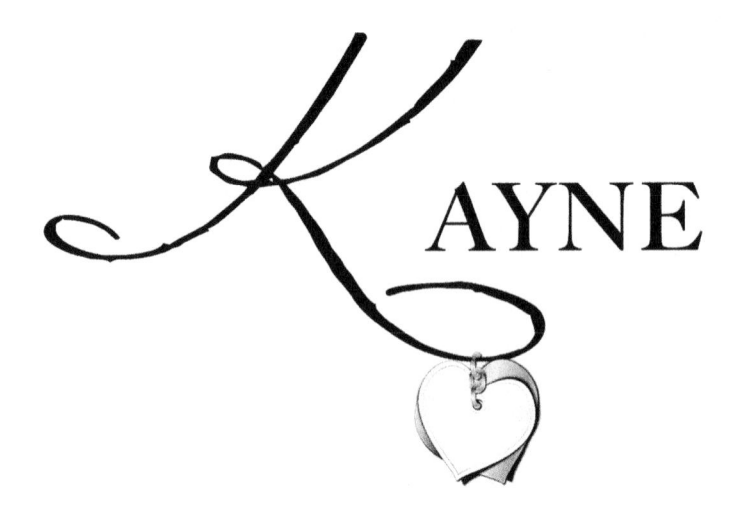

JUST FOR THE RECORD, I did not enjoy using Pilipo's daughter as a bargaining chip. I just did what had to be done. I did what I had to do to protect my own.

"Are you speaking to me yet?" Juice asks from the front seat of the Suburban.

"No," I growl. "You're lucky I haven't killed you yet."

"That would look bad in your personnel file. Killing a fellow employee."

I shoot him the most deadly look I'm capable of.

"I ran the background check like you asked me to."

"If you don't stop talking, I'm going to wire your jaw shut."

Juice huffs. It's mostly his fault we are in this situation. I told him to run a background check on Michael the second Ellie had a conversation with him. It came back clean. Not even a parking ticket. But there should have been something to tip us off as to who he was or what he was involved in. There's always something, and Juice missed it.

"The guy was tight. Clean as a whistle. Nothing to even suggest criminal activity."

"Or that fact he was a drug lord's son," I add vindictively.

"Come on. That identity was buried so deep, it took a hacker much more skilled than me to uncover it. We all know El Rey was a master at concealing his identity. So how far-fetched is it that he did the same with his offspring?"

"Just save it." I clench my jaw so tightly, I may just crack a molar.

I know it's not all Juice's fault. It's just easier to blame someone else at the moment. Maybe if I wasn't shitfaced half the time wallowing in my own misery, I would have done the background check myself and dug until I found something on the conniving little piece of shit whose head I'm going to gladly rip off with my bare hands.

"Is everything ready?" Jett asks, collected—always in control no matter the circumstance.

"As ready as it will ever be." Juice fiddles with the laptop on his dashboard. We are currently parked in the woods three miles away from Michael's compound. Satellite images confirmed this is where they're holding Ellie and surveillance shows there are nine guards heavily armed.

We were able to assemble a twenty-man team in under three hours with the help of Honolulu S.W.A.T.

"HSWAT come in, over." Juice talks into a walkie-talkie.

"Copy HSWAT," the commander answers.

"In position?" Juice asks.

"Roger. Falcon One. Diversion set for nineteen hundred hours," which is seven PM civilian time and in twelve minutes. "Men positioned on foot."

"Copy," Juice replies and the walkie hisses. "You two ready?" He turns to Jett and me in the backseat.

I pull on my brass-knuckled gloves, and the leather creaks. "Can't wait." I tighten my fist and curl my biceps ready to pound Michael's face in.

"Good. It should be fully dark by the time you emerge from the woods and reach the edge of the property. Don't breach the perimeter until you hear the explosion. That should divert all shitheads to the front of the house, leaving Ellie light on muscle." Juice tips the laptops so we can see the schematics of the immense structure in infrared. "It looks like they're keeping her in this back bedroom, which boasts well for you, since there's a trellis and slanted roof right underneath it. Easy in, easy out." Jett and I nod, memorizing the layout.

"Got it," Jett confirms.

"I'll be on comms the whole time," he puts in an ear piece, "so no pillow talk you two. I want to keep my lunch in my stomach."

"You're just jealous no one loves you that much." I grin callously.

"Insanely." Juice rolls his eyes. As much as we bust his chops, the man can run an operation like no other. He was mine and Jett's handler the six years we were undercover. He knew the ins and outs of everything, advised us in sticky situations, and basically saved mine and Ellie's lives by knowing where in the mansion we were and exactly how to infiltrate.

"See you on the flip side." The three of us bump fists, and then Jett and I are gone.

We jog straight toward the sunset, pushing brush out of our way as we go.

"Comms check, Alpha Green," I hear Juice say in my ear.

"Loud and clear, Falcon one. Roger."

"Test, test," he says again. "Come in, Charlie Blue."

"Copy," Jett responds. "You have such a lovely speaking voice, Falcon One."

"Can it," Juice responds.

"Just wanted to make you feel loved."

"Stay the course," he says seriously.

"I don't think you could divert Alpha Green if you launched a missile."

"Roger," Juice repeats, some amusement in his voice.

Jett and I cover ground quickly, keeping to the strict timeline and markers. We're two hundred yards out when Juice chatters in my ear. "Alpha Green we have movement on the south side, over."

"Identify, over?"

"Switching to satellite."

Seconds tick.

"Shit. It's Ellie. She made a break for it," Juice informs me.

"What?" Jett and I both pick up the pace.

"She's heading straight for you. Man, she's quick."

I can't help but smirk as I push my body to the max, flying through the woods.

"There's someone tailing her. Coming up fast." The hiss of the walkie-talkie echoes in my ear.

"HSWAT, we are a go," he yells. "Push the panic button."

"Shit. Shit." I run faster, branches catching me in the face and whipping my arms.

Moments later, we hear a blast as the car bomb is detonated.

"Check in, Falcon One," I huff.

Silence.

"Juice!"

"Motherfucker, he caught her." My chest explodes. "They're fighting. Damn, your girl has one hell of a right hook."

"Don't I know it." I can still feel the sting from when she hit me outside Mansion.

I see a clearing, the perimeter of the property. I burst through the trees onto a manicured lawn with Jett by my side. It's nearly dark, only a sliver of light left. I break out into full-blown sprint as my lungs burn and my leg muscles tear.

"Oh, man." It sounds like Juice winces.

"What!"

"He's beating her. Kill that cocksucker, Kayne."

"With immense pleasure," I pant.

Just as the last shreds of light disappear, Ellie comes into view.

With each breath, a montage of images flash in front of me one after the other.

Ellie on the ground, Michael standing over her. A gun pointed at her head.

"ELLIE!" Her name rips from my throat, and then a gunshot rings out.

"NO!" I tackle Michael to the ground, knocking the gun out of his hand. We roll over the thick lush grass, struggling for control. I pull a power move, grabbing under one of his legs and hooking an arm around his neck. He punches me in the head and kicks out of my hold. We both get to our feet and I don't waste a second going back at his body, grabbing hold of his chest and landing a kidney shot. He knees me in the stomach, but I barely register it. There's so much adrenaline pumping through my system it feels like I have wings.

"I'm going to let you be the first to see what happens when

someone fucks with what's mine." I smash Michael right in the face and his nose explodes with blood.

"Fuck!" He stumbles back making a go for his gun. He grabs it and points it at me, but I kick it out of his hand then punch him again. He drops to the ground, and I continue to pound on his face. Soon, it's barely recognizable. His cheeks are swollen, his lips are split, and his eyebrows are ripped open. I pull my fist back about to slam him again when he speaks.

"Do it! Kill me, you motherfucker! Just like you killed my father!" I pause to look at him mid punch. He thinks I killed El Rey? Everything begins to make sense now. Ellie, Endeavor, he was trying to get to me.

I lower my fist and respond harshly. "You're wrong about one thing. I didn't kill your father." He sputters blood as I speak. "But you're right about the other. I am going to kill *you*." I jerk a Glock out of my back holster and pull the trigger, shooting him square between the eyes. Then I pull it again—and again and again. I pull it until the chamber clicks.

Then I reload and repeat.

"Kayne!" I hear Juice's sharpened voice cut through my murderous rampage. "I think he's dead!"

"Not enough for me." I squeeze the trigger one last time.

"Heel man. Jett needs you. *Ellie* needs you."

"Ellie!?" I snap out of my lethal haze and turn to see Jett leaning over her body under the bright moonlight.

"Ellie? Ellie?" I crawl over to them. "Ellie?" I examine her face. Her eye is swollen, and her lip is bleeding.

"Give me your shirt!" Jett roars. It takes a second for my mind to catch up with my body as I process the scene in front of me. Jett's hands covered in blood. Ellie lying still as a statue, a pool of red staining the grass underneath her, growing larger by the second.

"Kayne now! She's going to bleed out!"

Without thinking, I rip off my holster and tear off my shirt. "I need you to hold here." He takes my hand and places it on his already soaked T-shirt pressed against her abdomen.

"I think it went straight through. I need to compress the exit wound." He tilts her body, assesses her back, and then applies pressure with my shirt.

"There's a medivac already on its way. The house is secured." He talks to me, but all I see is Ellie, dying right before my eyes.

We hear the chopper in the distance. "Two minutes max," he says.

It's going to be the longest two minutes of my life.

"Kayne," Ellie's faint voice calls my name.

"Ellie, I'm right here. Hold on." I wish I could scoop her up in my arms and hold her, but I know my hands need to stay where they are.

"You were right," she murmurs.

"About what, baby?" I try to keep her talking.

She doesn't open her eyes as she speaks. "I am a terrible judge of character." I nearly lose it. That's what I said to her when she was locked in the dungeon. *"I won't hold it against you for being a bad judge of character."*

"I don't know shit. I was talking out of my ass," I choke.

"It's so cold in the city." She shivers. I glance at Jett.

"She's hallucinating. She thinks she's in New York," I say, shaking.

"She's going into shock," he tells me as her eyes flutter and chest compresses just as the air ambulance hovers overhead.

"Shit! Come on, Ellie!" Jett yells over the propellers. "Be the strong girl we all know you are!"

The spotlight shines on us as the EMS helicopter lands. The door flies open and two flight paramedics dressed in all white exit with a gurney and oxygen.

They check her vitals as soon as they reach us and instruct Jett and me not to move.

"Ellie?" one of the medics asks. "Ellie, can you hear me?"

She doesn't respond.

I watch withdrawn as the two men work rapidly to bandage the bleeding, place her on the gurney, and cover her face with an oxygen mask. Right before they lift her, I whisper in her ear. "Ellie, if your hearts stop beating so will mine. Third rule of survival, fight like hell. Stay with me." Tears escape down my cheeks as she's carried away, leaving me helpless, hopeless, and in utter despair.

"Come on, come on." Jett pulls on my arm, lifting me to my

feet as the helicopter takes off. My entire existence is in that aircraft. Everything I have to live for.

He hauls me into the back of a Suburban I didn't even see pull up, and we speed off in the same direction as the transport.

"It's going to be okay. It's going to be okay." Juice's voice is distant compared to Ellie's in my head. *"Till death do us part."* She only said that yesterday. Yesterday was the start of our tomorrow and now tomorrow might not even exist.

"Put this on," Jett whips a shirt in my face while Juice drives like a maniac. "And here," he hands me a pack of wipes. Black op survival kit, a change of clothes and baby wipes. "We gotta clean up, they'll never let us in the hospital looking like we just left the scene of a massacre."

"Didn't we?" I tighten my fists and draw them into my chest. I don't want to clean Ellie's blood off my hands. It's the only piece of her I have to hold on to.

"Kayne." Jett chastises me as we speed through Honolulu. "Come on." He grabs my hands and starts wiping frantically in the dark. I look up at him, removed. I feel like I'm six years old again. Helpless, alone, and scared out of my mind. "If she dies, you're going to have to bury me with her."

Jett pulls his lips into a tight line. "She's not going to die."

"How do you know?"

"Because I know everything," he says, not sounding very confident of knowing anything at all.

Juice pulls up in front of the hospital, and Jett and I jump out. We're somewhat put together, but still look like we just walked through hell. Or maybe that's just me.

"Ellie Stevens," Jett asks the front desk guard. "She was brought in by medivac. Gunshot wound."

The elderly man in a security uniform punches something into his computer.

"Steven or Stevens?" he asks.

"Stevens," Jett answers. I pace.

"Ellie with a Y or i.e.?"

"I.e."

The man shakes his head.

"Female?"

I fume. What the fuck is wrong with this guy? I slam my fist onto the desk. "Elizabeth Anne Stevens. Female, with a fucking F!"

The man jumps.

"Kayne!" Jett yanks me back. "Re-fucking-lax. We're all worried about her, but giving the security guard a heart attack won't help."

"Fine!' I throw my hands up and walk away, leaving Jett to deal with the incompetent man.

"Down the hall, second set of double doors. Emergency medicine."

Finally.

At Emergency medicine, we don't find out much more except Ellie is in surgery, and all we can do is wait—which feels like a set of red-hot butter knives are slicing me open one long, slow slit at a time.

"I think we should contact Ellie's parents," Jett tells me. "If something happens, they should be here." There's a grave tone in his voice. I just nod. What else can I fucking do? I've done everything. Everything wrong. I drop my head into my hands. I should have never gone that night. I should have stayed away like my gut told me to. She wouldn't be here right now fighting for her life. She'd be out having fun, living the way she so desperately wanted to. And I took that all away.

"Hey," Jett puts his hand on my shoulder, "don't do it."

"Do what?" I look up at him.

"Blame yourself."

"Too late. Too. Fucking. Late."

He frowns. "I'm going to go arrange to have Ellie's family flown out."

I just nod despairingly.

Three hours. I have watched every second on the clock tick by for three agonizing hours.

"I'm looking for the family of Elizabeth Stevens," a man in light-blue scrubs and a mask hanging off his face announces in the waiting room. Jett and I immediately stand up.

"I'm Dr. Holiday. I worked on Ms. Stevens." He shakes both our hands.

"Jett Fox." "Kayne Rivers." We both reply.

"How are you related?" he inquires.

"I'm her fiancé," I answer with a thread of composure. "How is she?"

The doctor sighs. "Ms. Stevens wound was severe. She lost a lot of blood and coded on the way to the OR."

My knees nearly give out. Jett catches my arm and holds me up. "She—"

"No," Dr. Holiday continues. "We were able to revive her, but she was deprived of oxygen for nearly five minutes. She's stable, but in a coma," he says gently.

"So, that's good? Right?" I grasp at any tiny reassurance Ellie is going to be okay.

"It's promising, but there is a chance, Mr. Rivers, that she'll never wake up.

"Never?" my voice nearly disappears.

"The next forty-eight hours are critical."

I nod, barely holding it together.

"There was something else," the doctor frowns.

"What?"

"Our examination showed severe trauma to the vaginal region."

I blink rapidly at the doctor. "She was raped?"

He nods. "If she does wake up, a social worker will be visiting."

I don't hear the last part as rage explodes inside me like a nuclear bomb. I punch a hole right through the wall to relieve the pressure in my chest.

"Mr. Rivers!" the doctor shouts. "I understand this is distressing news, but please compose yourself, or I'll be forced to call security."

I breathe savagely in his face. "You don't understand jack shit."

"Kayne!" Jett yells at me for the umpteenth time tonight. "I apologize for my friend." He steps between me and the doctor. "He's had a very rough night."

Dr. Holiday acknowledges with a head nod. "Hearing someone you love was hurt is never easy."

"No, it's not," Jett agrees as I seethe behind him, wishing I could kill Michael all over again.

"Can we see her?" Jett asks.

"When *he* calms down." With that, Dr. Holiday turns and leaves.

NOT ONLY DID JETT ARRANGE for Ellie's parents to be flown in from New York, but he also arranged for her to have a private room with extra care.

Sometimes I don't know how I would function without him.

My first look at Ellie lying in a hospital bed, unconscious with tubes sticking out of her, was almost too much to bear. Knowing what Michael did to her was the grain of sand that tipped the scale. Alone with Ellie, as still as silence, I finally broke down. Her suffering will always be my fault.

"I'm sorry," I sob exhausted. "I'm so sorry. I wish I could take it away. I'd carry it all. It should have been me."

"Kayne?" I feel a hand on my back. I pick my head up off Ellie's mattress and wipe my face hastily.

"Hey. What's up, man?" I ask Juice, trying, but failing miserably, to pretend to pull it together.

"They found this when they swept the house." I turn to see he's holding Ellie's engagement ring. "I thought you'd want it."

"Thank you." I take the ring and slip it back on Ellie's finger and nearly start crying all over again. I'm really not sure I'm going to survive this. I lived through a lot of fucked-up shit in my life, but this? It's the worst of the worst.

"I'll be back in the morning. Ellie's parents are due in at ten. I'm picking them up and bringing them straight here."

"Okay. Thanks." I hide my face. "Have you seen Jett?"

"He's in the emergency room with London."

I snap my head back to look at him. "For what?"

"She was still sick. Couldn't stop throwing up, so he made her come in. They're giving her IV fluids."

"Why didn't he tell me?"

"Figured you have enough on your plate," Juice states the obvious. "Get some rest, man." He taps the doorframe then leaves.

Yeah, right.

I WATCH THE SUN COME up through the window. Bright yellow rays breaking through the dark sky.

Ellie hasn't moved a muscle, or fluttered an eyelash, or twitched a lip.

The nurses come and go—readjusting pillows, checking vitals, and taking blood. I never move from her side. I just hold her hand and imagine all the things I want to do with her when she wakes up. The wedding I'm going to give her, the honeymoon I'll surprise her with.

"Ellie, you have to wake up. There are so many things I have to tell you." My heart pinches in my chest. "All the ways you've changed my life. I want to tell you all my secrets. I want you to be the one to know." I caress her hand with my thumb. Always so soft. "I've been thinking. You know how you asked which last name we should use? Well, since I've never really had a family of my own, I thought maybe we could use yours? You're the closest thing to family I have besides Jett. What do you think? Kayne Stevens doesn't sound bad, right?" I'm just fucking rambling now, slowly unraveling.

"I want to know who's responsible!" a man's voice bellows from the hallway. I immediately stand up as the door to Ellie's room swings open. "I want to know why my little girl is laying in a hospital bed fighting for her life!" I stand there frozen as Juice walks in with three people I only know from pictures. Ellie's family.

"Alec, please stop shouting."

"Stop shouting! How can I stop shouting? Look at her!" There's obvious emotion in the man's green eyes. The same eyes as Ellie's.

"Kayne. Alec, Monica, and Tara Stevens," Juice introduces us.

"Kayne?" Her mother repeats my name as if she recognizes it. Tara eyes me suspiciously.

"Who the hell are you?" Alec snaps at me.

"Kayne Rivers, sir." I put out my hand over Ellie. He doesn't take it. The tension in the room intensifies. He hates me already. Can't say that I blame him.

"I see it's a party," Jett walks in a moment later whiter than a ghost.

"How's London?" I ask worriedly. I think this is the worst I've ever seen him.

"Pregnant." Every head in the room swings toward him.

"What?" My jaw hits the floor.

Jett just shrugs, dumbfounded.

"Mazel tov," Alec spits. "Now is someone going to tell me what happened here?" He motions to Ellie.

The room becomes deadly silent.

"I believe Mazel tov is used for a wedding." Jett breaks the ice.

"Whatever. I'm very happy for you, son. Your life just got a hell of a lot more complicated, but right now I'd like to know what the hell happened to my daughter."

"A very unfortunate accident," I answer. "She was in the wrong place at the wrong time," I lie. Lie upon lie upon lie. It's what my life is built upon. Ellie is my only truth.

"Has there been an arrest?"

"No arrest," I tell him.

"Why the hell not?" he barks.

"The perpetrator has been taken care of," Jett informs him.

"I thought you said he hasn't been arrested?" Alec looks crazily between Jett and me.

"He hasn't," I tell him menacingly calm.

"Then how—"

"He's dead."

"Who killed him?" Alec's face contorts.

"Me," I say evenly, staring straight into his eyes.

Alec glares at me for what seems like a lifetime before he nods, almost satisfied, then sits down next to Ellie. I look around the room; it's suddenly very crowded and very uncomfortable. Tara makes her way next to me and picks up Ellie's hand.

"Why is she wearing an engagement ring?"

All attention falls on me.

I clear my throat. I suddenly feel like I'm suffocating. "I asked Ellie to marry me, and she said yes."

"What?" Alec scowls at me, Monica gasps, and Tara scoffs.

"That is *so* Ellie." Tara laughs.

"What's so Ellie?" I ask her.

Tara tosses her long platinum hair over her shoulder and looks over at me. She's a cute girl. Big blue eyes and a nice smile. "Getting engaged to a man she didn't even tell us she was dating. I'm surprised you two didn't already elope."

I glance at Jett. "We didn't get the chance."

Alec looks like he's about to go into cardiac arrest, he's turning so many shades of red.

"Why don't we give Ellie and her family some time alone?" Jett suggests to me. I want to throw daggers at him. There's no way in hell I'm leaving her side. He gestures with his head. I shake him off. "Get the fuck out," he mouths strictly. I bare my teeth at him, but do as he says, begrudgingly.

"If you need anything, I'll be outside," I tell her family.

"Thank you." Monica grabs my arm and I flinch. She smiles up at me, but I don't understand why. I don't really appreciate her touching me either, even if she is Ellie's mother and my potential mother-in-law.

"Big daddy Jett." Juice clasps his shoulders once we're outside in the hallway.

"Yeah." He looks like he's in shock.

"You happy?" I ask him, keeping an eye on Ellie's room.

"Yeah." I think that's the only word he's capable of at the moment.

"You going to make an honest woman out of her?" Juice asks.

"I was planning to purpose when we got back from Tahiti."

"Why not while you were on vacation?"

"Too cliché." he laughs, regarding me.

I flip him the finger. "That wasn't planned."

But I'm happy as hell that it happened.

ELLIE HAS BEEN UNCONSCIOUS FOR three days.

I haven't left her side for one minute. I've basically moved into her hospital room. I eat, sleep, and shower here. I'll live here for the rest of my life if I have to.

We put Alec, Monica, and Tara up in a hotel nearby so they can come and go as they please. Presently, Alec is pacing the hallway. The man doesn't sit still. I now know where Ellie gets it. Monica is sitting beside me watching Ellie, and Tara is having lunch with Juice. Not sure how I feel about that. He says it's innocent, but we'll see. We call him Juice for a reason.

I've spent the most time with Monica. Despite my issues with women, matriarchal figures in particular, she quickly grew on me. She's nurturing and mellow and very non-threatening. All the same traits that drew me to Ellie.

"I remember that night," Monica says randomly, staring at Ellie.

"What night?"

"The night she was going to meet you. She was so excited, on another level even for Ellie." Monica smiles. Her dark-brown hair is pulled back in a low ponytail and her bangs are falling into her eyes. I don't think she's slept since she arrived. "Tara kept teasing her, and she and Alec were fighting over her dress," she reminisces.

"He didn't approve?"

"The man has died seven times over from the girl's wardrobe alone." She glances over at me amused.

"Really?" I say intrigued.

"Yes. Those girls drive him nuts. But Ellie is Ellie, and she does what she wants. She kissed us goodbye," Monica's eyes water, "then she disappeared."

Oh, shit.

"She went through a lot," I say softly, a mix of guilt and impenitence battling inside me.

Monica nods, wiping away a stray tear. "She did. I don't know how you two crossed paths again, but I'm glad. I could see how much she liked you."

"I sought her out," I tell her truthfully. "I really liked her, too. Now I love her."

"That's very clear."

"What was Ellie like as a child?" I ask, wanting to know as much about her past as possible. If I can't ask Ellie, I can ask the next best person.

"A pain in the ass," Monica laughs.

"What?"

"She was. She never stopped moving, she got into everything and was independent to a fault. We used to call her Hurricane Elizabeth."

I chuckle. "That is surprisingly a very accurate nickname." Considering the way she turned my world upside down.

"She was also very loving and so, so adorable. Like a living doll. She could knock you over with just one dimpled smile. I think that's how she survived childhood. She had us all wrapped around her little finger." Monica is now laughing and crying all at the same time. I'm not sure how to interpret that.

"It's how I survive adulthood, too," Ellie murmurs, and both Monica and I jump up. "How did you two end up in the same room?" she asks as she cracks her eyes open. I think *I'm* about to start laughing and crying.

"Were you eavesdropping on us?" I ask, as my heart starts beating again with short shallow pumps.

"Yes. You're not the only one who can spy," she responds groggy.

Monica shoots me a funny look. I grin uncomfortably. "Inside joke."

"Oh, well I guess that's a good sign that she's making jokes."

"Why does it feel like I was shot?" Ellie groans in pain.

"Because you were," Monica tells her kissing her forehead. "I have to go get the doctor and your father," she announces overjoyed. "I'm so glad you're awake."

Once she's out of the room, Ellie looks up at me confused. I want to smother her with kisses, but I brush my lips lightly all over her face instead.

"How long have I been out?" she strains.

"Three days." I kiss her lips, reacquainting myself with the feel of them. "I'm sorry, baby," I nearly weep, the guilt eating me alive.

"Sorry for what?"

"Everything. Every single second of suffering I've ever caused you."

"It wasn't your fault," she grimaces as she tries to move.

"That's a fucking lie, and we both know it."

"Kayne, don't. Just tell me it's over." She says exhausted.

"It is. He's dead."

Ellie's eyes start to cloud with tears. She's been up for five seconds, and she's upset already.

"Do you know?" Her lip quivers.

I nod solemnly.

"Do my parents know?" Her voice tapers off.

I shake my head.

"Good," she sighs with relief.

"Do you remember everything that happened?" I ask delicately.

"Yes," tears drip down her face.

I grab her cheeks in my hands and wipe away the wetness with my thumbs. My heart cracks in nine different directions. It's amazing how many times that muscle can be destroyed and still keep working.

"I killed him, Ellie," I tell her with conviction. Like somehow that's supposed to make everything better.

"Good. I hope it hurt."

"I can assure you it did."

"Can I please have some water?" She tries to sit up.

"Lie down," I order. "I'll get it." I dutifully pour her a glass and press the straw to her lips, allowing her take several long sips.

"Thank you," she smiles weakly.

"You're welcome." I skim my knuckles across her face. God, I can't believe how much I missed touching her. "I'm not going to leave your side. We're going to get better together."

"We?" she asks concerned. "Are you hurt?"

I nod, rubbing my chest. "Funny thing about pain," I laugh, not finding anything funny about it at all. "It's a hell of a lot easier to deal with the physical than it is to deal with the emotional. I could run twelve miles and ignore the burning in my legs or take a bullet and withstand the throbbing in my arm. But try to take away someone I love? There's no escaping that agony. I may not be lying in a hospital bed, but I'm still injured."

Ellie sighs trying to hold back the overload of emotion that is so clearly evident on her face. "What now?"

I smile. "We move forward. We can get married, have children, travel. Whatever you want to do."

"No children," she fires back at me spontaneously.

I look at her funny. "Why no children?"

Her dark-green eyes widen and completely well with tears. "Kayne, my mother needed more therapy than I did after I came home. And after going through what I went through—" she wipes her cheeks as large the reflective droplets fall, "there's so much evil in this world. I don't think I could handle it." She starts to cry so hard she can't breathe. "I don't think I could handle—" I wrap her snugly in my arms. "Okay, Ellie. It's okay. We don't have to talk about any of that right now." I let her sob on my shoulder, worried someone is going to walk through the door any second. I don't want her family to see her like this. "Shhhh..."

"You still want to marry me even though I don't want kids?" She sniffles, eyes puffy and face red.

"Of course I do," I assure her. "You are the only person I need in this world. Whatever makes you happy will make me happy. Okay?"

She nods sternly, burying her face in the crook of my arm.

"Please don't cry," I beg her. "Everything will be okay."

I hear the door swing open as Monica, Alec, Tara, Juice, and the doctor on rounds appears in the room.

"Where's my little girl?" Alec announces. I reluctantly let go of Ellie, and I have to give it to her, she puts on her bravest face. She really is the most resilient person I have ever met.

"Right here, Daddy." She rubs her eyes and smiles.

I step back and watch as she's showered with love, hoping like hell everything really is going to be okay.

IT HAS BEEN ONE VERY long, tiring, trying week. Ellie spent the last seven days recuperating in the hospital, and today she finally gets to go home. I watch as she signs the discharge papers the nurse hands to her and listens as the sweet older woman explains how to change her dressings and which medications she should take when. She's been prescribed so many antibiotics, pain killers and anti-depressants, she could start her own cartel.

"I'm going to get the car." I kiss her head once she sitting in the wheelchair.

She nods silently. Silent. That's Ellie these days. Her superficial wounds may be healing, but more often than not she's lost inside her head.

It's making me a lunatic. I worry nonstop. I don't eat, I barely sleep, terrified that Michael may have succeeded in taking her away from me. He might not have killed her, but her spirit is definitely broken, and I'm scrambling to figure out how to fix it.

I pull up to the front of the hospital just as Ellie is wheeled outside. It's another perfect day in paradise. Blue skies, white puffy clouds and rainbows in the distance. Ellie's parents went home yesterday, leaving her in my care. We may all be screwed. To say I'm not nervous would be lying. We've had this discussion—I've never looked after another person in my life. Never had anyone have to depend on me, or commit myself to caring for another person. But I'm going to do my damndest with Ellie.

I just hope it's enough.

I help her gingerly climb into the car, and then hop in the driver's seat.

She looks around the interior strangely.

"Whose car is this?" she asks mildly confused.

"Mine."

"You drive?" I almost think she's trying to be funny.

I snicker. "Of course I drive. Why'd you say that?" I punch on the engine and the Jag rumbles to life.

"Because I've never seen you drive a car before." She grabs her seat, surprised by the vibrations. "You always showed up in a limo when you came to Expo and we were carted all over the place in Bora Bora. Jett even drove the boat to and from the airport."

I laugh to myself as I put on my sunglasses. Oh, how little does she know. I can drive all sorts of thing.

"Well, I guess I'm full of surprises." I press a button and the roof retracts, Ellie squints as the sun shine hits her face. I open the glove compartment. "Sunglasses?" I hand her a brand new pair that Jett picked out especially for her.

"Thank you." She takes them, smiling shyly. "What kind of car is this anyway?" she asks, gliding her hand over the door handle.

"Jaguar F-Type." I hit the gas in my black V8 and take off.

"One of your toys?" Ellie inquires, as her hair blows in the wind.

"One of the many." I grin carefree, placing my hand over hers, and just drive.

I notice Ellie start to look around curiously as we drive through and then out of Waikiki.

"Where are we going?" she asks confused.

"Home," I tell her, not taking my eyes off the road.

I feel her staring at me peculiarly. I just smirk and continue to drive.

Ten minutes later we are rolling through the Diamond Head section of Honolulu.

"Seriously, where are you taking me?" she asks again, and I can't stop myself from smiling widely.

"I told you," I pull into a driveway. "Home." I throw the car in park.

Ellie freezes as she takes in the two-story stucco house.

"Exactly whose home are we going to?"

"Ours." I hop out of the car.

"Ours?" she repeats perplexed as I walk around the convertible, open her door and carefully help her stand up.

I think it's a record. That's the most she's spoken in a week.

"Yup." I take her hand and lead her to the front door. The walkway is landscaped with lots of bright island flowers and tall green trees. Once inside, Ellie gasps. Yeah, it's pretty insane. I fell in love with the house as soon as I saw it online. It was so different and modern, yet homey as well. The website boasted it was an award-winning design, inspired by the shape of a sundial, the back of the house curved with one hundred, eighty degree views of the ocean and mountains. Between you and me, I had already put an offer in prior to leaving for Bora Bora. It was some serious wishful thinking on my part, but I couldn't help myself. Every time I looked at it, I could see Ellie and me living here.

I walk her through the kitchen decorated with light cabinets and dark granite. I grab a small remote off the counter and continue straight back into the living room. I glance at Ellie taking it all in. Then I hit a button and the electric curtains rise. The entire room is made of windows, and as they lift, an unobstructed view of the Pacific blinds us, as if we're sitting right on top of it.

"Oh my God." Ellie puts her hand over her mouth as she looks out over the lani, curved swimming pool hugging the house, and vast blue water.

"Like it?" I ask nervously.

She doesn't answer, just stares straight ahead.

"Ellie?" I put my hand on nape of her neck and rub my thumb back and forth over her skin. "You don't like it?" I frown disappointed.

Like she snaps out of a trance she looks up at me, her eyes shining with unshed tears. I can't tell if they're happy or sad, but by the looks of it, it may be the latter.

"Oh no," she sniffles. "I love it. It's perfect. You're perfect."

"Then what's wrong?" I hear the distress in my own voice.

"Nothing. Everything," she contradicts herself.

"Well, which is it?" I search her face. "Baby, you can talk to me."

"I'm sorry," she blurts out.

"For what?" My heart stops.

"I keep trying to convince myself I'm stronger than what happened, but I just keep getting sucked down. It's like I can't breathe and I can't fight." She starts to cry. I pull her against me and let her sob into my chest. "I don't want to be broken, but I think that I am."

Thank god, finally she speaks!

I stroke her hair and hold her close.

"Ellie, if there's one thing I've learned being with you, things that are broken can always be fixed. They can be made stronger. You make me stronger, and I'm the most broken person I know."

She lifts her head and looks at me with soaking wet eyes.

"How am I going to get stronger?"

I smile down at her. "You're going to fight. And I'm going to help you. If there's one thing I know how to do, it's fight."

I hug her and she squeaks in pain, but she holds on to

me, inhaling me like I'm air, like I'm the oxygen she needs to breathe." Use me, Ellie. I told you before — get mad, scream, hit me, beat me, torture me if you want. I'll endure it all if it will help you get better."

She sighs heavily, "I think all I really need is for you to lay with me."

I chuckle. That's exactly what she said to me the first night in Bora Bora. The same words that opened the doorway for our relationship to heal. I'm hopeful for the first time in over a week.

"Whatever you need, Ellie." I reassure her.

"I have exactly what I need." She draws in a small shaky breath and gazes up at me. "You."

ELLIE

EPILOGUE

One year later

"TIME TO WAKE UP, SLEEPYHEAD!" Tara jumps on me.

"Umph." I jolt awake.

"Someone has to get beautiful for her wedding day," she sings, her blue eyes bright, platinum-blonde hair even brighter. She used to wake me up the same way when we were kids.

"Nice to see nothing has changed." I try to push her off me.

"You missed me, admit."

"I'll admit I missed pulling your hair when you annoyed me." I yank on her long strands.

"Ouch!" she laughs.

"Serves you right! Disturbing the bride's beauty sleep."

"You're going to need way more than eight hours to help you with your beauty."

"Bitch!" We both laugh as I hit her with a pillow. "And I can't believe you pierced your nose!" I grab her face and examine the tiny stud. It actually looks good on her.

"It's not the only thing I pierced." She pops her eyebrows at me.

"You didn't!"

"I did! Want to see?" She bounces around the bed overflowing with white Egyptian sheets.

"No!" I smack her with a pillow again. "Please keep your panties in their place."

"Who says I'm wearing any?" Tara laughs.

"Slut."

"Call me whatever you want. The orgasms are worth it! You should totally do it."

I pause, thinking of all the ways Kayne could possibly torture me if I had a clit ring.

My blood heats. I might consider it.

"This came for you, by the way." She hands me a box wrapped in silver paper with a white bow.

"When?" I sit up and take it from her.

"Just now. CJ dropped it off." She grins wickedly.

Oh no, I know that look.

"He's yummy." She sucks on her bottom lip like she can already taste him.

"Tara," I chide.

"What?"

"I noticed the two of you flirting last night."

"So?" She bats her eyelashes innocently.

"He's ten years older than you," I point out.

"So?" she repeats.

"I'm not sure Kayne would approve." Actually, I know he wouldn't approve since I overheard him threatening Juice's life if he touched her.

"Well, Kayne isn't my father," she argues.

"I'm not sure our father would approve, either."

"He doesn't approve of anything we do." She rolls her eyes dismissively.

She has me there.

"Look, this day isn't about me." She changes the subject artfully, clearly done with this conversation. "So open your present already so we can drink some mimosas and start getting ready!"

"Fine." I appease her. Besides, I think her and Juice sort of make a cute couple, even if it would be short lived—like four days long since they live on opposite sides of the country.

I open the card first. It's plain white with perforated edges and reads:

> *Your naked body should only belong to those who fall in love with your naked soul.* ~ unknown
> And I own both.
> Kayne

That he does, I think to myself as I grin like an idiot.

I rip off the paper and flip open the flat box. Tara curls her lip. "It looks just like the one you already wear, except with a white ribbon."

I touch the necklace with the little diamond heart. "It has a special meaning."

"It looks like a freakin' expensive collar if you ask me." I flick my eyes up at her and try to hide my smile.

"I said it has special meaning."

"Seriously, Ellie. I don't want to know what freaky shit you and Kayne are into. He's so possessive, I wouldn't be surprised if he made you wear a collar." I nearly lose it. If she only knew!

"I'm ready to start celebrating." Tara slinks off the bed.

God, me too. I fall back onto the pillow and stare up at the ceiling, balancing the box on my stomach. The last twelve months have not been easy. Kayne and I adjusting as roommates was the least of our problems. Not only did my body need to heal, but so did my mind. When Jett told me Kayne was more loyal than a dog, he meant it. He never left my side. He came to every physical therapy session and therapist appointment. He sat beside me as I recounted every horrific minute with Michael, held me as I cried every tear, and comforted me after every single nightmare. Sex was a challenge. Not because I didn't want it, but because intimacy was difficult. I was disconnected from my emotions and had somehow lost my sense of security. There was a time I thought I was never going to get out from under the depression and fear. It had taken a while before things started to get easier, before I started to feel more like myself. After about six months, my therapist suggested I find something positive to concentrate on. That's when Kayne and I decided to set a date. May sixteenth, to be exact. Some may think wedding planning is stressful, and I guess that's true in some cases. Not in ours. If anything, it was therapeutic. It gave us something to look forward to, it helped fortify our very new and fragile relationship, and sparked hope. So here I lay, in a penthouse suite on Maui, about to become someone's wife.

I've never looked more forward to a sunset in my life.

"Ellie!" Tara yells. "Get up!"

"I'm up!" I yell back.

After a morning massage, a nice long hot shower, and several mimosas courtesy of Tara, I'm ready to start the beautification process. Hair, nails, makeup, dress—in that order, apparently.

By midafternoon, my hotel room—and future honeymoon suite—is buzzing with people. My mother and sister, of course, the hair stylist and manicurist and Mark. Yes, Mark. Like he would be left out of all the girlie fun. Plus, he wanted a manicure. How could I say no?

"You know, it's because of me that Kayne and Ellie met." He grins at the older woman with long, jet-black hair filing his nails. She just nods and smiles. I roll my eyes. He's been telling everyone that. Like he hooked us up or something. In reality, he was just responsible for letting two strangers' paths meet, but we won't burst his bubble and tell him that.

There's a knock at the door.

"I'll get it!" Tara announces, hopping off her stool, hair half curled.

"Oh, hi." She sounds almost disappointed as Jett walks in. My mother and I glance knowingly at each other.

"Hey, sweet thing." Jett walks over and kisses me hello just as the stylist finishes pinning a white orchid into my hair. "Very nice." He looks at the masterpiece she's been working on for the last hour. After about a million trials, I decided to wear it down in loosely textured curls accented with the flower.

"Jealous you didn't do it?" I jest.

"Maybe." He laughs, his aqua eyes sparkling back at me in the mirror. "You finally got that haircut."

"Just a trim," I joke. "What are you doing here?"

"I come bearing gifts." He holds up a small wrapped box and a large card.

I look at him confused. "Juice already dropped off my wedding present from Kayne."

"He got you two." Jett takes my hand and helps me up. "And he asked that you open it in private."

I glare at Jett. I don't like the sound of this.

"Just need to borrow her for a sec," he announces as he pulls me into the bedroom.

"If you think I'm going to let you clamp any part of me, you have another thing coming." I cross my arms. "It's my wedding day, and I'm not going to walk around like a cat in freakin' heat!"

Jett looks at me like he's out to bust a gut. His golden hair is styled back, and he's wearing a white T-shirt and dress pants. "I don't know what's in the box," his lips twitch fitfully, "but I'm pretty sure it isn't a clit clamp. He wants you to open the card first."

"Okay." I take them from him. "If it's nothing kinky then why the privacy?"

"I never said it wasn't anything kinky, he just didn't tell me what it was."

I roll my eyes as I slide my finger under the flap. My eyes water immediately. The card has one simple picture on the front. A little boy holding a cupcake. I flip it open to a long, handwritten note inside.

Ellie,

I'm not very good with words. I'll probably never be able to express fully the way I feel, but I've wanted to tell you something I've never told anyone before. Not even Jett. It's not something I'm proud of and not something I talk about. Ever. But when I was seventeen, I tried to commit suicide. It was the darkest time in my life. I was alone, homeless, and just wanted it all to end. I don't mean to upset you by telling you this. It's just ever since that day, a small part of me has always wished my attempt was successful. I'm sure you're wondering why I picked today of all days to tell you this. It's because, for the first time since that day, I woke up and was thankful to be alive. Thankful I failed because the happiness I feel outweighs every bad moment in my life. Every. Single. One. And it's all because of you. You U a piece of me I never knew existed, never thought I deserved. You're the best part of all my sides, all my faces. You're the glue. Thank you for being everything. My strength, my light, my hope, my warmth.

I love you always,
Kayne

By the time I finish reading the letter, I'm a blubbering mess and Jett is consoling me.

"What the hell was in that letter?"

I just shake my head and wipe my eyes. "The truth." I smile.

"Are you okay?" Jett slides his hands up and down my arms and examines me closely.

"Yes. Fine, actually."

He stares for a few seconds more. "Do I need to beat him up for making you cry?" He sounds like an overprotective older brother.

"No." I laugh, glad my makeup isn't done yet. "A black eye would look terrible in pictures.

"True. Why don't you open your present?" he suggests.

"Yeah, good idea." I sniff as I rip off the silver paper and pop open the small gift box. "Oh!" I gasp as a pair of diamond earrings stare back at me—ones that look exactly like my engagement ring. Two cushion-cut stones with a halo of pink diamonds around them.

"Perfect. Just like the girl who is going to wear them." Jett smiles.

"You just always know what to say," I quip.

"It's a curse." He sighs dramatically.

"I'm sure," I respond drily as he kisses me firmly on the cheek.

"My work here is done."

I grab his arm. "Not quite yet."

I walk over to the closet and retrieve a large, white flat box and hand it over. "Make sure he opens it in private."

Jett frowns. "Oh, no. Is it going to make him cry?"

I shrug playfully. "It might bring him to tears."

I FIGHT WITH MY VEIL as it blows around in the wind. My stomach is in knots and my heart is pounding in my ears. I have been hidden in a small alcove for the last twenty minutes as the guests arrive and take their seats. I'm so nervous, I'm bouncing in my barefoot sandals.

"You still have time to run, kid," my father jokes.

"Kayne would find me." I laugh nervously. It's completely

true. Besides, I may be nervous, but I know I could never live without him. Now more than ever.

I check myself one last time in the reflective wall of the 'bride's staging area.' At least that's what the wedding coordinator called it. My hair is falling in perfect waves around my face, my makeup is flawless, and my dress is hugging and pinching in all the right places. I went for something simple and romantic—a diamond white, backless A-line with double spaghetti straps and an empire waist. My favorite part—it has pockets.

"Time!" the wedding coordinator pokes her head in and announces just as the procession music starts to play.

Here goes everything.

Clutching my bouquet made of white roses and blue orchids, my father begins to lead me toward the aisle. We turn the corner to an expansive view of the Pacific Ocean, several small rows of chairs, and an arbor draped with white fabric, strings of crystals, and two small chandeliers. But as magnificent as the setup is, it's only Kayne I see. Once our eyes lock, it's like I gravitate toward him, float almost. He's dressed in a white buttoned-down shirt and dress pants, the blue of his irises ablaze in the sunlight. His expression is composed, yet full of emotion all at the same time.

My father lifts my veil and kisses my cheek like we practiced at the rehearsal the night before and then gives me away. I take Kayne's hand with a shaky breath as I step under the arbor with him. The smile that suddenly beams from his face nearly knocks me over, and I can't help but laugh nervously, tears stinging my eyes.

"You look *so* beautiful," he breathes right before the officiant begins.

"Dearly beloved . . ."

"HAPPY, MRS. STEVENS?" KAYNE ASKS as we sway steadily to the encore of our wedding song.

"Deliriously, Mr. Stevens." When Kayne suggested taking my last name, I was a little stunned at first. But when he explained *why*, there was no way could I refuse. He finally has a home and the family he's deserved all along.

"You almost ready to sneak out of here?" he asks, his breath tickling my ear.

"Yes." I nestle up against him as David Cook sings about fading and colors bleeding into one.

"Me, too," he growls, pulling me closer.

I grasp onto the last seconds of the song, trying to memorize what's left of the night. Pink candle holders hanging from fishing wire over the round tables on the beach. The devoured red velvet cupcake tower, my parents talking and laughing, Jett holding his infant daughter, Layla, and Tara and Juice dancing way too close for comfort a few feet away.

When the song ends, Kayne still holds me close, kissing my temple lovingly.

We didn't accept any gifts for the wedding. Instead, we asked for donations to our foundation. To Catch a Falling Star. Kayne, Jett, London, and I started it a few months ago. It was my second positive thing to concentrate on. It gives victims of sexual abuse and human trafficking a chance to see paradise. We've already sent over twenty families on the vacation of their dreams. I plan to expand the organization once I finish college.

"Let's go." Kayne tugs on my hand to start our hurried goodbyes.

As we walk to the elevator, we catch sight of Juice and Tara huddled in a corner, kissing. Kayne tries to let go of my hand, no doubt to interrupt them, but I pull him back.

"Leave them alone. They're consenting adults."

Kayne frowns just as the elevator doors open. "That's what I'm afraid of."

I giggle and haul him inside. "I'm the only consenting adult you have to worry about at the moment." I pull his face to mine and kiss him passionately, dying for the feel of his tongue against mine.

"Mmm." He pushes me up against the wall, easily distracted as he devours me, running his hands all over my body, causing my nipples to harden instantly.

The doors ding open, and we break apart restlessly. Before we exit the elevator, Kayne lifts me into his arms.

"What are you doing?!" I throw my arms around his neck.

"Carrying you over the threshold. Duh." He steps out, and then walks down the hall to our suite.

I laugh freely as we walk through the living room toward the bedroom, then inhale sharply when he opens the door and we are engulfed in candlelight. There must be one hundred white pillar candles lit all around the room.

"Someone was busy," I muse.

"Who?" He responds sarcastically.

"Did we take a funny pill tonight?" I ask as he sets me down.

Kayne shakes his head. "A happy pill."

"Same differen—" The last syllable of the word is cut off as he smothers me with a kiss so deep, he actually forces me to lean back.

"As much as I love you in this dress, it's time for it to come off," he pants as he pulls at the straps, yanking the top straight down. I barely have time to unzip before he rips it completely off. Animal. He then starts pushing me toward the bed, our mouths fused together, his hands kneading my naked breasts.

"Did you like my wedding present?" I ask as he forces me down.

He pauses, ogling me wickedly. "I loved it. I had to go jerk off in the bathroom while I looked at it."

I smile. I wracked my brain trying to figure out what to give Kayne as a wedding present. The logical answer was me. So I had an ultra-sexy boudoir album made. Lots of lacy underwear, pearls, and bows. It was one step above a porno magazine.

"By the way, who took those pictures?" His eyes storm.

I bite my lip. "London."

"Oh, really?" his irritation turns to curiosity.

"She's really good with a camera," I responded apprehensively.

"I saw that. Several times." He bites my neck. "You two didn't do anything you weren't supposed to?"

I swallow thickly. "Can I plead the fifth?"

"You bad girls." He manhandles me, smacks my ass, and then pinches it hard. "Next time Jett and I will be the ones with the camera."

"Yes, Kayne," I purr.

"Damn straight." He caresses my behind and grinds his

erection between my legs. "Did you like my present?"

"Which one?" I lift my hips and press my pussy right up against him.

"Both of them," he groans.

"Yes." I kiss him gently. "The second one made me cry."

"I didn't mean to upset you." He tells me earnestly.

"It's okay. I'm glad you told me. I'm glad you're not carrying around those feelings anymore." I touch his cheek.

"Me, too." He chokes out the words, and my heart splits.

"I have a second present for you," I tell him. No unhappiness tonight.

"Oh really? I'm starting to enjoy getting presents."

I nearly gnaw through my lip this time. "Want it now?"

"If you want to give it to me."

"I do."

"Why do you sound nervous?"

"Because I am." I push him lightly so he rolls off me and retrieve another large white box from the closest. This one with a red ribbon around it.

I place it next to him. "Go ahead. Open it."

He pulls the box toward him inquisitively and unties the ribbon while I wring my hands together like a lunatic. Once he removes the top, his face falls. Oh, shit. He cocks his head as if studying the contents of the box.

"You don't like it?" I ask, feeling foolish. Maybe he thinks it's too soon.

"I . . ." He starts pulling out everything that's inside. White ears and a long bushy tail, a new white collar with my tag, matching wrist cuffs, and a studded leash.

He looks up at me silently, candlelight flickering on his face.

"We don't have to . . . I just thought . . ." I scramble, trying to stuff everything back in the box. How ridiculous do I feel?

"Ellie, stop." Kayne stands up and grabs my wrist, pulling me into his body. His erection like a stone slab against my thigh. "Are *you* ready?"

I glance up at him timidly through my eyelashes. "Yes. I'm ready. I'm ready to get back to *us*." And it's the truth.

"I don't want to do anything to upset you. To trigger anything."

"You won't. I want this."

He runs the pad of his thumb along my cheek, staring deeply into my eyes as if trying to read my soul. Ever since Michael, Kayne has been overly cautious with our sex life, fearful his dominance might spark a flashback or deter my progress in some way. It's not illogical — my therapist said it could happen. But it never has. If anything, I feel most safe when I submit, and I need that security. The same way Kayne needs to hear me say his name. I've been slowly hinting that I'm ready to move things to the next level; that I really am ready to get back to *us*.

"Please," I implore him.

"Please, what?"

"Unleash the beast. I need both our monsters to come out."

Kayne breathes heavily, no doubt at war with himself. He never has been able to deny me when I press him to take control.

"On one condition."

"What's that?"

"No begging or pleading tonight. I want you to come freely, like a waterfall. I want this night to be as pleasurable for you as it is for me."

"Okay," I agree, ready to attack him.

"Good. I love you." He kisses me tenderly.

"I love you, too."

"Now sit on the edge of the bed," he instructs.

I sit immediately. He pulls the flower from my hair then picks up the ears and places them on my head. His eyes dilate and something in my stomach jolts. "Stay." He runs a finger under my chin. I'm molten inside already.

He then steps back and pops open the bottle of champagne sitting in the ice bucket on the small table adjacent from the bed. He comes to stand in front of me holding it with one hand.

"Take my clothes off."

I scoot forward in just my white satin bikini briefs and garters adorned with a bow on the back of each thigh. I quickly unbutton his shirt and push it off his shoulders. It falls to the ground exposing his perfectly formed tattooed body. Yes, Kayne is human perfection. And why shouldn't he be? He works out like an animal. Ripped abs, strong chest, and chiseled arms — I can't wait to run my tongue over every pristine inch of him. I take off his pants next, bringing me face to face with the tip of his cock. I want to dart my tongue out and lick it, but I'll behave and wait to do as I'm told.

"You know, you missed something in the box," I tell him wetting my lips.

"Oh?" Kayne takes a swig of the champagne right from the bottle.

I reach in and pull out a tiny pill bottle. Kayne's eyes widen.

"Is that what I think it is?"

I nod. "I told you I want you to unleash the beast."

I open the top and shake out a little circular pill.

"You know there's only one way to satisfy the beast?" He takes it and swallows it.

"Yes."

"How?"

"Give it what it wants. Hours and hours submerged in my wet pussy and tight little ass."

Kayne nearly fries me with a scorching hot look. "That's right,

kitten. Are you ready for that?"

"Yes," I answer, my voice thick with desire.

"Good girl." He drops to his knees in front of me, placing the bottle on the ground. He hasn't even touched me yet, and my pussy is already throbbing.

He skims his hands up my thighs and slips his one finger beneath each garter. "These are sexy as hell. They stay on. But these go." He slides my panties off in one fluid motion. He licks his bottom lip and moans gutturally as he stares at my bare folds. Kayne then reaches into the box beside me and pulls out the collar. My arousal spikes as he fastens it around my neck, right over my new white necklace. He tickles the tag once it's secure with a bold blatant look of propriety.

"Mine," he says as he claims my mouth, stretching it wide as he rolls his tongue languidly against mine.

"Yours," I reply breathless once he pulls away. I watch engrossed as he picks up the bottle of champagne and pours it down the middle of my naked body. I jump from the cold and moan loudly from the abrupt heat of his mouth. Kayne rests his head on my thigh as he continues to pour the champagne, soaking the bed and my pussy. He licks up the wetness all while watching me get off on the feel of his tongue. That wicked evil tongue that's capable of so many perverse things.

"Kayne." I grab his head and lift my leg begging for more—deeper, harder, rougher. He pours another shot of champagne on me and licks a slow hot drag up my slit, his wide flat tongue covering every single inch of me.

"Oh God, please." I don't mean to beg, but it's my go-to response. He takes pity on me, burying his head between my legs and fucks me with his mouth until I fall apart, an avalanche giving way inside me as I grip his hair and scream out loud.

He makes sure to lap up every drop of my orgasm and the champagne before he flips my limp body over and pulls me up on all fours. Breathing like a mad man, I see him reach into the box and retrieve my tail. My excitement cranks. I'm nervous and aroused and scared all at the same time. Then I feel him sink one finger inside me. I'm still sensitive from my orgasm so it tickles. "Oh."

He doesn't waste any time smearing my wetness up away from my pussy and into my ass, pushing the same finger into me, and after a few seconds, adds another. I don't even have time to prepare for the bite as he scissors me open. My muscles spasm.

Then I feel him withdraw, his fingers replaced by the tip of the butt plug attached to the tail. I grab onto the comforter as Kayne works the spade-shaped plug past the tight ring of muscle. My stretched little hole tenses around the metal once all the way in.

"Holy shit." He strokes the tail now nestled in my ass. I turn to look at him, both sets of cheeks on fire.

He stares at the tail like he's starving with lust, then his eyes lift to meet mine.

"Hold still." His chest is expanding and contracting, his lips are pressed tight and his cock is the hardest I think I've ever seen it. The skin is pulled so taut his veins are visible even in soft candlelight.

"This is going to be hard and fast, kitten," Kayne says, shaking with need as he lines up behind me, nudging the tip of his unearthly erection against my wet entrance several times over.

"You look so fucking hot." His voice is gravelly. I brace myself as he digs his fingers into my hips and thrusts brutally into me. We both cry out as his cock slices through my pussy like a hot knife through melted butter.

"Kitten, kitten, kitten, kitten," he chants as he fucks me exactly the way he said he was going to, fast and hard. Like he's using me. I expel a breath with every clash of our hips, the butt plug playing on my need, forcing me to the edge faster and faster.

"Don't come. Don't come." It's not a demand, it's a request as Kayne beats into me from behind. I fight to control the sensations battling to take over as Kayne's cock twitches right before he comes.

"Fuck!" he yells as he traps my hips and pushes his pelvis forward as if trying to cram another half inch of himself inside me.

"Shit." He leans forward and hugs me, his chest to my back, breathing erratically.

"I guess you like the tail," I tease breathless, still on all fours.

"I fucking love it," he snarls, withdrawing from me and yanking my collar. "Turn."

I turn around. He's still panting heavily, a sheen of sweat on his chest.

Kayne picks up the bottle of champagne again as I kneel on all fours by the edge of the bed.

"Do you know what little kittens are good at?" He pours some

champagne over his still erect cock. "Using their tongues to lick things clean." He takes me by the collar and shoves his dripping wet dick in my face. I purr as I dart my tongue out and proceed to lick every drop of champagne off his shaft. "That's it, baby." He grips my collar tighter as I take him into my mouth and swallow him whole, the taste of crisp dry bubbles mixing with my saliva. I suck repeatedly, so turned on my gag reflex has completely disappeared.

"Enough." Kayne pulls his hips away, his cock popping out of my mouth. "Good kitten."

I eye him hungrily.

"Stay." He touches the tip of my nose.

I watch as he moves around the room, sliding the small loveseat near the window in front of the bed. Then he removes one of the large mirrors from the wall and places it against the footboard, directly beneath me. I look at him strangely, just like the curious little kitten I am. He sits on the loveseat directly across from me and strokes his cock.

"Come," he calls me.

I slide off the bed and onto the floor, crawling provocatively across the room until I am directly between his legs.

"Sexy little girl," he jingles my tag then slips his thumb into my mouth. I suck on it deliberately, swirling my tongue around it just to tease him.

"I know how fucking good that mouth is, but I want to be inside you." He withdraws his hand and pats his lap. "Sit on my cock, Ellie. I want to watch you fuck me."

With that, he pulls me off the floor, forces me to straddle him and impales me onto his erection. *"Oh!"* From this angle he digs in deep, reaching all the way to my navel.

"Ride me, baby. I feel how bad you have to come." He's right, I'm strung so tight I could snap in a second. The tail never giving my arousal any reprieve. He straightens so he can peek over my shoulder as I move up and down.

"Oh, God." I drop my head back as I use Kayne to chase my orgasm.

"That's it, kitten," he sounds distracted, "make yourself come."

I look down at him in a fog of lust and realize his attention is engrossed in the mirror behind me. I turn my head to see what he sees, and the image is erotic as all hell. My naked body straddled over his, the bows of my garters, the tail in my ass, my hair falling down my back and ears on top of my head.

I bob faster and harder as I watch us in the mirror, my orgasm coming at me like a heat-seeking missile.

"Kayne," I cry, I pant, I moan. "Kayne," I clench, everything inside me constricting.

"Let go, Ellie," he strains as he caresses every part of my body.

"Oh, God," my voice elevates several octaves, as the build-up pressurizes. "I'm going to come. You're going to make me come." I slam down onto his cock and the sensations give way, lighting every single one of my nerve endings on fire.

I ride out my orgasm, literally, until there's nothing left of me. Until I'm bare bones draped over a heaving man.

Kayne's feathery kisses on my shoulders, neck and cheeks bring me back.

"Did you enjoy the show?" I ask him lethargically.

"Immensely," he laughs. "You?"

"Yes. You know I love to watch."

"I love that about you." He gropes me gently.

"I love everything about you." I kiss him in return.

"Good 'cause you're stuck with me for a lifetime."

"I'm pretty okay with that. Did you have a good birthday?" I ask desirously, rubbing my entire body against his.

"The best one yet." He rocks his erection between my legs. "There is only one thing that could make it better." He puts both hands on my stomach.

I immediately snatch his wrist. "That is still up for discussion."

"I know." He skims his nose under my jawline. "I just don't want you to have any regrets down the line."

"You're starting to sound like Jett, you know that?"

"He was bound to rub off on me eventually." Kayne yanks on my tail and I jerk on his lap.

"Mmm. You better be careful." I warn.

"Is that a threat?"

"Maybe," I slide my arms back around his neck.

"What are you going to do?" he challenges me.

"So many naughty things," I nip at him.

"I can't wait." He claims my mouth, slipping his tongue fervently between my lips.

"I love you," I exhale, showering his face with kisses.

"I love you, too." He strokes my tail affectionately. "Good kitten . . . *Cupcake*."

The End

Missing Decadence after Dark already? Be on the lookout for Lie with Me (A Decadence after Dark Novella): CJ and Tara's story!

Acknowledgements

TO SAY CLAIMED WAS THE most difficult book I've ever had to write is an understatement. It ripped me open on so many levels. I worried that it wasn't going to live up to Owned, worried how readers were going to respond to Kayne's 'human' side, worried it wasn't dark enough, erotic enough, emotional enough. Kinky enough . . . How many people can say they worry about that?? Claimed read differently, felt different, but I wrote Owned because Claimed was the real story I wanted to tell. It was the real characters I wanted to share. The true Kayne was the man in the second chapter of Owned. The flawed, insecure, worrisome person who was just as nervous to spend time with Ellie, as she was to spend time with him. He's the man I fell in love with. He's the man who compelled me to write, and I wanted everyone to know that person. These characters will always have a special place in my heart, and maybe, just maybe, there's a little bit of K&E's story left to tell. Maybe.

Luckily, during the writing process I had some really amazing people supporting me. People I barely just met who fell in love with Kayne and Ellie just as I had (Serena, Amy, Alecia, Sarah, Jennifer, Jaime, Debbie). I wanted to give them the book both the characters and readers deserved, and I finally believe I have.

A special thanks to my editors, Jenny Sims and Candice Royer, you both bring something unique to the table and I enjoy working with you immensely. My beta readers, Jaime, Jennifer, Sarah, Debbie, Ashley, and Heather, you play such a vital role in the development of the story. Your feedback is invaluable. I'll repeat myself—INVALUABLE. The ladies at Perfectly Publishable, Nichole and Christine, you are both outstanding, and thank you for ignoring my idiot moments; it's only March and it's already been a long year! My cover designer, Marisa Shor,

I love love love working with you, but you already know that. Jaime Burns, lady, you rock, plain and simple. Your ass belongs to me! <3 All my Collared Cupcakes, you guys just have me in awe. I never thought I would have a street team, let alone the amazing bunch you are. You are truly appreciated. I hope you know that. To K&J's Sls — I know I'm not always part of the conversation, but you guys always make me smile. I see everything, remember that! lol. To all the ladies in my readers group, thank you for choosing me. There are thousands of authors you could follow, but you elect to spend your time with me. To my family, (mainly my husband) who puts up with me ignoring the laundry, and the dishes and the dust just so I can meet my deadlines and hang out with fictional alpha males. You'll always be my number one Alpha, babe. Think I'm forgetting someone? Never. To the READERS! Thank you for picking up my books, reading them, recommending them, and sending me messages of love (keep those coming!) I <3 you all.

#ILikeYouCollaredBaby

Playlist

Lights Go Out ~ Fozzy

Beast Within ~ Blood

Take Me to Church ~ Hozier

Control ~Puddle of Mudd

Gravity ~ Sara Bareilles

If You Only Knew ~ Shinedown

Fade Into Me ~ David Cook

Don't Tell Em' ~ Jeremiah

Freak On a Leash ~ Korn

Riptide ~ Vance Joy

About the Author

M. NEVER RESIDES IN NEW York City. When she's not researching ways to tie up her characters in compromising positions, you can usually find her at the gym kicking the crap out of a punching bag, or eating at some new trendy restaurant. She has a dependence on sushi and a fetish for boots. Fall is her favorite season.

She is surrounded by family and friends she wouldn't trade for the world and is a little in love with her readers. The more the merrier. So make sure to say hi!

Visit my Website: *www.mneverauthor.com*

Or find me on:

Goodreads
Facebook
Instagram
Twitter
Pinterest

Printed in Great Britain
by Amazon